What if a relentless predator—a parent's worst nightmare come true—dropped out of nowhere? He has, and now cynical Detective Richard Slater and reluctant psychic Kate Macklin are all that stand between death and life for the children targeted by this psycho. But can Richard and Kate piece together the puzzle before the killer comes for them, too?

Kate didn't want to know these things, but she didn't seem to have a choice...

Kate watched Captain Dennis Murphy stare at the small, still form on the metal table in the city morgue. Sweat trickled down his forehead in spite of the chilled dry air in the room. His silk shirt stuck to his back like a second skin.

She was in the middle of a terrible nightmare and couldn't wake up. The morgue was the last place in the world she wanted to be. Did knowing so much about the killings make her a suspect? Was that why she was inside this dream? Still, this was outlandish to her quiet soul.

"Here are the next two." The medical examiner pulled open two more drawers.

Murphy didn't need to turn around to know Detective Sergeant Richard Slater moved close behind him as the outer door whooshed open and then shut.

"God! What kind of—" Slater exploded, startled out of his usual composure.

Murphy sighed. "It's hard to believe, even for this city. Three of them. We have to nail this creep and fast. The medical examiner said they died peacefully," he added, as if this mitigated the evil of the murders somewhat.

The faces of the three little girls were bright red, the color of obscene rouge on the innocent faces of wax manikins, as if they'd never been live, warm-blooded human beings.

KUDOS for One...Two...Buckle My Shoe

P.K. Paranya tells a really good story. – *Brenda A. Snodgrass, Reviewer*

Paranya provides an electrifying thriller here, allowing readers a peek into the mind of a serial killer and his twisted yet surprisingly comprehensible reasoning for murder. Nicely developed characters, plenty of psychological suspense, and a shocking twist at the end will leave readers thinking about this book for a good while. – *Christy Tillery French, Reviewer*

Bernie is one of the most complex characters you will ever read about and Paranya's knowledge of psychology is obvious in this deeply disturbing psychological thriller with an ending so surprising it will take your breath away. You will not want to put this one down until you have read every word and then you will go back and read it again because you won't be able to sleep anyway. Definitely one of the best thrillers of the year. – *Kathy Thompson, Reviewer*

The psychology behind the motives of the serial killer was extremely well done. The characters are very complex and completely three dimensional. I was fascinated with all of them, from the heroine who is an agoraphobic and afraid to leave the house to the bitter and cynical detective, to the psychologically disturbed serial killer. – *Regan, Reviewer*

Paranya tells a chilling story. The psychology and characterization is amazing. I absolutely loved the book, chilling as it was, and found that once I picked it up. I couldn't put it down. If you want a book that will touch you, make you laugh and cry, and keep you riveted until the very last word, you can't go wrong with One...Two...Buckle My Shoe. – *Taylor, Reviewer*

ONE...TWO... BUCKLE MY SHOE

by

P. K. PARANYA

A BLACK OPAL BOOKS PUBLICATION

GENRE: THRILLER/ROMANTIC ELEMENTS

ONE...TWO... BUCKLE MY SHOE
Copyright © 2007 by P. K. Paranya
Cover Design by Jackson Cover Designs
All cover art copyright © 2012
All Rights Reserved
Print ISBN: 978-1-937329-53-2

First Publication: JULY 2012

Published by Black Opal Books **http://www.blackopalbooks.com**

DEDICATION

I dedicate this book to the excellent people who work at Black Opal Books. Lauri Wellington, Acquisitions Editor, has provided comments that have improved my books so much. And Jack Jackson, Art Director, bless his heart for his patience as well as expertise in figuring out what we want on our covers even if we don't know. All the people at Black Opal have made this the best experience I've had as an author.

CHAPTER 1

Katharine Macklin stared at the computer screen in disbelief. Little dolls stood in a parade in front of her, wrapped in see-through plastic. She rubbed her knuckles in her eye sockets, trying to clear her vision and bring back the bookkeeping program.

'*One...two...buckle my shoe.*' The snippet of nursery rhyme came clear, over and over, in high pitched, whispery little voices.

Kate's throat tightened and the muscles around her heart constricted when she realized they weren't dolls—but little girls. Why were they singing to her? An ominous dread settled around her shoulders. It was the psychic thing coming back to haunt her. It had helped to find her daughter when she needed it two years ago, but why was it here now?

The familiar chills ran from the back of her neck down her spine and something told her she would have to call the police again.

᠅᠅᠅

"We're facing a brick wall, Slater." Captain Murphy glared at the man in front of him as if he'd grown two heads. "What do you mean you won't come back to Homicide?"

The big man shrugged, towering over Murphy, causing him to move back a step. "I told you. I'm never doing homicide again."

"The chief wants it." Murphy struggled to keep the "God only knows why" sound out of his voice. "Don't you ever wear anything besides street clothes?" Technically the sergeant wasn't on duty, but Murphy's own men always wore neatly-pressed New York City blues and he liked that. "If the chief wants you back on this, it's not negotiable."

The two men glared at each other, neither backing down.

"No can do. That's why I left. Too much."

Murphy didn't want Slater on this case at all. He wasn't a team player and was difficult to work with at the best of times. But the chief was...well, he was the chief, and neither Murphy nor Slater had any choice.

"It makes no sense to anyone but that killing machine out there. It's a parent's worse nightmare. We ID'd the kids. So far each family thinks their child is the only prey of this psycho. When the news gets out there are others, the public will go crazy buying weapons—I don't blame them. Jesus!" Murphy sat behind his desk and slammed a drawer in frustration. "If you could talk to the parents."

"I'm not coming back. I like it where I am." Slater turned to go.

Murphy felt himself sputtering. "Hold on a minute, the chief didn't say pretty please. He said you'd do it, although I don't see how—"

"You don't see how I can do anything Homicide hasn't already done," Slater finished Murphy's sentence. "I don't either."

Slater's interruption showed an arrogant lack of respect. It wasn't Murphy's fault the sergeant hadn't progressed through the ranks.

Slater's mouth compressed into a grimace, a look that scared the hell out of rookies, and Murphy wasn't too comfortable with it either. "The chief knows, when I left Homicide I said no more. Nearly killed me."

The entire precinct knew how Slater's dedication to work broke up his marriage. Many times, when Murphy heard his men talking about their home life or lack of it, he was glad he never took the time to develop any relationships. Slater's next words jerked his attention back.

"I put my time in, got the flat feet to show for it. I'm good at what I do now, and you know it. The college boys, the button-down cops, are taught that any kind of mayhem to the suspect is to 'punish with extreme prejudice.' The older officers call it 'getting the perp's attention.' That's where I stand."

"Plain and simple, you can't accept progress."

On the phone, the chief had called the sergeant by his first name, Richard. It grated on Murphy's nerves to know the chief and the department troublemaker were on a first name basis. Only a few of the old-timers ever called Slater by his first name.

"I damn well don't want to talk to any parents. That's why I transferred to Robbery. I try reasoning with the suspect. If he won't cooperate, that's his problem. Pure and simple."

Murphy tried to hold back a comment. Slater had crossed the line several times in his career. Not far enough to get suspended, but he wasn't a stranger to Internal Affairs. In fact he came so close to the line he was never promoted beyond sergeant which didn't seem to bother him.

"Look, Slater. I told the chief I had plenty of men who could do the job on this one. Hell, I see your point. I'd jump at early retirement too. I heard you've been seeing the doc about those headaches. A nice cozy desk job should work it all out for you." Murphy swung his chair around, turning his back on Slater, dismissing him. Not easy, since the big man towered over his shoulder like a pile of rocks threatening to avalanche down a hill.

"You know that's a crock of shit. I never pulled down a desk job in my life and don't intend to. But that doesn't mean I'm going to work in Homicide again."

Murphy felt a glow of elation mixed with regret. He had Slater by the short hairs now. When a man began to justify his decisions, it was a sign he was caving in. You didn't get to be captain in one of the toughest precincts in New York and not know your men. Time for a swift kick to the *cojones* while Slater hesitated, even so briefly.

"Don't make me pull rank. I know you've been here longer than most of us, but I'm still boss. Robbery can wait, but the little girls out there can't." Murphy remembered that Slater had a daughter about the same age as these kids.

Slater opened his big fist and closed it again, cracking his knuckles. "Shit. Where's the paper work?"

"Problem is, I can't keep the news quiet much longer. We'll have to hold back some information—as much as we can."

"Yeah, I know. The copycats. They follow media coverage like groupies after a rock concert."

Murphy slid the file toward the edge of his desk. "We have one citizen who's anxious to talk to us about the murders."

Slater reached long arms for the papers and read for a moment. "Macklin. Is that the name of the woman I'm supposed to talk to first?"

"You should remember her. I looked up her file. A couple of years ago her daughter was killed in a hit and run. She led us to the body after having some sort of psychic vision. You were one of the investigating officers."

"Oh yeah. I remember. She was strung out all right, scared of her shadow."

Slater wouldn't have tolerated any lack of control. That's what made him so damn good at solving psycho cases. They didn't like to give up control either.

Murphy scratched his head, careful not to muss the few wispy strands. His pale reddish-blond hair was thick everywhere on his head but the very top. He figured he'd probably be bald at forty. "The point is, when she called, she told me about the plastic wrapped around the bodies— something few people know. She claims she sees things on her computer. That's how she knew where her daughter was—or so she said."

"Brother, that's all we need. Let's bring her in. Maybe she's the killer looking for her fifteen minutes of fame."

Murphy ignored the sarcasm in Slater's voice. "Kicker is, she refuses to come to the station. Insists on someone going to her house. One officer at a time. I told her that wasn't procedure. You'll have to question her. Sure, she sounds like a nut case, but we can't take a chance. I know of police departments that keep psychic detectives on retainer—like attorneys. But you wouldn't know about that, not having kept up with the times."

"Yeah, Murphy, right. They probably do that in California on a regular basis."

Leaning back in his chair, Murphy laced his fingers behind his head. "I've got an FBI buddy who says they don't officially acknowledge it, but they use psychics, too. All I'm asking is that you check this out. If you don't want to bother..." Murphy knew his tone of voice irritated the man, like a stone in the toe of Slater's shoe. He folded his arms across his chest and waited.

Slater glared at him and when that didn't seem to work, gave up, and stared at the message in his hand with distaste. "Oh hell. I'll do it on my way home this afternoon."

"What time you get here this morning?" Murphy asked. "You look like you've been dragged behind a truck on an unpaved road."

"Thanks. Came in about four. Couldn't sleep."

"I don't know about going over there alone. You should take another officer with you, even if she doesn't want it that way. We can't make her come in, although we could put on some pressure. If we do that, she might decide not to talk at all."

"Think she'll try to take advantage of me?"

The captain laughed. "You should be so lucky. But hey, all kidding aside, this one sounds strange. Sometimes it doesn't pay to stick your neck out."

"That's what I do best."

Murphy's shrug delayed the sarcastic comeback that had edged to the tip of his tongue. Slater wasn't known for his sense of humor. "I'll call Mrs. Macklin—let her know you're coming and fill her in about you talking to her before." He rustled some paperwork on his desk and felt rather than heard Slater's departure. For a big man, the guy was light on his feet.

Murphy got up to go to the john, still thinking about how the lab had analyzed the scrapings from the shoes of the victims with the results showing loamy soil and grass mixtures. The kids hadn't picked that up from a city sidewalk or street. Just one more fact to file away in his brain.

ev⬩ev⬩ev

A car pulled up in front of her house. She sneaked a peek from behind the drapes and watched the man inside the car. Her mind instantly connected with his. He was sizing up her place. It had been two years since he'd been there and bits and pieces were coming back from the past. She felt his reluctance to come inside—he thought she was neurotic. She watched him continue to stall, judging the surroundings. She knew his thoughts as clearly as if he'd spoken out loud.

Middle class, older people in the neighborhood. He could tell by the respectable vintage cars occupying most driveways in the afternoon that the owners were probably retired. The silence of the street said no children around. No toys or bikes cluttering the yards. Several streets down, the area was changing into a quiet warehouse district.

Her driveway was empty with no sign of an oil or radiator leak. Had she grown bored sitting around home listening to her soaps? She could be lonely and needing attention.

He intended to set her straight in a helluva hurry. He didn't have time to waste.

Kate pushed away the detective's sour thoughts, wishing that nice Captain Murphy might have come. He sounded so gentle on the phone. This man was the opposite. He was everything in the outside world that terrified her and kept her a recluse since her husband and daughter had died and left her behind. In a few moments, she would have to open the door and let him into her home.

CHAPTER 2

The bell rang and Sergeant Slater heard a commotion inside the house. When the door cracked open a few inches and then wider, he was surprised by the woman facing him. Murphy said he'd worked on her daughter's case two years ago. He did remember her, but now she seemed younger.

"Sorry it took so long." Kate Macklin was flushed and laughing. "It's my cat, Rasputin. He hates strangers. I had to put him in the bathroom or he would've hidden under the refrigerator again."

She stopped talking abruptly, as if realizing she'd been babbling. The heavy screen door was still between them and Slater saw with approval that she wasn't about to open it.

"Captain Murphy called to say he was sending someone out to talk to me. Can—I'd like to see some identification, please."

He took out his wallet, hoping she hadn't noticed that he'd made an error in judgment. He should have thought to show his shield before she asked.

After glancing at the proffered identification, she unlatched the door. Slater pushed forward, needing to show her that he could have shoved through with one shoulder, had he been so inclined. "I'm Detective Sergeant Richard Slater."

"We've met. I remember you now. It seems like a lifetime ago."

"Yes. Under very unhappy circumstances, I'm afraid."

She held out her hand.

He took it, moving with care this time, pity mixed with irritation at her fragility. Everything about her was washed out, like a bad photocopy. The woman was in her early thirties, tall and slender—plain, yet her features were appealing in an odd way. Nice mouth and nose, good skin, but almost a prison pallor. He was used to sizing up people, couldn't help it—part was training, part natural nosiness.

"My name is Katharine Macklin."

Slater imagined she must feel a little foolish, when she made a wry grin. He already knew her name. He filled the hallway with his bulk and moved back a pace, having the good sense to realize it made her claustrophobic.

She turned toward the living room. "Come in, please. I've fixed a pot of coffee."

"Sounds good." Great. He was afraid she was going to offer tea. He hated hot tea in thin little cups.

She smiled, a gentle, tentative smile, ready to cancel it at a moment's notice. "Rough day?"

He shrugged, not wanting to talk about it with a stranger—and a civilian. He looked around, noting the clean, uncluttered surroundings. "Nice place."

He would have taken her for a collector with rooms full of furniture and glass figurines. She was spinsterish in spite of the Mrs. attached to her name and having had a daughter.

The cat ventured out while they sipped their coffee, rubbing up against Slater's legs. "Rasputin! I must have forgotten to shut the bathroom door." She reached for the cat. "He never touches strangers. I hope he doesn't leave a ton of hair behind."

"No, it's okay. He likes me, I guess." Most cats did, but for some reason dogs never took to him. He liked cats better anyway, they left you alone mostly. Maybe that's why he didn't remember having a pet when he was a kid.

They sat a while, not speaking. It surprised Slater that he felt comfortable. It had been his experience that most women didn't care for silence. He was trying to do this by the book—the captain had warned him about messing up. Slater wanted this bastard bad. If he could collar this last one, he could sink into the ooze of early retirement like one of those prehistoric animals Murphy was forever comparing him to.

I.R.O.N.I.C. The initials came to him as in the police procedure manual Murphy had given him to read a week or two ago. Identity, Rapport, Opening statement, Narration, Inquiry, and Conclusion. That's the crap that's supposed to go into a witness interview. Jeezus, he should be glad to retire. He didn't envy the new guys just coming in.

Well, looks like he'd made it past the first three basics, and since the witness wasn't going to volunteer anything to get into the narration part without help, he might as well begin. "Mrs. Macklin, I'd like to hear your story. Why you called us." He flipped his notebook open, not that he expected to use it.

She swallowed hard. "This is going to be difficult to believe—I'm having trouble with it myself."

He waited, trying not to judge. Whatever her delusions, he guessed they were real to her, not designed to gain attention. It had to have been a tough decision to call the police.

"I hate to go into a long story, but I suppose it's necessary to give you a background."

"Whatever makes you comfortable, ma'am," Slater said with an inordinate amount of patience.

∽∾∽

Time filtered past while Kate stood and began pacing back and forth. The detective looked so damned smug sitting there. He probably hadn't remembered anything of the circumstances surrounding Annie's death. It wasn't important to him.

What a nightmare that had been, struggling with the closed-minded attitudes of the police when she tried to convince them to search where she saw Annie's body. She hadn't slept for a week, worrying where her daughter was, but by then she'd had the strong feeling Annie was dead. That had torn her up bad enough, but to not ever know what had happened to her—where she would lie for the rest of eternity—that was intolerable.

"Why don't you refresh my memory about your daughter? That might get us on track," Slater suggested.

Kate nodded and took a deep breath. "You'd think a twelve-year-old girl would be safe walking five blocks from school. She'd be fourteen today. For a long time I punished myself for being a bad mother, for letting Annie walk home from band practice those five blocks. I punished myself by remembering every detail, every day."

Slater sat still, attentive.

"If only I'd given in to my premonition that day and gone to meet her. I hate this second sight. I've denied it all my life. I saw my parent's car crash and woke up screaming. But it didn't help to know when it happened. I didn't have time to warn my husband either, when he had the accident at work."

"Yes, ma'am," Slater said.

It was apparently meant to keep her going. He must be experienced enough to know once the floodgates opened, she couldn't stop talking until it was over.

"Two years ago, when Annie hadn't come home after practice, I went to the school to check. Someone told me she had argued with the girls she usually chummed with and walked off alone. Poor Annie, a chip on her shoulder as big as the moon after her father's death.

"I called the police department. You and another man came to talk to me. Both of you seemed impatient and not as sympathetic as I'd hoped you'd be. At first you insisted my daughter was a runaway. Annie was all I had left, and while we didn't always get along, we loved each other, no question."

She paused.

"I remember," Slater said and punctuated the small silence.

"When days went by and no word came, I thought of the worst circumstances possible. Late one night, after a week of insomnia, I sat at my computer, trying to concentrate on my bookwork. I must have dozed off because the screen was blank. When I touched my finger to a key, the familiar ledger with its column of figures didn't appear. I remember staring at the screen for a long time, watching the static and listening to the sound of the fan running inside the computer. That was when the pictures came. I saw Annie as if the television was on without sound. She was walking across the street when a junky old two-door sedan came out of nowhere and struck her broadside.

"I screamed a warning, even though I knew I was watching something that had already taken place." Kate shuddered and pulled her sweater closer around her middle. "I felt the terrible crunch of metal against her fragile flesh and bone.

"The driver opened the car door, stood a moment staring down at the small, crumpled body lying on an empty street lined with nothing but closed warehouses. He picked up Annie, laid her in the back seat and sped away." Kate closed her eyes for a moment, feeling the nausea rising in her throat from talking about it for the first time in two years.

"The car disappeared in the yellow fog of the monitor. That told me some time had passed. Oh God, I was sure I was losing it. I pushed aside the panic and concentrated hard. Suddenly the vehicle reappeared at the side of a highway, parked, and then the doors opened. I waited, sure that it would come to me. The man had dumped Annie at the edge of the turnpike, under a viaduct that looked unused. It was sort of a landfill area. Trucks would come and dump garbage on top of her and no one would ever find the body."

She had tried to reach for feelings of pain and suffering from Annie, but none came over the computer screen. Annie had died instantly. It wasn't enough to know that. Kate had to put her daughter to rest, next to the girl's father.

"I concentrated really hard, and that's when I saw the exit sign, so far away up on the hillside." Her heart tripped in her chest as the vision slipped away. Kate closed her eyes again and prayed, opened them and concentrated as hard as when she'd given birth to Annie.

"I finally made out the sign that told me where Annie's body lay. I had no car and no idea how far away the off-ramp was, that's when I called your Captain Murphy again. He sent you and a policeman I'd not met. Surely you remember now. At first you wouldn't listen. I saw you sneak looks at the file in your hand, which probably had notes of a neurotic, hysterical female. But I finally convinced you to take me to the off-ramp where we found Annie, just as I'd seen on my computer."

For weeks after that she had been consumed by a thirst for vengeance. Although willing it to happen, she'd never come close to seeing the man's face or being able to identify the car. Finally Kate had accepted that to be able to bury her daughter was no small miracle and she reconciled herself to being grateful.

Sergeant Slater made an impatient click of his pen. Kate stopped pacing and sat down across from him. He seemed interested in what she'd told him, although some of it must have been familiar to him even after two years. His eyes were sympathetic.

"I finally accepted that I'd been born clairvoyant, and I might as well give in to it." She paused, smiled. This psychic thing—it's supposed to be a gift, sergeant"

He nodded. "I'd sure as he—heck hate it."

She smiled at his quick change of words.

"You stay indoors a lot, don't you, Mrs. Macklin?"

She looked down at her hands clenched into fists in her lap and flexed them. Narrow, bony fingers, pale like the rest of her. "You're patronizing me. I knew you would. The police department had a hard time believing me then. I was afraid they wouldn't this time either." She leaned forward to clutch his knee but pulled back at the last moment.

"I've checked the papers and haven't seen anything about missing little girls. Yet I saw children wrapped in plastic. Clear plastic wrapping so that some of the color of their clothing showed through."

"Yes, ma'am. The captain said you mentioned that."

"They were wrapped very carefully. As if someone didn't want bugs and...and rats and animals to get at them. He wanted to protect them until they were found."

Slater's mouth tightened, his eyes narrowed to a speculative stare. "Go on, I'm listening." She had his full attention now.

Realizing she had nearly touched him in her effort to get him to listen, Kate clenched her hands more tightly together. "I don't know how or why it happens. I don't *want* it to happen. It's just that when I sit at my computer—

I think it comes mostly when I'm tired or sleepy—I see things. Sometimes."

He flipped open his notebook. "Tell me how it started, from the beginning, when you first saw the children on your computer."

"I heard them—then I saw them."

He snapped the pen in and out, annoying her. He was waiting far more patiently than he usually did. She recalled how impatient he'd been with her two years ago.

"Heard them? So, you hear as well as see things on your computer?"

At the touch of sarcasm in his voice, she was ready to give up before she made more of a fool of herself. But there had to be something to this business with the missing children or they wouldn't have sent a detective to talk to her.

She decided to pretend she hadn't noticed any derisive tone in his voice. "Yes. Sometimes. Actually this is the first time I've ever heard anything, and it's only been a snippet of a nursery rhyme, one line. '*One, two, buckle my shoe*' the song went. After I heard them singing, I saw what I thought were dolls. It was like they stood in a row, *willing* me to see them. I couldn't see them clearly though, not at first."

"Go on, please," he told her, gently now, as if concerned she might stop talking.

"I saw the last one, a figure paler and smaller than the others and way in the back of the line. I saw the empty housing development where he left her. I realized they weren't dolls at all. Poor dear little girls." Tears came to her eyes and she fumbled for a tissue from a box nearby.

He waited until she wiped away the tears and hiccupped a few times before he spoke again. "Can I get you a glass of water?"

She felt his impatience change to pity and couldn't decide which was harder to take. "Thank you, no. It's a relief to talk to someone."

"Are you saying it's like watching television? Did you see anything else on your screen? Any background? Trees? Bushes? Streets you'd recognize?"

Again his thoughts collided with hers. What was happening here? She'd never been able to read anyone's thoughts. Kate tried to block them out. It felt so smarmy, like eavesdropping, but his thread of inner conversation wouldn't be hushed. He didn't want to believe her. It was so out of line with his straight-thinking, logical mind. Yet she knew she didn't fit his profile of a loony. He accepted that she was eccentric, but he was thinking that after what happened with Annie, who wouldn't be a little neurotic?

"I'm afraid I didn't notice the surroundings. I get so agitated when it happens, usually I turn off the computer."

"I can't tell you details—you know almost as much as we do—but a killer's out there and we have to catch him. No little girl is safe otherwise. Sometimes these killers move on to another location, another unsuspecting city, but that's even worse, because then it starts all over."

"How can I help?"

"By concentrating on what you're seeing the next time it comes."

Kate still wasn't certain he believed her, according to his thoughts. She tried not to tune into them any more. She was curious to try and glean more, but that was a dreadful invasion of privacy. Was he merely humoring her? "But—"

He raised his hand, palm toward her, to stop her protests. "I know it'll be hard, but to tell the truth, we aren't making much progress. No witnesses at the abduction or drop sites, it's like the guy's a shadow. He's either very lucky or he knows how we conduct our investigations and what to avoid. I think he's just lucky."

"I never liked this sight—this second sight," she said. At his raised eyebrow, she continued, "My mother had it and her mother, too, or so the story goes. They came from Scotland, where I understand it's pretty common. My mother always called it *the gift*, but as far as I'm concerned, it's a curse."

"I wouldn't like it," Slater admitted. "But it did help you find your daughter."

"Too late to save her. Same with my parents. If I have to be saddled with this so-called gift, why can't it be of real use?"

"Maybe it can, now. Tell me how it works."

She knew it went beyond anything he wanted to know, but at this point he was willing to listen. Kate moved the cat onto her lap and began to pet him absentmindedly. "There's what's called *distant viewing*. That's moving into the awareness of a person, seeing what he sees, feeling what he feels. That's mostly what I do."

"You checked it out—what you do?"

"Yes. After Annie, I bought books and studied dozens more on the paranormal at the library, trying to understand. Besides distant viewing there's something called *psychometrics,* where a psychic is supposed to hold an object that has touched the person. I've never tried that." She took a deep breath, waiting for his impatient interruption. When he didn't make a sound, she continued. "Then there's *astral projection*. Sounds ominous, I know—a space alien kind of thing. It's where part of a psychic's personality—some might call it the soul or spirit—travels. I'm pretty sure I've done that, with finding my daughter."

Slater put away his pen and note pad. When he stood, he bent forward a little, as if trying not to loom over her. He was plainly uncomfortable at her revelations. "I'd better go. Here's my card. Call me anytime, day or night, doesn't matter. I don't live too far away. I can be here in minutes."

"When I get the—the visions—they don't last long. I have no idea if anyone else can see them but I'd doubt it. The images I had with Annie—they only lasted long enough to see—certain things I needed to."

"That's all I ask. Do what you can. Be alert to surroundings and the environment. Anything might give us a valuable clue." He regarded her for a moment as if deciding to speak. "I'd get out more if I were you, Mrs. Macklin. You look as pale as any lifer I've ever seen doing hard time. It's not good to be alone."

At first, indignation rose in her throat. She wanted to lash out at him. The truth of what he said punctured her skin like tiny needles. She gathered her courage to look up into his face, but all she saw was a rough kindness, no contempt or ridicule.

He ran thick fingers through his dark brown hair, which was graying at the temples. His pensive, coffee-colored eyes somehow went with the slightly flattened nose that he probably got playing football in his youth and never bothered to have set. His jaw was square and belligerent looking even when he smiled.

"Thank you for your consideration, sergeant," she said stiffly, holding back the tears. "I'll try. I'll really try."

His eyes showed genuine concern and she looked away, unable to cope with that honest expression.

"There is one more thing," she said. "The first night I saw three little girls."

He paused, a hand on the door knob, frowning.

"Last night I saw four."

                                        ☙❧☙

Out in the street, Slater started the car, shifted gears and sucked in the moist spring air. Wouldn't be long before the heat came, but after this past winter, he was ready for it. He tried to put his thoughts in order but the strangeness of what he'd just been through boggled the mind.

What the hell was going on? This woman was privy to information no one outside the department knew. He had to believe her strange story. There was no way she could know these things—unless she was the killer. He shook his head at the notion. Women seldom committed serial killings. They weren't *that* liberated, yet.

How in the hell was he going to write this up in a report? He should just get it all down and let Murphy figure out the procedure. The captain had been the first to believe she had something to say. For his part, Slater would write it up as a routine visit, leaving out the more offbeat aspects of her story.

Unless she was right and there was a fourth victim.

CHAPTER 3

Kate woke with a gnawing in her stomach. *It's going to happen again tonight.* Since Annie died, she'd been afraid to go out. Now even her computer was scaring her.

Maybe if she changed her routine, worked a while in the daytime instead of night, the images wouldn't return. She positioned her thermos of coffee next to the computer, on a little tray so it wouldn't mess up the desk. Awareness of these compulsive routines every time she sat down at her work, offered comfort, keeping her safe.

"Rasputin. Where in the world..." Mealtimes went by when she forgot to eat, but she never forgot to feed and water her cat, mainly because he always lay within arm's length of wherever she was. He was nowhere in sight at the moment. How strange. Now that she thought about it, ever since the visions had started, he hadn't lain in his special place. She'd check on him later. Right now, it was time to get to work.

Kate turned the machine on and loaded the spreadsheet program. That was what she had liked about the computer—until these visions appeared. Everything had to be done just so, no choices, no decisions, just the exact same routine every time she used it, or it didn't work. She could put her thoughts on automatic pilot and let go. When she finished her work and e-mailed it to the businesses, they transferred money to her account. She never had to see anyone.

That was the way life should be. Otherwise it was like creeping through a long, dark hallway. If she didn't make a sound, didn't touch the walls, didn't scuff her feet, she might make it to the end without someone catching her— without that grab on the shoulder from behind. If she just stayed small, quiet, and invisible, she'd be safe. Kate wished this insight had come sooner. Maybe she could have protected her husband and daughter.

Once into her work, she let it take over her thoughts, losing herself in the spreadsheets, the comforting columns of figures lining up in obedient sequence. Hours must have passed. Her head jerked once or twice when she nearly dozed at the keyboard until a funny tingling sensation crept into her fingertips.

'*Look at me. Look at me.*'

Reluctantly she looked at the screen, her throat tight with fear. The now-familiar golden fog swirled, mashing the words that had been on the monitor to a soft mist. She stared into the center, fascinated.

This time she saw a youth in a yard, sitting on the ground. She couldn't make out his face, but by the size and set of his shoulders, he was probably eleven or twelve. The same age Annie had been. He was crying, sobbing his heart out. No words came from him as she watched, hypnotized by the strangeness of the scene, relieved that the little girls hadn't shown up in their macabre parade.

Her fingers froze over the Escape key, wanting to touch it, get out, but she couldn't move.

The boy turned toward a tall redwood fence covered with vines just beginning to change to green from stringy wintry brown. Her eyes saw through his—saw what he saw, felt what he felt. A garden surrounded the boy. He hated the garden, which wasn't a sunny, happy place, but dank and shadowy. Her tidy nature cringed at the profligate waste of beauty. Lush landscape, overgrown with climbing roses, cried out for pruning and mowing. Everything was neglected, everything unkempt, except...

His eyes, with her captured inside, turned toward a soft swell of earth covered with grass, neatly trimmed. The mound reminded her of a grave site.

The boy continued to sob, tears running from his open eyes. An awareness came to her, with a sudden force, that he didn't want to look in that direction, but *had* to. Fear sent spasms to her empty stomach, and the skin tightened on the back of her neck, causing her to shiver and fold her arms across her chest in an effort to keep warm.

The boy's gaze shifted—like a camcorder zooming in close.

Shoes. Tiny shoes placed just so on the mound of green. Not pairs—the odd, unmatched presence of the single shoes made ominous whispers breathe up and down her skin, rippling the hairs on her arms.

'*One...two...buckle my shoe.*'

A red-checked tennis shoe, a black patent leather with a strap across the center, a ribbony bow on top, a little white sandal. Tears clouded her vision; *his* tears, not hers.

He didn't approach the shrine, for that's what it was, some kind of shrine. He sat and sobbed, as if he were an element of the scene, but yet not *in* it.

Finally, exhausted and drained, Kate willed herself to crawl away from the computer and lie on the couch. Hours later when she awoke, the computer still hummed but the screen was blank. Touching a key to bring the scene back, Kate cried out as the parade of little dolls, leaped onto the screen. This time all the children were clear. The fourth was no longer the shadowy figure she'd seen before. And their voices sang softly, sadly, '*One...two...buckle my shoe.*'

⌀ↄↄ⌀

After days passed with no more bodies discovered, Slater considered the possibility that the murders had been flukes. A spur of the moment derangement—a crazed urge some lunatic might never repeat. Even though the Macklin woman had said there would be four.

He sat at home in his recliner, the TV remote in his hand, idly staring at the blank set. Why didn't he believe this was the last killing?

Because the killer *couldn't* end it, Slater's instinct warned. Whatever the killer set out to prove, whatever his deranged logic told him were the reasons for his frenzy of killing, he wouldn't end it now.

Slater realized he thought in singular terms. Psychos, by their very natures, were loners. Years of police work, years invested in Homicide and Vice, left him with savvy he thought he'd forgotten.

Damn, but he didn't want to be sucked into this sewer again. He hated nuts and weirdoes. Most robbery scenarios were straight stuff, with greed the motivator, not an evil malignancy that could rip your guts out.

The phone rang and he considered not moving. Although he hated that answering gizmo, it came in handy sometimes. Good thing his ex-wife left it behind. No one ever called but people wanting to sell something, poll-takers, or the captain. In the case of Captain Murphy, it always meant bad news. He decided to answer it.

"Yeah, Slater here." He kicked the recliner back to upright. It was the captain. He should have known. "Okay, meet you at the morgue."

The clothes Slater had worn since morning felt wrinkled and lived in. He longed for the shower he'd thought of before the phone rang. The TV dinner still sat in the microwave and the lukewarm can of beer on the kitchen counter.

Hell, he wasn't hungry anyway. He should have stopped at The Office for a beer. The new owners of the bar down the block from the station named it with the idea that it could serve as an alibi. When you got home to the little woman and she beat her gums about where you were, you just said, at the office. Stupid idea—why would a man need an excuse to get a beer? He knew he was evading his thoughts, but it worked until he pulled up at the county morgue.

The captain met him in front of the brick building and they entered together. Neither had to show ID. Murphy looked calm, unruffled. The cuffs of his white shirt sleeve always showed an exact half inch from beneath his jacket. Jeeze, did they teach 'em that at the academy?

"Another kid?"

One at a time. *Small consolation.* Slater's mouth twisted at the irony of the phrase that popped into his thoughts. The Macklin woman had seen it coming.

Glancing at their reflection in the window separating the visiting area from the hallway leading to the back, Slater thought he and Murphy looked peculiar walking side by side. Like Mutt and Jeff in the old Sunday comics. He was brawny, tall, and creeping toward heaviness. The captain was shorter and slender, younger by quite a few years. He tried to hide his premature balding by combing wispy hairs over the top so that it resembled a grate with something flesh-colored trying to poke through. He had, in Slater's opinion, an unbearably optimistic disposition.

But not tonight.

Neither spoke until the assistant pulled the drawer open and they stared down on the remains.

The sound of the two men swallowing hard echoed in the cold, still room. "Same deal?" Slater asked.

"Yep. Same M.O. and same killer I'd bet." Murphy signaled to the assistant who brought out three large storage bags.

Slater opened each one to look at the neat pile of clothing.

"The killer wrapped each body," the assistant commented.

Murphy's glance chastised the assistant for speaking out of turn. "We're aware of that."

"To protect them. The first thing is, find a pattern," Slater said more to himself than anyone else. His gut instinct told him this was an unleashed psycho's work, the work of one man.

The girls were the same age. Blonde, with fair complexions. Their clothes didn't tell much of a story. They had been well dressed, their garments clean. One bag held orange-colored slacks and matching top with neon green socks.

Slater's lips thinned across his teeth at the T-shirt emblazoned with "Grandma's Girl" across the front. The second bag contained denim overalls with suspenders and the third held an expensive-looking wool plaid dress. Nothing special there. The usual coats and mittens. What was he missing?

"Let's see the shoes."

Murphy grunted a reluctant approval at Slater's quick perception. He gestured to the coroner's assistant who handed them another, smaller bag.

Slater looked inside the bag and let out a low whistle. He picked up a tiny black slipper that barely covered his big palm. It had a little blue bow and a buckled strap.

"One shoe for each kid," Murphy said. "My guess would be the killer kept the matching ones."

Slater turned the shoe over and over in his palm, knowing the lab had processed the bag's contents for prints already. "A killing is one thing, but a wacko who kills little girls for no apparent reason, protects the bodies from rats and bugs after they die, and keeps one shoe from each of his victims—that's way beyond weirdo status."

Murphy had studied abnormal psychology in college, would know about deviant behavior, and had probably witnessed it all. "Exactly. We don't know the killer's agenda. He may never stop unless we find the key to why he's doing it. Could be the missing shoes are accidental, maybe he forgot to include them."

Murphy was more savvy than that—so he was baiting him again. "That's a crock," Slater said. "Why would he take one off in the first place, without touching the other clothing?" He looked at the captain and figured Murphy was close to boiling over. He liked to prod him out of his usual composure.

"Slater, I'm leveling with you. I don't like your kind. You're trouble. You don't follow orders unless you want to, you don't work on a team—hell, you're a goddamned dinosaur. I give thanks everyday there are only a handful of you left on the force."

"Save the speech, Captain. I don't like you either. You suits taking over the department are screwing it up good and proper. You can't do a damn thing without looking it up in your procedure manual first. But get this straight, because I never repeat myself. I'm willing to shelve our differences. For now. The case is what's important."

"You're right," Murphy sounded grudgingly respectful.

Slater felt as if the captain was about to clap him on the back but had decided at the last minute to forgo the familiarity.

"Sawed Off wants you on a joint determination between their department and the head of the investigative team as to the cause of death." The medical examiner everyone called Sawed Off behind his back had left the room to answer a call.

Slater made a wry face at Murphy's pompous statement. "You mean he wants me to rubber stamp his findings. I know the drill." He'd gone through this routine many times while he was in homicide, but never with a child. Well, a body was a body, he supposed. Was that in the procedure manual?

"Let's get out of here a minute, while he gets her ready."

They moved from the depressing chill of the building out into the bleak sunlight.

Looking upward at the sparse limbs of the leafless trees in the park across the street, with spring still struggling to push away the cold winter, Slater's thoughts turned as bleak. No children playing out there. The wind whipped through his trouser legs, chilling him to the bone. He thought of the little girls who would never see another winter or summer, never play in another park.

Murphy spoke. "Ready for this? The M.E. says the first one ate ice cream and cake just before she died. And a sedative—Valium. The sonofabitch made sure she died happy."

Weird, Slater thought. He had never heard of anything like it. Usually a killer like this got off on hurting the victims. The control thing provided a turn-on in every multiple killing he'd come up against.

"There'll be others, won't there?" Murphy's voice was flat with discouragement.

"Sure as the next sunrise."

"God, you're so cheerful."

"Have you contacted the parents of this last one?"

Murphy made a face as they walked toward his car. "They put in a missing child report three days ago. A jogger found her in a grove of trees at the rear of a new subdivision."

"Wrapped in a sheet of plastic?" Slater asked.

"Everything identical. A killing machine, for chrissake."

"Hold on a minute. Did the jogger mention if that was his usual itinerary? Most times they run the same place every day."

Murphy narrowed his eyes a minute, concentrating. "Yes. Matter-of-fact he said he ran by there the previous morning and...oh, I get it. You're saying the killer wants them to be found."

"Bingo. Secluded enough so no one sees him make the drop, but not enough so the bodies won't be found before they can decompose."

Murphy wiped the back of his neck as if he felt something crawling there.

"How about NCIC?" It wasn't so much a question as a verification. The National Crime Information Center had a list they could draw on like known child molesters, serial rapists, serial killers. He'd used it many times in the past.

"First thing we did, ran it down on the computers."

"This guy doesn't fit any known M.O. does he? So much for that computer shit. He doesn't *do* anything to them," Slater said.

"Outside of killing them, you mean. No, not a mark on them. None were touched in any way, clothing all intact."

Murphy wiped his brow. Slater watched him sweat even though the shrill wind pummeled his back, whipping through the city street.

"One reason we haven't let the press in on more of the details yet. This could turn into a freaking epidemic. Copy cat killers could come out of the woodwork and we'd end up with more false confessions than we can handle. We have to stop this one or force him to move on."

Slater shook his head. "We both know that isn't what we want, to turn him loose on some unsuspecting community."

Murphy kicked his shiny shoes into a dank ridge of brown grass. "No, I'm blowing steam. I wouldn't wish this on any other city. One more thing." Murphy hesitated and then plunged on. "You should talk to the parents. Tomorrow's a good time. It's Saturday and most likely they'll all be home. Ah—I want you to take Mrs. Macklin with you."

"The hell you say!"

"No negotiation on that. Whoever goes to talk to the parents has to take her. She may get a feel for something we don't know about. Maybe one of the parents did it to his or her child for—hell—insurance, maybe, and then did copycats to throw off suspicion."

"That's the stupidest comment I've ever heard you make and believe me—"

"You've heard plenty coming from me." Murphy finished Slater's sentence, his expression showing he took no joy from beating him at his own game for once.

"If I'm lucky, if I get a feel for the case, I don't worry about time. I'll get the bastard." Slater spoke with more assurance than he felt. He touched his finger to his forehead in a motion of leave-taking and turned to go back inside.

Murphy watched the big man amble away, loose-jointed, as if he didn't have a care in the world. The captain knew better. Out west Slater might have been a Texas Ranger. He had that look. The problem would be jerking Slater's leash if he found the killer. Rumor had it there was no stopping him when he really got into a case. He had to play it out to the end. For that reason most of the brass sighed a collective sigh of relief when he transferred from homicide to robbery detail. It could turn sour if Slater got carried away. They needed to catch this guy alive, to find what made him tick. See if he'd killed anyplace else.

No damn wonder Chief Jacobson was desperate for help. Was Slater up to working homicide again? Murphy wondered if he could control the detective enough, keep him from going off on some game plan of his own. The pathetic faces of the little girls jarred something deep inside him, and he knew he had no choice.

They would have to depend on Slater.

☙❧❧

In the cold morgue, Slater stood close to the stainless steel table, his gaze glued to the sheet-covered corpse, so small it barely raised the material. He didn't want to look again. Same size as his daughter.

The M.E. called Sawed-Off behind his back, motioned to an assistant to pull up his specially-made metal box to stand on. A short man with a chip on his shoulder, nothing new. But in Sawed-Off's case—no wonder. Hell of a depressing job.

"Sergeant Slater? I remember you from Homicide. Thought you quit. You got heavier."

"Yeah. And you got shorter."

The M.E.'s assistant snickered, the sound incongruous in the icy cold room with the blazing fluorescent lights shining down.

The pathologist pulled the sheet slowly back and Slater looked at the tiny naked form, a lump in his throat he could hardly swallow past. He thought he'd seen everything and hadn't had any tears left, but he fought against them now.

"What we have here is a classical example of carbon monoxide poisoning, note the cherry-red complexion of the upper extremities." Sawed-Off's formal, deliberate speech, as if he were addressing a body of neophyte medical assistants, made it somehow easier to listen to.

"Percentage-wise it's probably fifty percent blood saturation," he continued. We'll make certain of that, of course, with the toxicology report." He handed Slater a pair of gloves the same as the ones he wore. "By the way, no prints on the skin, the killer wore something like these, I'd imagine."

Or maybe he didn't touch any skin. The clothing of the girls looked normal when the police unwrapped the plastic. Slater tried to keep his thoughts on an unemotional level, but it wasn't easy this time.

The M.E. continued to drone as if to a room full of student doctors. "The pathologic examination revealed microscopic hemorrhages and necrotic areas throughout the subject. The brain, liver, kidneys and spleen were also congested, with edema ensuing. There is extensive nerve cell damage in the cerebral cortex. Your victim Number Two had myocardial damage."

He rolled the girl on her side. "See the purple on her back and buttocks, what does that signify?"

The little bastard wanted to see how much he remembered from homicide days.

"Postmortem lividity," Slater answered without hesitation. If Sawed Off wanted a textbook answer, he'd get it. "When a victim's heart stops, the blood settles, leaving a livid, or purple discoloration at the lowest level of the body. After a couple of hours in the same position, the purple color stays the same no matter how the body is moved."

"So. What does that tell us?" Sawed-Off prompted.

"That they died on their backs, as if asleep, and he leaves them that way until he dumps them."

"Exactly." The M.E. hummed while he worked, a tuneless, joyless sound that did not offend.

"Bruises?" Slater asked.

The M. E. shook his head, barely a movement. "The children ingested a drug. Benzodiazepine or to be precise, diazepam."

"Valium." Slater knew the name well. He took it for headaches, even though the doctor had told him it would only relax him, not get rid of the pain. He was always careful never to overdo. The thought of being hooked on any substance made his skin crawl.

"Manipulate the jaw," the M. E. commanded.

Slater did as he was told and then his gloved fingers touched the elbow and abdomen. "Looks as if she's been dead around thirty-two hours, give or take."

"Excellent. The rigor mortis has moved down to the extremities and is resolving. So far it's progressed to the jaw and elbows. Abdomen still hard. It was mild last night, 50 degrees."

"I took that into consideration," Slater said.

He watched Sawed-Off for signs of emotion, but the medical examiner never allowed an extra blink of an eye. Maybe that was what made him so good at his job. And maybe that's why coming back into Homicide was so damned hard. Keeping emotions away, especially when it came to kids, wasn't easy to do. He'd noticed that in the other officers, case-hardened as they were.

The medical examiner flipped through his notes on a clipboard. "This body, same as the others, has no sign of *cutis anserina*. Of course, this one wouldn't have, due to the time element. They found the others sooner."

Slater tried not to show his annoyance at the smug tone. Sawed-Off had him. "*Cutis- anserina*? If that's a joke, it isn't a good time—"

The man laughed, a bloodless, joyless laugh like his humming. "It only means goosebumps. When a victim is put in the cold air, they'll have goosebumps for twenty-four hours after death and then they disappear. These kids were killed indoors. A warm place."

"Yeah. A warm place with ice cream and cake and a long, cozy sleep to last forever." Slater didn't want the M.E. to have the last word. "I guess if carbon monoxide did them in, a closed building or car would tend to be warm," he commented dryly.

"Touché." The M.E. started to lick a finger to stick up an imaginary star, looked at his gloved hand and changed his mind. "We'll do a blood test next, to make the manner of death official and also to verify the drug ingested."

Slater stepped back and wiped his forehead with the handkerchief from his pocket. He spared a thought for Kate Macklin, wondering how she could cope with what she was seeing on a nightly basis. It might not take much for her to slip backward over the edge.

The M.E. stripped off his gloves and motioned for his assistant to wheel the body away. "Any questions?"

"I don't think so." Slater pulled his attention back when Sawed-Off kicked away the step he used to stand on. It scraped back against the smooth tile, causing a shudder to run up Slater's back. Nerves, raw nerves. He'd better get a grip if he wanted to catch this bastard before Murphy scratched him from the case.

"I'll sign the papers later. Send them to the captain." Slater began stripping his gloves, thankful the formality didn't require that he look at each of the bodies.

He figured he'd see the next one soon enough.

CHAPTER 4

Kate watched Captain Dennis Murphy stare at the small, still form on the metal table in the city morgue. Sweat trickled down his forehead in spite of the chilled dry air in the room. His silk shirt stuck to his back like a second skin.

She was in the middle of a terrible nightmare and couldn't wake up. The morgue was the last place in the world she wanted to be. Did knowing so much about the killings make her a suspect? Was that why she was inside this dream? Still, this was outlandish to her quiet soul.

"Here are the next two." The medical examiner pulled open two more drawers.

Murphy didn't need to turn around to know Detective Sergeant Richard Slater moved close behind him as the outer door whooshed open and then shut.

"God! What kind of—" Slater exploded, startled out of his usual composure.

Murphy sighed. "It's hard to believe, even for this city. Three of them. We have to nail this creep and fast. The medical examiner said they died peacefully," he added, as if this mitigated the evil of the murders somewhat. "This isn't your ordinary chicken-hawk. No sexual, weirdo stuff, the girls were never undressed according to Sawed-Off. We're supposed to get the full report—like, yesterday." Murphy's frown directed toward the M.E. hinted that he'd be in the drawer, too, if he didn't rush the report.

The faces of the three little girls were bright red, the color of obscene rouge on the innocent faces of wax manikins, as if they'd never been live, warm-blooded human beings.

Kate watched Slater take a crumpled handkerchief from his back pocket and wipe his forehead. "How'd they go?" he asked. "All at the same time?"

"No. One was killed twenty four hours ago and the other two—well, it could have been weeks ago. The killer packed snow around each one—dropped them off in separate places. Vacant lots, not out of the way. Looks like they were supposed to be found."

"He use carbon monoxide?"

Murphy knew the tell-tale cherry-red extremities told the story.

"He? She? It could have been a gang for all we know. But you're right, it was carbon monoxide." Murphy winced as Slater cracked his knuckles, each one separately. The sound ripped through the silence.

Kate tried to blend into the wall, as if they knew she was watching. How could they not know, the feelings were powerful, all around her. The room held so many frightening impressions, she didn't want to think about it, yet she felt compelled to let her thoughts travel back to when this nightmare started.

Whispered voices had chanted in a childish sing-song when she stared at her computer screen. '*One...two...buckle my shoe.*' The song thankfully broke her dream apart.

She awoke then, covered in perspiration, in spite of the covers she'd thrown off as if trying to run away. It was two forty-five in the morning. She walked into the front room, not wanting to look in the direction of the computer desk, but unable to look away. The computer was on, and she'd definitely turned it off after her work the night before. The familiar screen saver rolled across the screen, and she felt a relief that no pictures appeared. She'd been through enough, damn it! Was living alone, fearing to go outdoors finally playing havoc with her mind?

"Good Lord, Rasputin. I'm a basket case, that's what I am." She leaned down to pet the fuzzy gray cat close by her side. The fur along his back stood up, spiky. He spit at her and moved away from her feet. What was the matter with him? He seemed to sense the visions on the screen, but he couldn't know what she'd been dreaming.

Kate went into the kitchen, liking the feel of the cold tile on the bottom of her feet. She needed to put on a pot of coffee—sleep was lost to her.

ოჳ€ჳ

The next night, when she sat in front of the columns of figures, working on her bookkeeping jobs, the childish voices swirled out of a pale yellow fog that immediately enveloped her work on the computer screen. The nursery rhyme whispered over and over in high-pitched chanting.

'*One...two...buckle my shoe...One...two...buckle my shoe.*' She put her hands over her ears, but still she heard it. Voices of children who'd lost something, the plaintive sound, questioning, sorrowful.

"Do you hear that, Rasputin?" Kate looked down at her cat, but he wasn't curled at her feet anymore. He must have heard it too and bolted for another room.

On the monitor, the wrapped dolls slowly slid forward. Kate tried to swallow, but her throat felt like it was filled with sand. Drawing on her willpower, she closed her eyes and shut off the computer.

She dumped the dregs in her cup. Too much coffee and forgetting to eat half the time, played havoc with her nerves. What did it matter that she was getting too thin? She had no one in her life to care.

"Ah, there you are, cowardly cat." She pulled him from behind the refrigerator and held him close. His heart was pounding, she felt it against her cheek.

Lately she slept only a few hours at a time, knowing she had to work on the bookkeeping accounts that earned her a living, but hating to turn on the computer. The gray machine began to resemble a monster from her worst nightmare, with one eye focused on her every move. When she covered the monitor, the plastic cover reminded her of the plastic on the victims in her vision.

Kate closed her eyes tightly against the vision of the dolls turning into children as they lined up on her computer screen. '*One...two...buckle my shoe.*' The parents of the poor little kids must be nearly out of their minds. Were the children frightened when they died?

"Ah, Rasputin, this'll never work. I've got to finish Melody Cleaner's monthly statement, and I promised Gracie I'd have her inventory done yesterday."

Kate thought of the two missing people in her life. The memory of her husband had softened around the edges so that she could call it out, stroke it a few minutes, and tuck it away most times without pain. But her daughter had been gone a shorter time and the ache in the empty place wouldn't let up. Gradually, she had managed to pull the shards of her life together after the pieces had gone every which way. Feeling scraped raw and naked when she ventured out in the streets, more and more she chose to stay inside. Terrible things happened out there. And now even worse things had come to haunt her.

CHAPTER 5

Kate stared into the computer monitor, half afraid to turn it on. She hadn't seen anything unusual lately. It took long hours to get out the quarterly tax figures and catch up on work she'd let drag. All because, even though she'd promised, she didn't want to see anything or hear anything unusual from the computer.

She'd lost several customers during the last weeks. Missing deadlines and not keeping in touch made small-business people impatient. It didn't matter that much. Her remaining clients were faithful. Kate knew she could probably get by comfortably without the extra money, but since her daughter died, she needed the work to keep her occupied. Keeping busy had saved her sanity.

Sergeant Slater's last visit had left her on edge, restless, and unable to concentrate. He was right. She needed to overcome her debilitating fear of leaving the confines of her home. Get outside more. His comment about her prison pallor made her think about it.

Spring was coming and she'd hate to miss another one. The soft wind in the trees outside the windows told her the day was nice and warm, waiting for her. She stood and stretched. An overwhelming desire to go outdoors seized her.

She coaxed Rasputin outside, where they sat on the back step, the door ajar behind them. The cat was as fearful as she, though only a butterfly and a quarrelsome hummingbird offered any threat. Maybe she should put out the feeder again. She remembered the enjoyment of watching the graceful little birds from the kitchen window.

This fear of going outside wasn't normal, but so far she hadn't cared. What difference did it make to anyone? Delivery boys brought groceries to her door. She paid for everything by check through the mail. What reason was there to go out into the streets?

She inhaled the heady scent of lilacs. If this turned into a false spring, most of the emerging flowers would die, unable to cope with another snow. Spring had come and gone several times without her, and suddenly she missed them.

"Hey, old fellow. I think I'm going to unfold that lounge chair and catch me some rays." She giggled at the phrase heard on a late show a couple of nights ago. One of those California beach movies, a mindless pleasantry to help pass away the night. Kate watched everything on television, even sitcoms she hated, just to stave off the silence.

Her reflection in the mirror this morning had shocked her. Her hair looked tacked on as an afterthought. Dull and dry, it hung about her face in shreds, like bark stringing from a dying tree. Her complexion had a sallowness that went with her shapeless duster and the fuzzy slippers. Is this what she had looked like to that police sergeant?

The thought of Sergeant Slater brought a twinge of guilt. Lately she'd slept in starts and fits during the night, working days again. That hadn't happened for years but she felt the need to normalize herself. She'd been going too far over the edge. The truth was she didn't want to see any more little girls on her computer. This wasn't doing her part to help the authorities—she knew that. The sergeant hadn't wanted to believe her. She wasn't sure he *did* believe her, but he'd asked for her help.

His kind made her decidedly nervous. He was probably overbearing, opinionated, and condescending. Strong and honest came to her unbidden and she pushed the thoughts away. She didn't want to like him.

Kate did care what happened to those children. The sergeant said they weren't molested or tortured, which made her feel a little better. But still, they *were* dead, leaving grieving families behind. She knew about grieving. Did it ever end? She vowed to work late all this week to see if the visions returned.

The sudden shrill ring of the telephone startled her. No one ever called. She did most of the work with e-mail and the fax machine. She ran inside to catch it.

"Hello, Mrs. Macklin?"

"Yes, sergeant?"

"I called to see if you were busy tomorrow."

Oh no, he wanted a date. How terrible. She wasn't ready for anything like that, and he would be the last person...

"Why do you ask?" Stall for time until she could think how to let him down gently. He wasn't the sort of man one would care to insult.

"The captain asked me to talk to the parents of the dead children. He mentioned he'd like you to go along."

"Me?" Her voice rose to a squeak and she coughed to get it back down to normal. Relief and disappointment hit her at the same time.

"Yeah. The captain has this idea that you may be able to read between the lines, so to speak. See if anything's going on with the parents that we should know about."

Good Lord, did they think a mother or a father would...

"Well? What do you say?"

He bulldozed over her thoughts. She wasn't used to that.

"I don't go out, sergeant"

"Christ sake, I'm not asking for a date!" His voice was hoarse with indignation.

Well, screw it, I'm not going. Did she say that out loud? She'd never even imagined thinking those words. But now, she'd really like to say them. Out loud.

"Something funny?" his voice held a growl.

"Tell the captain I don't go out," she said and hung up. "I guess we told him, huh, Rasputin." She cradled the big cat in her arms and turned up the volume on the television.

In less than fifteen minutes the doorbell rang. The cat skittered one way and she went toward the door. Looking through the peephole, she recognized him from a visit he paid after they found Annie. He had been very kind, if a bit stuffy. "Oh my. Hello Captain Murphy. Please come in."

"Thank you, Mrs. Macklin."

They sat on opposite couches. He seemed nervous, which made her less so. He resembled a corporate executive, on his way up the ladder of a boring job, not a captain in the busiest police precinct in the city.

"Can I get you anything? Coffee, tea?"

"No. I was on my way home and thought I'd stop by and clarify something."

She waited, making him do all the work.

"Ah...Slater said you refused to go with him tomorrow. Something about you never go outside."

He was wrong about that. She and the cat had been out on the back porch. Once they ventured onto the lawn and yesterday she stepped out on the front porch and waved at a neighbor. At least she supposed it was a neighbor. The woman waved back, anyway.

"I'll level with you, Captain. I have agoraphobia. It's fear of going out of the house. I'm working on it, but—"

"That puts a different light on the subject then, doesn't it? Slater will have to go on his own."

"What do you think my presence might add?"

"I can't say exactly. It's just a hunch that if any of the parents had something to hide, not that we think they do." He held up a hand before she could protest. "It's only that sometimes Slater is kind of...well...heavy-handed. Losing a child is a very difficult subject to broach, even for an investigative officer. I thought you might be of help that way, what with your daughter..." His voice trailed off uncertainly. "You might pick up vibes, so to speak."

Did they still call them vibes? The captain would be the last to know if the word went out of date, she supposed. Kate took a deep breath and began talking so she couldn't change her mind. "I want to help. But the sergeant isn't the most patient man in the world."

"Well, it's his case. He won't like it, but I could tag along if that would make you more comfortable. It might overwhelm the parents, though, to see two cops and a civilian on their doorstep at a time like this."

Kate thought it over. A lot of time had disappeared without her making good use of the passing years. That had been her choice. She couldn't blame anyone. Why had she given up her life? How did that help Mac and Annie? They wouldn't have liked her withdrawing this way. That concept hadn't occurred to her before.

"I want to help. These poor little murdered girls. My God, their families must be going through hell." Annie's memory was always there, just a little beyond her consciousness.

Murphy stood, as if impatient to leave, not wanting her to change her mind. "Slater said he was going about ten. That okay with you?"

"I'll be ready." Kate watched him drive away in his dark gray BMW. A quiet, understated car, like the man driving it. Not like Slater's beat-up old Chevy that spit out exhaust and jerked down the street as if it had a mind of its own.

❧❧❧

Just before midnight, when Kate could no longer sleep, she sat at her computer. The screen fuzzed up again and she leaned on her elbows, this time forcing concentration, pushing away apprehension. A chill entered the room, settling against the back of her neck like someone blowing an icy breath. She refrained from clasping her hands behind her neck, not wanting to give in to the fear.

Rasputin flew out of the front room in a gray blur. She heard his nails slide on the kitchen tile as he made for his hiding place behind the refrigerator.

The whimpering came first. Then big, racking sobs that caused goose bumps to raise on her arms. A breaking heart. No, a broken heart. Then the boy appeared on the screen, sitting on the grass, his head bent over his knees. What happened to make him carry on so? Was this all there was to him? As though fixed in time, forever crying?

Kate fumbled near her keyboard for the card the sergeant had left with her, but stopped. There wasn't that much to call him about. The image would vanish as soon as she left the computer. Watching was like spying on a stranger's personal grief. She reached to switch off the computer, but then she heard the whispering voices singing their sad little song. '*One...two...buckle my shoe.*'

Now she knew what it meant. Behind the boy, in solemn procession, marched little doll-like figures. Closer and closer they came, until she recognized the dead little girls. Their eyes were closed, as if in sleep; their expressions serene and composed.

Kate held her breath, waiting for the boy to look at them. He never did. The images of the boy and the row of children might have existed on different planes in time or space.

There were still four figures. The fourth was no longer faded and distanced from the others, but on the same plane as the first three. In the background, behind the fourth, she could barely make out a shadowy form. The number was going to change—soon.

She dialed Sergeant Slater at home.

His answering machine gave her no satisfaction, but she left the message and turned back to the computer monitor. The picture hadn't vanished this time.

The boy sat on the lawn sobbing. *'My name is Bernie— Little Bernie. He calls me that. We can't let him know you can see us. He'd...he'd have to kill you.'*

Kate sucked in her breath. Was he talking to her? Did she actually hear a voice or was it inside her head? "Who? Who would have to kill me? Why?"

His cries gradually died away and the boy looked directly at her. *'He takes care of the girls. He fixes it so they'll go live with Jesus. He says if they aren't pure...they can't go.'*

"Who are you talking about? Do you know who kills the little girls?"

'I gotta show you something. Promise not to never tell.'

"I'm not sure I can promise that. Not if you know who is responsible for killing the children." Later she could never be sure if she spoke out loud or thought the words.

'You gotta promise. If you tell anyone about me, I'll leave and won't come back.'

Kate nodded her promise, secure that she could find a way around the promise if she had to. She crossed her heart as she used to do with Annie.

The screen cleared and Kate was inside the boy, walking in his shoes, using his eyes to see a scabby old tenement row house looming in front of them, ugly and narrow. When she walked up the stairs, still looking through the boy's eyes, she smelled ancient odors of cabbage and garlic embedded in the walls. His steps began to drag, hers inside of his, slower and slower. As they passed one closed door, she recognized an old rock and roll tune. Good Lord, she hadn't heard the Shirelles in light years. Behind another door, a baby cried fretfully, in harmony with the monotonous squeaking of a rocking chair.

There was a newspaper leaning against one doorway. She tried to see the blaring headlines, but the boy passed by quickly. *LYNDON BAINES JOHNSON, 36TH PRESIDENT OF U.S.* Kate got that much, but that didn't make sense.

Bernie hesitated at a door, obviously not wanting to enter. The sounds of slamming pots and shouting struck him like a blow. Kate could feel his pain and fear bursting through his bloodstream with every explosion of his heartbeat. He waited a moment for the sounds inside to fade. Then he straightened his narrow shoulders and, taking a deep breath, opened the door.

"About time you got home. I need you around here. Your father's in another one of his tempers, drinking again. Stay out of his way if you know what's good for you. And get two glasses of milk out for the girls."

The boy looked at the disheveled, pale woman—his mother. She was trying to fix food for the twins. Her movements were repetitive, agitated. The boy had heard the neighbors whisper about her "female problems," but he couldn't figure out what they meant, and there was no one to ask. All Bernie knew was she had changed so much over the past months she was almost a stranger.

Bernie wanted to help with the housework as much as he dared, but if his father caught him at it he whipped him with the belt, taunting him with ugly names. He wanted the boy to quit school, come down to the docks and work alongside him. "You don't need that sissy school stuff. I never had it and look at me, I'm okay," he always insisted.

"Ah, there you are." The man entered the room— Bernie never called him Father, not even in his thoughts— just him or he, or the man. He usually smelled sour, like a washrag that wasn't rinsed out. The twins were by his side as usual, like two delicate bookends holding up a mountain.

Bernie looked at his sisters with so much love in his heart, he felt near to bursting. Love and fear and shame. They had just turned five a couple of weeks past. Like peas in a pod they were, except for the one different shoe it pleased their father to make them wear so he could tell them apart. He assigned them a different left shoe every day. He issued it like a sergeant outfitting troops.

Bernie thought it disgusting and weird.

But then, everything about the man was weird—and disgusting. God, how he hated him and his mother, too, for being so weak. All the time guilt ate at him for his hatred. Honor thy father and mother, didn't the Bible command that?

Bernie hated the way the man taught the girls to help make his boilermakers every night. It was a big joke to him. He set out the heavy glass mug, filled it part way with beer and the girls took turns dropping a shot glass of whiskey in the mug, their pale little faces solemn, as if they'd done something important.

Every night Bernie went to sleep with the same nightmare tormenting him—of the scene he had witnessed. He hated nights, but days were not much better. The only respite was school and he didn't even like that. His shabby clothes and shy manner kept him in constant discord with his schoolmates.

The stutter when he became frightened or nervous didn't help him to blend in with his classmates, either. The bullies never let up, but he took everything they poured on him with stoical silence. From Bernie's experience with his father, he knew fighting back would only prolong the misery.

The scene ran over and over in his brain, and he wondered how he could have stopped it. Someone smarter and stronger than he could have stopped it. The pall of guilt and impotent rage never let up.

Bernie had come home early one morning, dismissed from school because of an upset stomach. The apartment was quiet for once, the radio wasn't blaring out his mother's soap operas. The door to his parents' room was ajar. His mother lay stretched out on the bed, asleep or doped up with those little white pills the doctor gave her for pain.

He tiptoed to the room he shared with the girls, hoping they were napping and would stay that way so he could lie down for a while. He felt so tired.

As he pushed against the door, he stepped back in shock, the skin crawling on the nape of his neck. He felt the acrid sourness of vomit rising in the back of his throat.

There on his bed lay his father, grossly naked, black hair on his body standing out starkly against the pasty white of his skin.

Bernie's mouth opened in protest, a protest he was never able to utter. Although the boy was frozen in space for a brief time, Kate felt every ounce of his agony. The man pressed one of the twins close to his side, her blonde head underneath his hairy armpit. The little girl's face screwed up in a horrible grimace of fear, tears rolled down her cheeks, but she never made a sound.

The man kept whispering, "Don't cry, honey. Daddy don't want to see his little girl cry. Daddy loves you." As close as she could get to the wall, the other twin sat in her rocking chair, clutching a teddy bear, sucking her thumb, eyes closed and waiting. Waiting her turn in resigned silence.

Kate closed her eyes, unable to witness any more. Still Bernie's thoughts ran rampant through her brain. The boy didn't know what to do. It would forever torment him that he hadn't known what to do.

His first feeling was shame. A terrible gut-wrenching shame for his father and for his sisters and for his mother in the very next room, letting this happen. Then he felt rage. He wanted to kill the bastard. Smash his head in, destroy him. But Bernie had been beaten too many times. He knew the crunch of fists pounding into his body, the feel of the belt against his bare back. As much as he wanted to stop the evil, he couldn't. And if he told—who would believe him?

Bernie's hands trembled when he eased the door shut and went outside to sit on the front steps. There weren't even any tears inside him to offer comfort.

༄༄༄

Once outside that terrible house, Kate closed her eyes and with a supreme effort, wrenched herself from inside the boy's head. She pushed away from the computer and ran into the bathroom, kneeling in front of the toilet to vomit bitter bile. Her rubbery legs made her want to lie down, but she gathered the effort from somewhere deep inside herself and stripped off her clothes to step into the shower. The steaming hot water played over her skin until she turned red, and yet she barely felt the heat.

"Oh my God. Oh, my God. Did that really happen?" Kate tried to block out the horrible scene. She never wanted to go inside this boy's head again, feel his anguish and suffering and guilt, feel what he felt. How could she make it stop?

How could one little boy bear all that hatred, that burden of shame? But why had he come to her? It was all mixed up. After toweling off and climbing into her pajamas and robe, she lay exhausted and drained, dozing until Sergeant Slater rang the bell.

CHAPTER 6

D etective Sergeant Slater, ma'am," he said through the door.

"Would you hold on a minute, please? I need to change clothes." Kate sensed his nod, and he turned around to look over the lawn and out into the street.

She rushed to take off her pajamas and slipped into a shift hanging on the rack in the bathroom. At the last moment she thought of something more presentable, but decided it didn't matter all that much.

It was crucial to her sanity to distance herself from that appalling scene she had been made to witness. Her legs threatened to buckle under as she walked back into the living room to open the door.

"What's wrong?" He reached out his hand to steady her. "Better sit down, you don't look so good."

Kate managed a smile of gratitude for his perception. "Thanks. I've just come back from hell."

Looking at this big, self-possessed man, into his open, honest face, her horror gradually ebbed into something bearable. There was no way she could share her experience with him, even if she wanted to, without breaking her promise to the boy. She wouldn't do that.

Not until she had to. Not until she found the connection between him, the killer, and the dead little girls. Kate glanced at Rasputin. The cat had come into the living room as soon as Kate shut off the computer. His eyes were closed. He slept with an equanimity that she envied. How quickly he accepted the detective.

Summoning every bit of reserve strength, Kate motioned Slater inside. In spite of the energy she'd lost on her mind-journey, it would be a relief to talk to someone. How far dare she go? Would the boy know if she told on him? Was he tuned into her mind? He appeared to be, since he called her out to help him. How did he do it? Without her computer, anything psychic came to her only occasionally. Lately, if a person was thinking hard, some of that drifted into her consciousness as it had with the thoughts of the detective when he came to her house the other day. Perhaps that was because she was getting used to her gift.

As close as she could figure, the static electricity of the computer reacted with the psychic energy field surrounding her and formed the picture on the screen. Although that wasn't very scientific, it was the way she thought of it. Who could explain such a thing? It just was.

She shivered, wrapping her arms around herself in an effort to keep away the chill.

For the past two years she hadn't accepted any responsibility, even for her own life. Because she'd heedlessly ignored her psychic powers, her daughter had died. If she'd acted on her premonition, walked those fateful five blocks to meet Annie that night—but she hadn't. Annie was gone from her life, but maybe she had another chance. A chance to help this boy and stop more children from dying.

"Cup of coffee?" she asked, motioning him to take a seat.

He sat in Mac's big recliner, filling it up as Mac had done. "You sure it's no trouble?"

"No. I'm all right, really I am." She walked toward the kitchen, keeping her back straight, knowing he was watching.

"Four sugars, then. After that, we'd better hit the road."

When she came back with their coffee, she sat across from him and wondered how to begin. He knew something was wrong, but he was letting her handle it. For that she felt grateful.

"Sergeant, I saw something last night—early this morning, and it scared me."

Slater looked toward the computer on the desk near the back wall.

The room grew quiet. Only the cat's loud purring disturbed the silence. It was one of the few times Kate had turned off the television in years.

Slater stretched his legs and leaned back into the heavy chair. It had been Mac's favorite and she couldn't bear to throw the ugly thing away. Slater looked right sitting there.

"I don't suppose you'd have another cup of coffee handy?"

She nodded. "Always. I'll get it."

"Let me help." They went back to the kitchen and he put more sugar on the tray.

"You take a lot of sugar in your coffee."

He grinned. "Yep. Only way I learned to tolerate the stuff. I'm not sure I like it yet, but I'm addicted to the energy boost."

I know about that, she thought.

When they settled again in the front room, she skittered away from the reason he was there.

"Do you have children, sergeant?" Surely he'd guess she was stalling. It didn't matter. Just so it worked for a time, to give her a chance to get back to normal.

"A daughter. Michelle. She'll be five soon. Time passes so damn fast." He reached into his wallet and flipped it open to show her the picture of the smiling little blonde girl standing close to a very elegant, lovely woman.

"She's precious. This your wife?" It wasn't the sort of woman she'd have expected Detective Slater to attract. She looked cool, sophisticated, moneyed. The wife must have been at least twenty years younger than him.

"Ah—well—" he cleared his throat.

"You're separated, aren't you? Divorced? It's been hard for you," she said gently.

"Yes, divorced. Did you see that in your crystal computer?"

She laughed. It sounded odd to her ears, so seldom had she heard herself laugh. What a drag she must have been to sweet Annie. Oh, God, she wanted so bad to do it all over.

"No. No crystal computer this time. You sort of have that abandoned look some men get when they lose their mate." The traces of bitterness around his mouth, the wariness in his eyes already told her it was a divorce, and not a pleasant one.

He looked embarrassed by her frankness.

"Please excuse me. I study people. It's sort of a hobby of mine, or was before I quit going outdoors. By the way, Rasputin and I sat outside yesterday afternoon, catching rays in the back yard." She was proud of her ventures and needed to share them with someone.

"Good. There's got to be a first step and then another." He refrained from mentioning today's journey out into the world. "Pretty soon you'll be mall hopping like it was second nature."

"Did your—did your wife enjoy shopping?" Kate didn't know how far to go. He had an open face but still, she sensed an inner core of isolation beyond which he retreated.

"Yeah. It was one of Margaret's hobbies, you could say. An upstairs bedroom was dedicated to her clothes, the ones she sneaked inside."

"Sneaked? Why'd she have to do that, if you don't mind my asking?"

He shrugged. She wondered if he ever played football when he was in high school. He had that rugged masculinity football players have and that slightly askew nose.

"She thought I wouldn't know. When we married, we agreed to live on a cop's salary. She said it would be an adventure. That lasted about three or four months, then the honeymoon was over. When she got pregnant with

Michelle, her fantasy was done. Reality is the pits to face when you've never had to."

Kate felt as if he wanted to talk about his ex-wife. That was fine with her. She needed time to distance herself from her emotional upheaval, so she could figure out how much to tell him.

"You don't go out at all?" he asked politely.

"I do—did—like to go to malls, and to the library, I liked to sit on the benches and watch people. At least I used to."

"Shop 'till you drop is the operative phrase. All women like to do that."

"Don't generalize, sergeant," she scolded. "All women never do the same stuff. I guess I'd rather shop for a book than a dress any old time." With that stupid boob tube off, she vowed to get back to reading again. Why had it been so important to stave off the silence all these years? She wanted to inhale the stillness like heady wine.

But the important thing now was to decide how much to tell him. Little Bernie warned her if she told anyone, he wouldn't come back. She couldn't take the chance that he wouldn't know. Not yet, not when there was so much to learn. She felt very strongly that Bernie wasn't the killer, if for no other reason than it would have been physically impossible for the slight boy to have accomplished these murders. But he knew who the killer was.

"Do you want to tell me what you saw?" Slater prompted.

She jumped a little, guilty when his thoughts collided with hers. The cat stretched out a paw to chastise her for jostling him.

"I saw the next little girl in the row. She was more real than she'd been when I saw her before. Her figure came up from the back, from the haze surrounding her." The idea of another dead child was hard to say out loud.

Slater ran his fingers through his thick dark hair. A small cowlick stood up in back.

"Ah...Mrs. Macklin."

"My name's Katharine—or Kate."

"Okay, Kate it is. Then you have to drop the detective bit. My name's Richard. No one calls me that anymore."

"Of course." Odd, she'd wanted to keep everyone distant for so long, it had become habit. Until now.

"I've decided to trust your instincts, or whatever it is you have. So by God, that means he's done another one." Slater leaned toward her, pushing away his cup and grasping her cold hands between his big and warm ones. "Are you sure you don't see anything else? No background? Nothing that would give us a clue as to who or where or how he picks his victims? Jeezus, all this time, and we've no place to start."

Her heart went out to him and his agonized admission. That must have been hard for him to say to an outsider. He pretended to be so gruff and tough, but of course he worried about these children. It had to be more than just a case to him, looking at the babies lying in the cold morgue. He had one of his own.

Slater released her hands and leaned back, swiping a palm across his forehead. "We've gone over and over what little we've been able to learn. There's no pattern. No logic, nothing to grasp onto. Most serial killers form a pattern early on. It's just a matter of fitting the pieces into place, more like cracking a code. This one is different."

"Can I ask what you've got so far, or is that classified information?"

Slater regarded her with a steady gaze. A handsome man in his youth, he'd worn a lot of it off as he moved through life. Yet there was still something about him that impressed her now, in spite of not liking him at first sight.

"I guess it'd be okay to tell you. You've leveled with us when you didn't have to."

She squirmed a little in guilty uneasiness.

"I've narrowed the odds down to race and size. He's probably white, sturdy, disciplined, unremarkable looking—enough to blend and not attract attention. He has to have some appeal, some way to charm these little girls to go with him."

"Do you—do you have any idea why he does it?"

"The captain brought in a police profiler, but even he hasn't come up with an idea as to the motivation yet, unless the killer's just an out and out crazy. That's the worst scenario, because it's impossible to out-think a nutcase who may not even have a motive but acts on some kind of instinct. I'm afraid that's what we're up against."

"But of course one would assume he is insane."

"Sure, insane—it's got to be. But in my line of work, there are degrees of insanity. You might say all serial killers are insane, make a generalization as you accused me of doing before, but still, they operate under certain rigid rules."

"Rules?"

"Rules known only to themselves. If you examine the patterns, most times you can figure out what makes them tick. Why they do it. Sometimes they even beg you to catch them, to stop the killings. They leave clues like you wouldn't believe. But not this one, not so far."

"Is it true he—he doesn't molest the children?"

"That's the hard part to figure. He takes good care of them, even after he kills them. If he was a former child molester turned killer, we'd get his previous record out of the national computer."

Kate was impressed. She'd put Slater down as one of those dense authority figures—big, dumb and arrogant— but he continued to surprise her more every minute.

Slater began to cite the statistics that gave them a tentative profile of the killer then went on to explain how they reached the other conclusions. "He has to be strong and agile—able to carry the victims from his car to the drop sites. We never found any tire tracks, so he parked a distance away each time. He has to be disciplined to sit for hours watching and waiting, selecting his victims."

Her guilt at holding back information lightened a bit, knowing Little Bernie could not physically accomplish these murders. But the detective's next words brought the guilt right back to her.

"He has to be appealing in some way to these children, or he couldn't coax them to come with him."

That sounded somewhat like the boy. She patted her cat and he nestled into her side, purring. It couldn't have been Bernie killing those children. He was just a child himself, a defenseless, pathetic little creature who had been crushed by the world, crushed beyond recovery.

"Ah—there is one more thing," she said.

His sardonic look told her he had been waiting for something else.

"He's going to put the next body..." She closed her eyes and took a deep breath then continued. "...in an abandoned warehouse somewhere downtown. I couldn't tell what streets or what kind of warehouse."

"You saw that?"

She wriggled uncomfortably, unable to look into his eyes. "No, not exactly. I—it's hard for me to sort it out, much less explain to someone how the visions come to me. A flash of the idea actually came to me just now, while we are talking, to tell you the truth."

"Uh huh," Slater said, his voice skeptical. He stood to go, his smile casual, his eyes wary. She knew he wasn't ready to trust her completely.

"Well, Mrs. Macklin—ah, Kate, I guess we'd better leave."

"I don't think I can go out there. Talk to those people...no, I don't want to." She walked to the window, looking out.

So much world out there...so dangerous. So safe inside.

He came up behind her, keeping his distance, as if afraid of intimidating her. "We need you." He spoke simply. "The captain thinks you can find out if any of the parents know more than they're letting on. At this point everyone is a suspect, but it goes beyond that. The parents may even have seen the killer at some point. He had to be stalking some of his victims."

"Oh, for God's sake! Captain Murphy thinks there's a possibility that one of the parents killed his child for insurance or something like that, and then killed the others to cover up? That's just not true! What kind of inhuman person would do such a thing?"

Slater's eyes narrowed. "Did the captain tell you that?" His voice was hard-edged, his police voice.

Kate wiped her hand over her face in a weary gesture. "No, I don't think so. I don't know where I got the idea, but it's crazy."

He touched her elbow, barely. "Please Kate. Let us be the judge of that. There has to be some link between these children, some common ground to help us figure out how and why he picks the victims. That would be a start. I promise I'll bring you home if you can't finish it."

"Then I'll have to change. I don't suppose the latest style is fuzzy slippers and a housedress." She managed to laugh at herself, not daring to look at what might be pity in his eyes.

When she came out, he grinned in approval. "Hey, that's quite a switch. You look real nice."

She mentally reviewed her A-line dress with a challis print, topped with a chenille jacket. Not so bad, the colors were good for her, but she must be hopelessly out of date according to the TV and magazines. Maybe she'd get a mail order catalog and look through it, find some nice things to wear. Or she could order from the web too. The idea of caring what she wore was so unusual, that it made her feel suddenly adventurous and strong. "I'm ready, sergeant. Behave yourself, Rasputin, I'll be back soon." The words had a good sound. She hoped the feeling would last until she returned.

CHAPTER 7

S later took Kate's arm when they stepped off the porch. Maybe the neighbors watched. She hoped so, since they had never seen her step out with anyone. The car in the driveway was a newer model than the one she saw previously, which surprised her.

When he reached across her lap to make sure she was buckled in properly, she took a deep breath. His sudden closeness nearly made her forget her terror of being outside.

"Do you have two cars?" she asked, to still her heart's silly runaway beating.

"Nah. This belongs to the department. You wouldn't want to ride in my old jalopy. But I'm comfortable with the heap, like an old friend. Margaret accused me of keeping it around just to annoy her." He laughed, a good strong sound that made Kate want to laugh too.

It was a brilliant Saturday morning. Kate hid behind dark glasses and a floppy hat until the feeling of exposure began to lessen gradually and she could take off the hat. It helped being insulated inside the car.

"You okay?" he asked a few blocks down the street.

She nodded, gulping the fresh air as it came rushing in through the window.

"You can roll the window up, if you're afraid of blowing your hairdo."

She snorted. As usual, she'd fixed her hair back at the nape of her neck with a barrette. Why would he think it would blow?

"Say, that's quite a look, suits you," Slater said.

She giggled. "You mean the hat? And sunglasses? It just seemed as if I'd have something to hide under if I needed it."

"You make me feel like I'm riding with ah...what's her name...Greta Garbo. Ever catch her on late night TV? Say, those ladies—her and Marlene Deitrich, and Lauren what's her name, they don't make classy dames like that anymore."

Kate turned away to hide her smile. No, indeed they didn't, and there probably weren't many like Richard Slater left either. Men who said "classy dames."

Their first stop was in the city, a nice section where tall condos melted into the skyline that surrounded a large green park. Kate made the concession of leaving her hat behind and tried to stop her arm from trembling as Slater led her up the steps to the front foyer.

Slater had to show his ID to the doorman before he would call to let the couple know they had visitors. How had the killer managed to get the child? The parents had lost their greatest treasure. Kate knew exactly how that felt. A thread of panic found its way up her backbone and she struggled to hold herself tight in place so she wouldn't crumble.

She put her hand on Slater's arm and, by his concerned look, knew he must feel her tremors through his suit jacket. Was it possible for a man to be sympathetic and impatient at the same time? That seemed to be the case with him.

"Buck up, Kate. You can do it. It's too late to go back now."

He'd lied. He said they could quit and return to her house when she chose.

By the time the elevator took them upward, Kate had managed to conquer her fears again by the need to know more about the little girls. To help the police, she must find out all she could.

"Did you call—make an appointment?" she asked.

He shook his head. "Nope. Thought I'd surprise them. Maybe we'll get lucky, if they drop any hint that might tie the children together. A thread, no matter how thin, can unwind the whole ball of yarn."

The door squeezed open with chains holding it in place.

"Mrs. Gardner? Is your husband here?" Slater showed his badge.

"Yes, he's on the phone. Please come in."

It was clear Slater had no idea how to introduce her, so Kate made it easy on him. "Hello. I'm Katharine Macklin, working with the police as a psychologist." She didn't look at Slater, but knew he was frowning. Well, she certainly had studied all of the self-help books in the world. That should qualify her for some kind of title in psychology. She couldn't very well tell the parents she was a psychic, and she didn't look like any policewoman she'd ever seen on TV.

When the husband entered the room he showed outright hostility toward them. "Why isn't the police department doing more? We don't know what's going on."

"I realize that, Mr. Gardner. It's hard to keep everyone up to date. We have every available officer on this."

"Did you call in the FBI?" The wife wanted to know.

Slater shook his head. "No, Ma'am. We've got New York's most competent investigative team—best in the country in fact—right here in our precinct."

"He's a maniac. He needs to be stopped. When can we get our daughter's body so we can lay her to rest?"

Kate looked at the couple and felt her chest tighten with sorrow for their loss. "I am so sorry for you both. I lost a daughter. She was killed by a hit and run. A child shouldn't have to precede a parent in death. May I look at this picture?" At the couple's nod, she picked up a photograph of the family of four and stared at it. No vibes came through. She'd never tried that before but it was worth a chance.

As angry as the father was, the mother affected Kate more with her quiet sobs into a handkerchief, her pale features and red eyes. Their agony made it tough to be here in the same room. It felt as if someone had ripped off the scabs to her own wounds, leaving them open and bleeding again.

Children deserved to be protected and cared for and loved.

A child of perhaps three peeped around a corner and ran to her mother's lap. The woman held her tightly and Kate knew Mrs. Gardner would have a hard time letting her go outside to play any more. This sister to the dead child would have to fight for freedom from now on, challenging her frightened parents at every turn in order to live a normal life.

Kate hadn't been paying attention to Slater, but by the tone of his voice, she knew he was ready to leave. The father had finally calmed down, only his eyes showed the bewildered anger which someday would turn to grief as he shook their hands and let them out of the apartment.

Slater steadied her on the marble steps going down to the car and turned her toward him at the edge of the sidewalk. "That's about all for you."

She took a deep breath, grateful that he knew how much this was costing her. "Did you see how the mother responded with their other child? That poor kid will be a captive in her own home. I'll lay odds they put her in a private school, take her there every day and pick her up afterward. Their lives are shattered."

His look was morose. "I know. That's the toughest part of this. It's like the ripples from a rock thrown into a pond. When the killer finishes with his victims...that's just the beginning for everyone else. Statistics show that a good percent of marriages end in divorce, some turn to suicide, and often spouses disappear and the families never hear from them again."

"How do you stand it on a daily basis?" They continued to move toward the car.

"I don't. Not anymore. That's why I got out of homicide, into robbery. Coping with families is someone else's job, unless we get a hostage situation. But the chief and me, we go back a long ways. I owe him big time. He stood up for me—a lot. He wanted me here, and so I came back."

"You've already been to see the other families, haven't you?"

They climbed in the car. She waited for him to answer.

He sat for a minute, his hands gripping the steering wheel, his knuckles white. "Yeah. I didn't think you'd make it all the way around. It's a mess. One was a single mother, thought her ex had taken the child away as a joke. After she finally called 911, she found out the kid's father was in another state. Guess she blames herself. Tried to slice her wrists, but the neighbors caught her in time."

"Oh, God. The others?"

Slater started the car and pulled into traffic. "One couple has split up. Waited years for a baby, tried all the new pregnancy things people do and finally made it. Now the kid's gone and the marriage didn't make it either."

They lapsed into painful silence. Kate felt a terrible anguish for the devastation of these lives. Why? Why did the killer do it?

Slater echoed her silent thoughts when he finally spoke. "Nothing seems to link the girls together, except their coloring and age. Whoever he is, he's a certified nut case and we don't have a clue how to stop him."

Kate knew thoughts and ideas were swarming through Slater's brain. Thankfully none came through to her.

"I'd better get back to the station. It'll be a long night, waiting for the call—if you're right about the warehouse. I'm ordering every available officer out there looking in the logical places, to see if we can't catch him at it, the dropping, I mean. Wish to Christ we could have stopped him before he picked her up, this little one..." Slater's movement of his powerful shoulders was an admission of facing overwhelming odds and losing out.

Kate touched Slater's arm, sharing his fear for the children. "You'll catch him. I know you will." She didn't know anything of the kind, but she couldn't bear to see him so dejected. "You've got a lot more to go on than you think. He'll make a mistake."

"I hope so."

Slater dropped her off and shook his head at her invitation to come in. Kate was relieved. There was too much going on inside her head to talk to anyone right now. When he drove away, she sank down on the couch and soon fell into a troubled slumber.

As Kate slept—Bernie, the shrine of little shoes and the tormented twin sisters mixed together like a tornado— spinning out of control inside her head.

CDCD

In the car, driving in traffic, Slater thought about the families left behind in the destructive wake of this madman. He'd never had a problem scoping out the slime he dealt with on a daily basis when he worked in homicide, but he couldn't figure this one. The bastard had to have a motive. Not even a small percent of serial killers offed their victims without causing them pain. They typically had an underlying motive, some hate/love attachment to the victim.

When he began a job, he needed to be alone—let all the information and perceptions in his head sift down to where he could touch them with his tongue, feel the bite of it on his back teeth. Like when a spoon touches old fillings.

Thinking of marriage and parenting turned his thoughts to Margaret and Michelle. Michelle—God, how he missed his daughter. Conjuring up her delicate pink face, the soft blonde hair, he could feel the splitting headache start between his eyes. He thought about Kate and how she handled herself today, even though he knew she was scared down to her skivvies. He liked her. She would make someone a good companion and wife if she ever got her act together. He wasn't thinking of himself. He felt too old and washed out to go that route again, ever.

He remembered the feel of the blood stirring in his veins when he went to work each morning in the beginning of his career. This time the feeling was not so much a stirring as sludge moving through a straw.

He knew the time between killings would get shorter.

When he arrived at his driveway, he was surprised. He'd driven home and not to the station, clear across town through the traffic without even realizing it.

CHAPTER 8

S o, the Medical Examiner's made it official. The victims died of carbon monoxide poisoning." Captain Murphy leaned back in his chair, his voice too loud in the early morning. He'd asked to see Slater in his office early.

"Christ on a crutch, what kind of bastard..." Slater looked at his hands, clenching them as if they squeezed the neck of the murderer.

"It's the shits. I don't know how much longer we can keep the details from the media. I've asked the more responsible ones to play it low key—give us some time. Sooner or later it's got to blow. Trouble is, I don't know if I am doing the right thing by keeping a lid on the killings. Suppose that makes it worse? Suppose we could have warned an unsuspecting parent?"

The captain wasn't really talking to him. A feeling of empathy intruded. Slater tried to push it away. He didn't envy Murphy the job. "That kind of thinking just rattles your brain. Most psychos thrive on publicity. The longer we play down the press coverage, the longer we delay a copycat."

"I know, I know. But we're running into dead ends. What about you, hot shot? You're supposed to be the expert."

Slater grimaced. "I told you what Kate—Mrs. Macklin—said about the drop site." He pulled out his note pad and flipped through it. "It's tough. The guy doesn't molest kids, so he's not likely to turn up in the FBI files. The only link in the victims is their race, sex, coloring and..."

"Age," Murphy finished for him. "All are about five years old except the last. She was six. Small for her age, according to the M.E."

"That's something. It shows the killer probably doesn't know the families. He's guessing at the victim's age, but age is an important factor to him."

"The girls come from varied backgrounds, so he's not into any economic connection," Murphy pointed out.

"How in the hell does he grab them without anyone seeing him?"

"Beats me. Most parents are aware of monsters in today's streets. What do you think? Random grabs or is he stalking his victims? What did the parents say?"

Slater didn't need to consult his note pad. He knew the information by heart. "He stalks. Maybe random grabs too. Number One was picked up in front of her yard, playing with her dog while the mother went inside to get them a snack. He grabbed Number Two from a vehicle while the father dashed inside a convenience store for a six pack. Number Three—"

"Hell, Slater, do we have to use numbers?" Murphy broke in.

Slater studied the captain with that familiar calculated stare which never failed to make the recipient damnably uncomfortable. Murphy was no exception.

"It's the way I operate. Learned long time ago not to get personal or the job'll wring you dry."

Has wrung you dry, Murphy wanted to add, but didn't. "Okay, okay, I see the point. It's just so goddamned cold. Like calling the killer the Shoe Man. I hate that."

Slater agreed. "Me too, but you know the guys use nicknames to ease things. It's only in the department."

"It had damn well better not get out. The chief mentioned you're a cool bastard. I see it now."

Slater accepted the chief's remark as a compliment. "That's what it's going to take if—when we bag this one. He's not killing these kids in a frenzy of violence. He's a cold-hearted, dead-souled freak who is methodically eliminating them for a reason."

"And if we find out the why, we'll be closer to the who."

"Right. I'm not into psychiatry or crap like that, but you don't work as a cop a couple of decades without picking up on what's in a perp's head."

"That's what makes a good cop, and why the chief wanted you in on this. So what about Number Three?"

"He got her at playtime in a day care center. Don't ask me how. The attendants are still hysterical at that place and no help when I tried to talk to them. Number four, she..." Slater faltered for a second, struggling to suppress the remembrance of that little body on the cold morgue table—the soft little mouth pursed as if in sleep, the long eyelashes against the pale skin. He shoved the emotions down, displacing them with hardened detachment.

"Number four played with friends in a park, supervised by a few maids gossiping on the bench." He smacked his fist into his open palm in angry frustration. "No one saw a damned thing. Can you beat that? As if an invisible killing machine dropped from nowhere and..."

"Created a parent's worst nightmare," Murphy finished the sentence. "The only reason we've been able to keep a lid on the details so far is the papers think we've given them everything. When it gets out that we've held back—there'll be hell to pay."

"You said it," Slater agreed. "I'm going to re-check each of the grab sites, try to pick up on something the investigators might have missed."

"I can't give you more than forty-eight hour's leeway. The chief agreed. Then, if there are more victims, it'll have to go public with additional details. Just on the off-chance someone witnessed something."

"Not much time. How about this DNA stuff? Any chance of that helping if we catch him?"

The captain shook his head. "Not a chance. No fingerprints, none of the usual semen and saliva deposits. Nothing to go on unless the bastard gets careless."

Slater's tightening lips would never be construed as a smile. "Not likely. He probably uses plastic gloves to move the bodies. No blood, no body fluids, clean kills."

The telephone buzzed, causing them both to jump. "I told them to hold my calls," Murphy growled.

Feeling his scalp begin to crawl over his ears, Slater recognized it as a sure sign bad news was coming.

Murphy picked up the phone, his forehead puckered in annoyance. "Yeah? Yeah? Holy shit!" He slammed down the receiver and turned to the sergeant "She was right. In an alley behind the old factory warehouse on Tenth Street. Better get over there."

Was this a site he'd checked out? Had they missed something?

The killer might be going for a score. A certain magic number of victims and then he'd stop. That's the good news. On the other hand, a situation might have set him off so that he'd never stop on his own. Slater kept his morose thoughts to himself as pushed open the door.

 споса

Murphy sat thinking after Slater left. He needed a more detailed psychological profile before going any further. Murphy wished he could bring in a crew of younger men, but he had to give Slater a chance. Some said Detective Sergeant Slater was burned out, over the hill. Jeeze, is that all a cop had to look forward to after twenty years on the force?

Slater had commendations galore. He'd solved ninety percent of his cases, a higher percentage than any detective before or since. Of course Internal Affairs Division had him on the carpet more than a few times. His file was bulky, for "excessive zeal" in questioning suspects. Nothing ever stuck and IAD left him alone with the passing years.

Murphy knew Slater worked by instinct, gut reaction. Those kind of cops were like saber tooth tigers and mammoths, all but extinct. About time. They were a real pain in the ass with their opinionated single-mindedness, but Chief Jacobson was from the old school too. And he was the boss. Murphy hoped that when City Hall turned up the heat, he could put his own men in charge and get rid of Slater.

He hoped it would be soon.

◈◈◈

After dealing with the body, Slater decided he'd better check the abduction site of number four, the one before this last killing. There was something that nagged at the back of his mind. Murphy had complied with Slater's request not to cordon off the little park with the bright yellow plastic. Instead, plain clothes detectives had roamed nearby, watching the perimeter for days. Sometimes, like arsonists, killers came back to watch proceedings. Nothing came of it.

Slater drove to the upscale area of the city. Condos pushed upward against the sky, each with fancy balconies. Margaret would have been right at home here. He wondered why he thought so suddenly of his ex-wife. Slater was never comfortable moving backward through his memories.

No one ventured near the place where the child was snatched. No children played on the swings, no gaggle of maids pushed baby strollers through the maze of shaded sidewalks. Word got around fast.

The doorman recognized Slater and buzzed the condo. Slater took the elevator upstairs. When the maid peeped out of the cracked door, she recognized him. "Are Mr. and Mrs. Kingston home?" Slater asked.

The maid shook her head. "Mrs. stay with *madre*— Mister work."

Maybe something had come to the maid that she didn't think was important the first time he talked to her.

Slater perched his butt on the edge of a couch that looked very old and very fragile and very expensive. The maid wrung her hands and wiped at her eyes.

"You say you didn't hear screams or the sound of a struggle?" He had a gut feeling about this crime scene. It could be the one that would start the ball of twine unraveling. Maybe the killer had grown a little overconfident. Then there was always the remote possibility that the Shoe Man *wanted* someone to stop him.

The maid spewed off a barrage in Spanish and when he held up his hands, she calmed somewhat and spoke in hesitant English. "I hardly take my eyes off the little one, *quierda mia*. I don't see nothing. We women, alone with *los ninos*. None of us see anyone."

"You didn't see anyone passing by? A man in a uniform like a meter reader or a mailman? How about a man walking a dog?" That could be one way to lure a little girl. But then there would have been dog hairs on the victim's clothing. Forensics would have picked up on that right away.

The maid shook her head, dabbing ineffectually at her reddened eyes. Slater struggled with impatience, feeling time ticking away with every heartbeat. "No car—an unfamiliar vehicle parked over there at the curb?"

She shook her head again. No hesitancy in her answers.

"How about the other children? How many played there?"

The maid screwed up her face in an effort to remember. She ticked the maids' names off on her fingers, counting the children by the maids. "*Seis*. Four *criadas*— maids—and six *ninos*. Two babies, in..." She made a gesture of pushing a carriage.

Slater walked to the balcony and looked over the wrought iron fencing to the grassy, tree-enclosed park below. The killer could have hidden anywhere, lying in the bushes, waiting. Stalking his victim like a jungle animal.

After Slater walked out into the street, he began to check the perimeter of the park again. Squatting down, peering at the ground, he ignored the curious stares of the few passersby. Just where the edge of the park eased off into the noisy beginning of the street, he touched his fingers gingerly to the damp earth.

Knee prints. By God, knee prints and broken branches. Slater felt his heart trip a few extra beats and he leaned back on his heels.

He'd watched the children from up here, selecting his victim from this little promontory at the edge of the park. How many hours, how many days had he observed her? Slater knew the man had carefully selected his prey, isolating her from the other children.

Slater crept gingerly around the site, careful not to disturb a possible shoe print. Something crackled beneath his foot. He stepped back and looked down at the crisp wrapper from one of those huge all-day suckers. He remembered his daughter being crazy about them.

Michelle. As if his nerves weren't strung out to the breaking point with this deadline, Margaret and her—he couldn't say husband even though he was her new husband—Margaret and Vincent had come back from France weeks ago. She hadn't called to let him know until guilt finally moved her.

It was good news, knowing Michelle was back in the U.S. now living just across town, although she was as inaccessible to him as ever, if Margaret's father had his way. Margaret told him her father had pulled strings to get Vincent a fine job here in the states. The old man was good at that. He'd wanted to do that for a certain homicide detective, but Slater had been too stubborn and proud. Besides, being a cop was not just *what* he was—it went deeper than that—it was *who* he was.

Was Michelle in danger because of her age and coloring? He grunted a denial out loud. Now he was growing paranoid. The city was huge. It would be too much of a coincidence. Anyway, Margaret never let their daughter out of sight.

Slater crept closer, seeking more. A week had elapsed but the weather had been cold with no rain and no wind to screw things up. He sniffed the brush, checking for smells that might linger on the damp leaves. Shaving cream, a special soap, the sour smell of a schizo.

He felt the juices flow inside him, the intensity that made him a good homicide detective. It wasn't enough to think like a cop. You had to think like the bad guys. Walk in their shoes. That was what had alarmed Margaret more than anything, he supposed. When he was nose-to-the-ground on a case, he tried to slip inside the skin of a killer. He was getting good at that, maybe too good to suit Margaret.

Slater opened his pocketknife and speared a corner of the candy wrapper, putting it in the evidence bag tucked away in his pocket. He shifted forward to look at the trunk of a tree overhanging the little hill. Measuring by his own height seated, he peered close at the bark for any sign of a hair, a tiny spot of hair dressing or fibers from clothing. He'd need a flashlight and a magnifying glass to check that out. If the guy leaned back against the tree waiting, which would be only natural, he should have left some tell-tale mark behind. Slater flipped open his pad and jotted down notes.

Ready to go, he paused and turned to look down on the empty playground. Yes, this had to be where the man waited and watched.

Now he only needed the who and why.

Later that day Slater checked out the homes of the other children who played in the park with the victim. One child was a red-head, two Hispanics and the blonde girl.

Slater finally had to accept the emerging pattern. It wasn't a good sign.

CHAPTER 9

S later sat in his big chair and looked around the room. He seldom had a chance to kick back with a beer and a moment of quiet. Maybe that was a good thing, because his spare thoughts lately had been turning more and more toward Margaret and Michelle. He'd managed to push his personal problems aside for some months, especially since this psycho killer began. Talking to Kate had dredged it all up again.

It wasn't the first time the division between work and his personal life had blurred together since he married Margaret, but it was the first time since their divorce. He'd thought, with a guilty comfort of freedom, that he'd moved beyond that.

Michelle. She would celebrate her fifth birthday in only a few weeks—without him, if Margaret had her way. Just Margaret and Vincent what's-his-name, a cozy little family. The pressure behind his forehead increased and he forced his thoughts to center on the meeting a month ago with his ex-wife. That meeting had left him with a festering hole in his gut. The worst part was, he had no idea why it should do that to him.

❧❧❧

Margaret had called from her father's mansion in Long Island, saying they were coming for a visit. She had a way of tucking in a secret, just at the edge of her voice so you'd know it was there. It used to tantalize him, now it merely irritated.

Slater ran a towel over the furniture haphazardly, thought of cutting some of her precious roses to stick in a vase then changed his mind. They were probably all dead. He hated this place, shouldn't have let her old man pick it out for their wedding present. He never went into the back garden, damp and gloomy with huge shade trees. Any flowers she'd planted had surely died away by now, choked by waist-high grass. He had no special use for the outdoors, it was just a place to pass through to get somewhere.

Margaret loved her roses. Slater decided at the last minute to rush to the nearest florist, buy a bunch of roses and put them in the big oriental vase in the foyer. Maybe she'd think they were from the back yard. When he came back, he straightened his tie, brushed a hand over his cowlick one more time and waited.

When the shiny silver BMW pulled into the circular drive, he opened the front door and watched Margaret stretch those elegant long legs to get out. It made him feel considerably better to realize that the sight didn't bother him one way or another.

"Richard. So happy that you're looking well."

He hugged her, but she didn't hug back. Instead she stretched to give him a token kiss on the cheek with her lipstick-coated mouth. The hug and kiss reminded him of a soft, limp handshake, the kind he hated to receive. She waved to the darkened windows of the BMW and the rear door opened with a sigh.

Michelle walked toward him—a little lady—with a stranger holding her hand.

Slater frowned and then tried to wipe it away as he greeted his daughter. He bent to lift her and she wrapped her arms about his neck, hugging him with enthusiasm. "I missed you, Daddy," she whispered against his shoulder.

He swallowed past a lump in his throat and held her while he waited for what was coming.

"I'd like to introduce Vincent. You might as well get rid of that frown, Richard." Margaret deliberately flashed a diamond solitaire under his nose. He'd naively given her a set that he could afford on a cop's salary and she had claimed to have "adored them." It was the same as comparing a five-alarm fire to a birthday candle. He should have known she'd never be content living on his wages. How stupid could he have been?

"Are you sure this time?" He studied the tall, thin man at her side. He looked like a damned insurance salesman, for God's sake. As they shook hands politely, Slater caught the snake-swift movement of Vincent's eyes as they acknowledged him and then shut him out.

"Yes, I'm, quite sure. Can we go inside?"

Slater remembered relaxing a little when she avoided remarking on the sadly neglected lawn, although her expression said it all. The little cluck of her tongue let him know she hoped the inside wasn't in such bad condition.

Slater ushered them through the door. "Did you let all the help go?" she asked.

He shrugged. "I didn't want anyone rattling around, waiting on me."

They sat in the living room. It looked reasonably tidy. Slater thought of himself as camping out, although he'd never done that in his life. He'd made the den into a bedroom. He rarely ventured beyond the kitchen into the other rooms or upstairs.

"Vincent, do be a sweet and take Michelle outside for a bit. She has a slide in the back and the swing set's still up in front, but don't let her get mussed." Margaret motioned toward the door.

Vincent looked as if he wanted to say something and then clamped his lips tight under his thin little mustache. So, she was training the new man right from the beginning, something she hadn't been able to do with him.

Before the door closed behind them, Slater spoke. "If you don't want her dirty, better stay in front. The back's full of spiders, snakes, and weeds up the wazoo."

Margaret's pouty lips straightened, a look came over her lovely face as if one of those creatures crawled up her patrician nose. She glared at Slater. "Goddamn it, you let my prize roses die too?" Along with our marriage, her undertone said. "Never mind, darling." She turned to Vincent. "Take her to the car and she can play with her doll."

Michelle turned to stare at her father with a strange, grown up expression, that shocked him.

As if she thought he'd abandoned her.

"Hey, I want to see Michelle. I haven't been with her since—"

"I know, I know," Margaret raised her hand, brushing away his objections with barely-contained irritation. "You can see her later. I need to talk to you now. It's important."

"Go along, sweetheart. You heard your mother. We'll get together later." It was a promise he meant to keep this time.

When Vincent closed the door behind them, an odd apprehension gripped Slater. He didn't have time to analyze his gut feeling before Margaret cut in, dispersing the residue of anxiety with her words. "Pay attention, for God's sake, Richard. For once in your life, listen when I talk to you."

"What's going on, Maggie?" He knew that irritated her. She didn't tolerate nicknames any better than he. Was that trivial thing all they had left in common?

They sat together, a discreet space between them. He felt a remote desire to touch her hand. He used to love those long, slender fingers. She could always dig his heart out with a look if she wanted to. He didn't feel like chancing it by touching her.

"I can put on a pot of coffee, or I may have some left from breakfast."

"No, thank you." Her tone was icily formal as she waved away his offer. The fingers he had loved to look at were notched with rings. Expensive rings. "I suppose you've guessed by now. Vincent and I are—well, he loves me. He wants us to be a family. And I love him." She added this vehemently as if he challenged her.

Slater considered her for a long moment then looked away, his heart in his shoes. She was lost to him, he'd never get her back. "I guess he's just what Daddy wanted for you." He let the sarcasm creep into his words. He had that right, at least.

She flinched but her eyes, so like Michelle's, held steady. "As a matter of fact, yes. Daddy is pleased. Vincent is considerate and kind. He talks to me. What's even more miraculous, he *listens*."

He's everything you never were, her words implied.

"His career as a translator at the Paris embassy is never more dangerous than an occasional misinterpretation." Her lips turned up in smug amusement at the inside joke that sounded as if she repeated it often. "His job is prestigious, his home is fabulous, he loves us, I adore him. What more is there?"

What more indeed. Slater could see them in their elegant apartment overlooking the Seine, no doubt. Vincent would come home every day at the same time. Margaret could entertain with expensive china, white tablecloth—the whole schmere. All the things she craved from life, but hadn't known with him.

In spite of his bruised heart and ego, the loneliness that crowded in on him at times, he wasn't sorry they'd had those few happy years together. And Michelle came out of that marriage.

Slater remembered pushing desperately at the familiar headache threatening behind his eyes. "I wish I could be a good loser—to congratulate you. I wish I could be more like your crowd, cool, polite—so we could remain friends, but hell, that's part of the problem. We never were friends, were we?" He touched his hand to her knee. "If we can't ever be a couple, I want the best for you. We shouldn't have tried it together."

Her expression softened, like the old Margaret he'd loved. "Richard, I swear to God I'm not sorry we married. We had our moments, the first years with you were..." Her strident tones oozed away, her lemon-sucking expression eased. He knew she was remembering. "It's just that reality finally hit on your last trip to the hospital. Why do you always have to play hero? Let someone else go first once in a while."

"We've been over that a hundred times. It's my job. What I get paid to do."

"No, it's more than that. You know better. It wasn't only the shootouts. I couldn't take the hours of neglect, of not seeing you for days at a time while you were on a stakeout. Of hosting dinner parties alone. Then the worry of when that call would come from the hospital or the obligatory two officers at the door to tell me the really bad news." She shook her head so the fine-spun honey blonde hair fell across her cheek.

He'd enjoyed brushing her hair. She used to giggle at his clumsy, gentle hands with the brush. "Hell, our fights were mostly about money. I wanted my wife to spend mine—not Daddy's. How stupid of me."

"Forget it, Richard. What's the use of beating those old bushes again?"

"And Michelle? What about our daughter?"

Her eyes flashed anger for the first time. "I love the way you say 'our daughter.' Why the hell are you so concerned at this late date? You weren't a real father, it isn't in you. I knew you cared, cared a lot, but I doubt the child ever did. Just because you had such a shitty childhood you can't even remember it—that's no reason. When did you ever hold her on your lap or cuddle her?"

"I did. When she was a baby I—"

"Oh yes, I remember so well, that's what hurt both of us. As soon as she began to walk, you turned into Mr. Cold. What happened? Be honest. Did you so badly need a son?"

He gazed down at his shoes, wishing he'd polished them. She always looked at people's shoes in judgment of the entire person. Learned that from her father, probably.

"Lord no. Michelle is a perfect child, like the little blonde angel on top of a Christmas tree. It just seemed as if she—she grew up so fast."

"Grew up? For God's sake, she's not even five yet. Has all that ugliness you deal with finally rubbed off—made the future so hopeless? Or were you just afraid of being a teensy bit human? A father's allowed to be mortal instead of that robocop identity you've taken on over the years."

Robocop, that hurt. His first reaction was anger but he counted to ten then another ten before he spoke.

"Okay, okay, we could go on fencing like this all day, but let's call a truce. When do I get to see her? Maybe there's an outside chance she and I can become friends as she grows older."

Margaret held her hands together as if to keep from showing her agitation. "I wish it were that simple. We'll be in Paris, you'll be here." She shrugged, a European shrug, if he ever saw one. No doubt she practiced in front of a mirror.

"Daddy wanted to pull strings to get Vincent a job here in the city, but he had a contract to fulfill in France. I promised Mums and Daddy that I'd visit New York on Christmas and their birthdays, maybe a few other holidays. I guess that will have to do for you too. Unless you care to fly over and see her in Paris. You're more than welcome."

Liar. She knew he couldn't afford it, nor would he take time from his work even though he could have. He was close to retiring. He curled his hand in a ball, fighting the desire to slap her lovely, smug face. "I'll contest it. No judge would yank a father's visiting rights."

"No one's yanking *anything* from you." Her voice tensed and revved into high gear, as it always did when her patience wore thin, when her attention span ended. "We both agreed to this divorce. It was supposed to be friendly. I didn't move away and take Michelle on my own. We both wanted it that way."

Margaret sounded as if she'd rehearsed those points over several times before she met with him today.

"Friendly?" Slater shook his head. "There's not a damn thing friendly about our marriage or our divorce, don't kid yourself. Or try to bullshit me."

Her lips tightened. "You know my father plays golf with most of the judges in the state. Can you match any two-bit lawyer a cop's salary could buy against the attorneys from Daddy's corporation?"

Slater looked out the window. The grass *was* brown. The only green things growing were probably weeds, her flowers long since gone. He regretted allowing this beautiful home to deteriorate, but he didn't have time for it. He should have moved out—given it back to her old man, but

stubborn pride held him. It was *her* home too. She was the
one who left it. Had he thought she might come back if he
stayed?

Margaret stood, clutching her purse as if to steady her
hands. He got to his feet, feeling heavy, used up.

"I don't want to hurt you." She moved close, touching
his arm. As she looked up at him, all his bitter anger
dissolved. He only wanted to lean down and bury his face
in that glorious hair tumbling in waves of fragrance around
her shoulders.

She pulled away. She had seen the look of banked
passion in his eyes.

Her voice was cool. "That's all we had, you know. We
had great sex but in the end, that's all we had. No
friendship, no mutual respect, nothing to base a
relationship on."

"You're talking like your shrink. You can't deny we
had a good thing going."

"We can't talk. Now any more than before." She
gathered her coat from the arm of the couch with
unmistakable finality. As if Vincent read her thoughts, he
opened the door with Michelle in tow.

"Are we ready to leave now, my dear?" His voice was
softly sibilant with an accent Margaret predictably would
find irresistible.

Slater didn't like the way the man held Michelle's hand.

Seeing Michelle, flushed from playing, her curls tangled
with dry leaves she must have picked up from the swing set
in the front yard, made Slater's heart clench in his chest at
the idea of losing her, losing his family. A thin layer of dust
clung to the back of her coat. Her shiny shoes looked

scuffed. Her mother glared at Vincent but made no comment. Beckoning to his daughter, Slater knelt in front of her. "You're gonna be happy, honey. I'll miss you but Mommy says you can come visit me."

Michelle smiled a wobbly, brave smile—wide gray eyes filled with innocent trust. Margaret must have had such a look once upon a time, long before he met her.

"I'll miss you, too, Daddy." Her voice quivered just a trifle as she turned to her mother, ignoring Vincent. "Why can't I stay here? I could live some days with Daddy and some with Grandfather."

Slater hugged her close, wishing to God he'd done it more often. He felt her heart beat a mile a minute under her coat. The poor kid was agitated to the point of hysteria. He lifted her chin with his forefinger and looked in her eyes. "Sweetheart, is something wrong? Something you don't like? You can tell Daddy. I'd like to talk to her alone for a second." He directed the statement at Margaret, ignoring Vincent's obvious irritation.

Michelle slid a glance at Vincent standing close with his hands on his hips. He resembled a cat that ate the canary and had swallowed the feathers for evidence.

"She's a little high strung, like her mother. Thoroughbreds, both of them." As Vincent spoke, his accent strung together the words of triumphant possessiveness. "We must leave soon, my dear." He looked at his watch—a Rolex, of course. "Your parents expect us for dinner, then we fly to Paris. My leave of absence will be over all too soon." He smiled ingratiatingly in the direction of Margaret but turned back to look at Michelle.

Shivers of alarm rippled over the hairs of Slater's arm. The headache began to pull the top of his head tight, his eye sockets felt empty. He fought it off.

"Baby, don't be a ninny. Your father can't take care of you, even if he wanted you to stay here with him. Richard, we don't have time for this right now. I'll bring her to you soon." Margaret interrupted impatiently, glaring at Slater as if he'd caused the entire disturbance.

Slater clenched his fists, trying to quell the rage welling up inside, threatening to explode. If he lost his temper, he'd lose everything. He sensed that Margaret would be even more vengeful if he embarrassed her in front of her lover. He might never see his daughter then.

He rose, lifting Michelle close, wiping her tears. Every tear that touched his skin turned to acid, biting his flesh. "Mommy promises to bring you to visit, honey. Soon you'll be a big girl. You can live where you want to." At her age, the notion was devoid of meaning, an adult's transparent attempt to push her away. He cursed himself for the lost time, the passing months when he was too wrapped up in work to see that his family had fallen apart.

Slater watched the three of them walk away. Michelle did not turn to look at him. He could feel the soft tears on his fingertips and suspected the struggle within her to hold back more tears.

The thought of a man touching his daughter, abusing her innocence—no, he was going off the deep end with jealousy and anger. It was this godawful case he was working on that made him see things crazy.

෴

Slater shook himself from the past, moving away from his memories. The present crisis demanded all of his attention and focus. That first and last visit with Margaret and Vincent had been over a month ago. They were married by now, a new family. Why couldn't he get past it?

His splitting headache told him reliving it didn't help a bit. He would heat a cup of left-over coffee in the microwave and then he had to get back to work.

Slater's thoughts turned to Kate. It always consoled him to know she had as many problems as he, maybe more, but she dealt with them one by one. Quite a woman, Kate was, even though his first image of her had been entirely different.

He drank the coffee, straightened his tie and pulled on a jacket, locking the door as he left. He tromped down on the accelerator, anxious now to get back to the precinct and get on with his job.

CHAPTER 10

CHILD KILLER CLAIMS ANOTHER VICTIM! The morning headlines leaped out at Slater when he opened the paper and spread it on the counter top.

Murphy must be freaked. They'd hoped the newspapers wouldn't put it all together until they had a clue as to who, how, or why this was happening in their city.

The thought of what this could do to the case made Slater queasy, and he forced down the dry toast with sugared coffee. If the killer was a news fanatic, it could push him to more killings. It could foster copycat killers.

As soon as the phone rang, he knew who it was. "Get your ass down here, Slater. We just ran out of time."

"Be there in ten minutes." He lived far enough out in the suburbs to take at least twenty minutes to get to the station but with the siren and blinking lights he could shave off ten minutes easily.

The large room buzzed as Slater entered the station. Reporters and television cameras stood three deep in front of the captain's door. Slater took a sharp right to a dinky little closet office in a corner, the captain's hideout. Some called it the Ready Room.

"Christ, man, shut that damn door." Murphy and several detectives sat in the windowless room, blank faced—waiting.

"You gotta face it sooner or later," Slater commented.

"Thanks. I know. But later is better. We have to get organized on what to let out."

"Think the M.E.'s office will leak about the Shoe Man leaving only one shoe?" one officer asked.

"For Christsake, enough with the Shoe Man," Murphy gritted between clenched teeth. "If that name gets out I will personally track down the leak and see that..." Words failed him for once, and everyone sighed, as if relieved for small favors. "We keep that missing shoe thing inside the department. The parents aren't even aware of it. We let them assume both were missing. It's not much of an edge, but it'll prevent us from going off on tangents with all the sickos who are going to turn themselves in and confess to the killings."

Slater agreed, without mentioning it had been his idea to begin with. Any kind of margin could only help right now. "Anyone could've put two and two together and come up with the serial killer idea. If a reporter interviewed all the parents, well, it doesn't leave much to the imagination to see that they could add it up without our help."

"Yeah, right. So I'll have to go out there and set them straight before they get it mixed up," Murphy said. He pointed his finger at the detectives around him, stopping with Slater. "I want this to take precedence over any of your other cases. Slater's the one you match findings with."

"You saying Slater's in charge?"

"Ah, hell, Kolaski, zip it up. Don't put words in my mouth. I'm just saying rather than run to me for every little breakthrough—and there'd better be some—just get with the sergeant and he'll correlate the findings and we'll go over it together. You can use this room, it already has a map of the city and a blackboard. You'll need them. I've got to go face the bottom feeders." He raised his shoulders, and sucking in his gut, closed the door firmly behind him.

Slater didn't know them all, some were newcomers, transferred from other districts. He walked to the front of the room to the map on the wall and stuck the blue tacks in place. "These are the abduction sites. As you can see, there isn't much of a pattern. At least not that we can make out yet." He reached down and took a handful of red tacks. "Here are the body drops. But if you notice—both sites are separate—as if he wanted to keep them apart yet in the same general area. Between the two sites is where we want to concentrate. His comfort zone."

They studied the large city map. The five red pins stuck out like drops of blood.

One of the rookies had a frown like a basset hound. He was sure to have some dumb question or a statement to make, afraid to say it out loud yet. Slater swallowed his sigh and continued. "The comfort zone is typically in the area of the serial killer's home or business—somewhere he feels secure—familiar. That's his operating arena. We have to zero in on it, spread out and ask questions."

He moved to the blackboard and wrote in quick, choppy strokes.

1. Why this particular weapon of death, carbon monoxide?
2. Why select these particular victims, five-year-old blonde girls?
3. How does he lure them—and without witnesses?

"Questions, questions, ask yourself questions. You've got to get inside the killer's head."

"Sarge, about question Number One. Could he use this as a means of killing because it'd be painless? I mean, pills are one thing, but you can never be certain with them. Unless you're a doctor. What if he used too little and the kid woke up or went into a coma? The carbon monoxide is painless and a done deal."

Slater regarded the detective with admiration plain in his expression. "Davis, by God, I think you've put a finger on it. Not that it solves anything right now, but it's part of the puzzle. Thanks."

The detective grinned. Not many officers received compliments from the sarge.

"Think there's gonna be another one?" an officer asked.

Slater nodded. "Sure as tomorrow's coming. This one won't stop killing until he's caught."

"Pick up on any kinda timetable on this?" an officer asked, pointing to the pile of notes and the blackboard. "Like maybe the Shoe Man operates on full moon or low tide or something."

"I don't like nicknames. I know why you do it, and I can't stop you, but it sure as hell trivializes the perp." Jesus, he was sounding like Murphy. He'd better get a grip.

Slater's frown touched each man in turn until he felt them squirm. "Good question, but no. Unfortunately the killer doesn't seem to operate from any timetable that we know about. That's the worst part of this situation. We can't be everywhere."

"We got nothing to go on that maybe sets him off?" a voice came from the back, the speaker a new officer he didn't know.

"Not yet. We don't know where he'll strike again. Maybe while we're sitting on our asses, he's stalking his next victim. He could be taking a goddamned vacation for all we know. We just suck each little clue like a hollow tooth. When he does another one, we got to be on the scene as quick as we can. We could overlook something important—miss a reluctant witness."

The men made sounds of agreement.

"The main thing is, keep it to yourselves about the missing shoe. Sooner or later a bunch of fruitcakes are going to start confessing. Serial killers rarely turn themselves in, but we can't take a chance that he won't try some sick joke on us. We have to weed each of them out."

The detectives began talking together and Slater stood staring at the map. True, these types never gave themselves up, but they were known to offer tantalizing clues, as if they wanted someone to stop them, or to play out their games. It could go either way.

ↄ∕ↄↄ∕ↄ

Slater walked uptown to meet Margaret and Michelle for the first time since their last encounter at the house. His mouth felt dry and his heart pounded like a kid on a first date. This came at a bad time—he couldn't give them his full attention—but he didn't dare let Margaret know. She would zero in with those eyes, screw into his brain and pick up on all his distractions and preoccupations. Never mind the reasons; she'd pull away again, taking Michelle with her.

He hurried, wanting to get there first, but didn't make it. They were waiting in the restaurant.

"Ah, Richard, good to see you." Margaret blew a kiss while sneaking a look at her little diamond watch.

Slater nodded and pulled up a chair. He bent toward Michelle. "How's my favorite girl?" His hand dwarfed his daughter's as she stood on tiptoes to bestow a kiss on his cheek.

"I missed you, Daddy. Missed you lots."

"Me too, sweetheart." He looked over her head at Margaret. "You getting settled in?"

She made a little face. "I guess so. Personally, I prefer Paris, but Vincent is infatuated with America. Can you imagine? He's keeping our place in France, just in case we decide to stay there. We'll figure all that out. Of course Daddy encourages him shamelessly. He'd like to have us next door if he could manage."

Oh, I'm sure he could. For once Slater didn't come back at her with the sarcastic remark on the tip of his tongue. He studied Michelle. At the first mention of Vincent, she withdrew, deep into the little world kids have for their own.

No use asking how they got along as a family. Margaret was a good person and a damn good mother, but her perceptions were skin deep. Funny he'd never noticed that until now.

They talked while Margaret teased her salad and Michelle ate a second helping of ice cream after he persuaded Margaret it wouldn't hurt the kid.

"You still want to see her sometimes?" Margaret asked. "Weekends or holidays or when you have some free time." No mistaking the sarcasm oozing out of every word.

"God, yes." He looked toward his daughter who was sipping her milk and folding her napkin in that prissy way that always made him grin. He knew the look she wore when she pretended not to hear the grownups.

"Yes, I do want to be with her. I've missed her. The only thing is..." He felt like a fool admitting it, but he would be a little uncomfortable alone with her—at least for a while until they got to know each other better. How would he keep her busy, entertain her? She was like a stranger, growing up so fast.

Margaret sat there with that shit-eating grin, one narrow eyebrow up into her hair line almost. "But?"

"Yeah, but," he said belligerently. "You saw the headlines this morning." Not that she ever bothered to read the paper. "It's my case, I'm in charge of it and—"

"Homicide again? I thought you graduated from that."

"Christ on a crutch, woman. These little kids..." he subsided at her warning frown toward Michelle. "They need me."

"I know, Richard, I don't mean to bitch. I don't have anything to say about your life now—except when it comes to Michelle, of course."

"I want to take her shopping for a few hours today, for starters. I can get off a while. I pick my own hours to work. We'll meet you here later."

Margaret looked at him with knowing eyes. "You want to grill her about our home life, don't you?" It didn't seem to bother her.

He managed a grin, embarrassed at her outspokenness in front of Michelle. "Nah. I just might not get much of a chance in the coming weeks and I'd like to try and explain to her."

"Well, don't throw too many gory details at her. She's only a child, remember."

Jeeze, as if he needed reminding.

Slater held Michelle's hand when they walked through the crowds on the sidewalk, shifting his bulk in front at times to protect her. They found a mall where he bought her some toys and a funny looking bear she picked out. Then they sat on a bench inside the mall and watched the birds in an aviary. Away from the dirty, crowded streets, it was like a different world.

"Is everything all right, honey?"

"I guess." She looked down at her feet, dangling.

"Do you like Vincent?" Directness, that was all he knew.

She moved away, and looked up into his face. Those troubled gray eyes, that pouting little pink mouth, God how he loved her. Why wasn't it easy to tell her that?

"No. I don't like him." Her voice was calm and decisive.

His heart skipped a few beats, his mouth dried to cotton. "Michelle, why don't you like Vincent? We've been over this before. You never said."

"He wants to hug and kiss lots. You never did. I don't like it."

He thought a moment, counting to ten. "Honey, some people show affection more than others. You can love someone without a lot of kissing and hugging. But some people don't think so." Was she getting any of this?

"I don't like to hug."

"Maybe I should talk to your mother, explain how you feel."

Her eyes grew wide in panic. "No Daddy! Mommy won't like that."

Slater sat back, alarms going off in his head. Strange how the killings began just when this guy came into their lives. *Oh, come on, jerkface, you just hate him for taking over your family.* He sighed in relief after he stopped to figure it out. The second victim discovered, which was really the first killed, happened before they returned from France. When they came to the house, Margaret had mentioned they would go to Paris so Vincent could check on his work. Slater remembered the day Margaret called, telling him they were back. They had been in the States exactly two weeks, she said.

"We won't talk about it anymore, but if anyone ever touches you in certain places that you know are wrong, you have to tell me or..." He wanted to say tell your mother, but would Margaret believe her? "...tell me. Promise? It's very important."

She nodded. "Promise."

"Do you like it here or in France better?" *Change the subject, go ahead and make yourself more comfortable, you're good at that.*

Her expression lightened and she smiled. "I like both places, Daddy. I had a nanny there. That's a grown person I can play with." Her high pitched childish voice sounded funny coupled with that prim tone she used to explain things to adults.

"Did you enjoy the plane ride?"

"We didn't come on a plane, Mommy doesn't like planes. We rode on a big ship."

"Vincent too?" He didn't seem the sort to enjoy long, leisurely inactivity.

She shook her head. "He came early—to talk to Grandpappa."

Slater's pulse began to throb in his temple and he could feel a headache coming on as danger signals flashed. "Can you remember when he came?"

She frowned. "'Course. He left on Mommy's birthday. Made Mommy mad."

Margaret's birthday. Two weeks before the first killing. Right after he first met Vincent. Slater recalled every nuance of that visit as if it happened yesterday. His headache grew so intense he didn't remember taking Michelle back to Margaret or saying goodbye to them.

Afterward he sat in his chair, thinking. Of all the millions in the city, surely he was mistaken about Vincent. Michelle didn't say this guy had ever touched her inappropriately. Europeans were used to displays of affection. He knew Margaret ate that up. The Margaret he had known would also sense something wrong with her daughter. But she'd changed so much since they were together.

Damnation! He got off on a tangent and it would haunt him until he overcame it. As a cop, he was violating everything he believed in, letting his personal feelings come into a case like this, clouding his judgment. He was wrong. Had to be.

Otherwise Michelle was in terrible danger.

CHAPTER 11

The next morning on the way to the station house, Slater thought about Kate and what she'd claimed to see on her computer. The idea of her hearing the children chanting a nursery rhyme never failed to send goosebumps over his arms. He thought nothing could do that any more. He had a hunch, a very strong hunch, that she was holding back on him. But why? She wanted this bastard caught as much as he did.

Slater rolled into the parking lot and eased into the chief's spot. He knew Chief Jacobson was out of town for a couple of days, but Murphy probably didn't. The captain would look down from his window and see Slater's beat up old car in the spot and throw a fit.

The tension around his eyes eased, if only briefly, while he allowed himself a small grin of satisfaction.

It was five a.m. when he strode toward Murphy's door.

"You're early," was the captain's only comment.

"Yeah. Haven't slept yet."

The captain's eyes narrowed, his bland features hard to read. His words were loud and clear. "How's it coming with Mrs. Macklin?"

"She's a decent sort, not ditzy like I thought in the beginning."

"So? What are you finding out? It's like pulling teeth, damn it."

"I honest to God am convinced she sees something in that damn computer of hers." Maybe now wouldn't be the time to mention she also heard things.

"I'll be surprised and disappointed if the psychics and seers don't come out of the woodwork now that the case is busted wide open."

"She's different. Not one of those publicity grabbers. But she's got problems."

Murphy raised an eyebrow that spoke sentences.

"You know she's agoraphobic." Slater grinned as if ashamed to know a five syllable word. "She's afraid to go outside—"

The captain held up a hand to stop his explanation. "Spare me. I know what agoraphobic means, I'm just surprised that you do. You convinced her to go to the parent's homes, didn't you?"

"We only went to one, but yeah."

"Well, get on with it. Did she give you anything we could use?"

"She hears the victims singing a nursery rhyme."

"Holy shit! You kidding me?"

"'Fraid not. First she sees these children lined up on her computer screen." Slater took a deep breath before continuing. "She hears them chanting the first line of a nursery rhyme. My ex used to sing it to our daughter."

"And?" Murphy prompted impatiently.

Slater remembered the captain was single, never had a family.

"It goes, 'One...two...buckle my shoe,'" Slater whispered the ditty self-consciously in a rough baritone. "She'll know when and where he'll drop this next one, I'd lay odds."

"For God's sake!" Murphy exploded.

"I know, it rattles my brain too. She told us about seeing them wrapped, and the way the killer doesn't want the children exposed to the elements. She told us we found only one shoe for each victim."

"Go on." Murphy leaned back in his chair, almost to the window.

"She knew about us finding a body in the abandoned housing project."

Murphy sat slack-jawed for a long moment. Coming out of it abruptly, he banged the desk with his fist. "Maybe you weren't so far off when you jokingly mentioned that she might be suspect."

"Nah, you're off the track there. She's got nothing to do with it, besides seeing the visions." Slater had started thinking of Kate as a wounded bird; soft, fragile, and easily harmed by rough handling. It disturbed him to realize that vulnerability in another human being didn't annoy him as it should have—would have in the past. Her saving grace as far as he was concerned—she had an inner strength she wasn't even aware of, but he saw it, buried somewhere inside her.

"What then? You thought she might be holding out some information."

"Maybe. Maybe not. But she's trying to help us. She told us about the one dropped in a warehouse district."

"Anything else?"

Slater stalled for time, looking at the walls, at Murphy's credits and trophies. The kind of crap Margaret would've been proud of.

"I'm not sure."

"What's that supposed to mean? You said she's on the level."

"Yeah, I said so, didn't I? Up to a point."

"You think she's holding back? Intentionally?"

Slater turned away to hide his resentment. He was uncomfortable that this upstart could second-guess him so well. Was he that transparent? Margaret used to call him Buddha when he wouldn't talk to her. The inscrutable one.

"I don't know. She comes across as a straight shooter. Could be she doesn't realize she's holding back, but I'd lay odds she is."

"Could we try our hypnotist expert? Maybe he could get something more."

"I already suggested it. She doesn't believe in that, or want anything to do with it."

"She's a psychic and doesn't believe in hypnotism?"

"It's not like she does this for a living or a hobby. She doesn't ask for it to happen—says she hates it. I got the impression it kinda runs in the family."

"Still, if she's keeping something back, I'd watch my butt, this could backfire on you."

What did Murphy care? He'd be relieved to have him off the case. "She's formed a link with this particular case, maybe because of what happened to her daughter, I don't know."

"Jeeze, Slater, you don't have to be so defensive. You were the one who thought she might be tired of watching soaps and wanting some attention."

"I know I did, but hell, I was wrong."

Detective Sargent Richard Slater, admitting he was wrong. He knew Murphy wanted to gloat, but refrained. Slater hadn't slept all night and was strung pretty tight; Murphy had to have guessed he wouldn't take kindly to any razzing. Captain Murphy leaned his elbows on the desk, tented his fingers and rubbed the bridge of his nose. It was a gesture of weariness that moved Slater, even though he fought against it. The captain apparently hadn't been to sleep either.

"Kate—Mrs. Macklin says the killer will drop the next body in an abandoned housing project that the city condemned but didn't demolish yet. That doesn't narrow it down any, we got hundreds of them around, big and small."

Murphy grunted and leaned back in his chair. "It's a start. Let's get on it. I'll get with City Planning to give us a map of the abandoned sites. Meanwhile alert the troops to search all the deserted developments we know about now. You talk to the detectives, have them use their snitches to watch out for a wrapped object. We'll have to let a little more information out so they know what to look for. What the hell else can we do?"

Slater knew there weren't many options left.

෧ඁඁ

When three days went by without a killing, the city breathed a sigh of relief. Tension was thick in the air, as if the residents waited. Murphy only let out the bare essentials. How many victims but not where they were found.

Slater had finally reconciled himself to the idea that he'd overreacted about Vincent. He didn't dare put a tail on Margaret's husband, not without probable cause. Knowing his ex's vindictiveness firsthand, there was also the power of her old man to consider. Her father held a few judges and maybe even cops in his pocket. If Slater was wrong about Vincent, he would never see his daughter again.

He walked toward the kitchen window. The long winter appeared to be ending and buds emerged on barren trees outside his windows. Long bare stems of some kind of foliage poked out green tendrils along its edges. He hated spring. Mushy ground, not cold, not warm, as if the weather couldn't decide what to do. The snow that hid all the dog poop and trash along the streets melted into an obscenity. No, he much preferred winter.

Slater sighed, straightened his tie and made for the door. Fifteen minutes later he pulled into his parking space. Uniformed men nodded when he entered the building. Down the hall, Murphy's door was open, the light on.

He went in and sat in a chair across from Murphy, tempted to put his feet up on the captain's neatly arranged desk top.

"Been interviewing men with records. The sickos weren't exactly cooperative." Slater and the other detectives had questioned dozens of known child molesters. They used arrest records from the city and also drew on NCIC records.

"Hell, Slater, you can't blame them." Murphy leaned back in his chair and put his hands behind his head.

Slater hated that. It was a special attitude, as if he practiced it often.

"They did their time in prison. When something like this comes up involving a child, they get their asses dragged in for questioning. That's a new start for them?"

"A crying shame!" Slater mocked the captain's indignation. "What a crock of bleeding-heart shit. The bastards get a nickel or a dime, five to ten years, as a freaking pervert. Then they're free to do it again."

"Ever hear of rehabilitation? It's what our prison system is supposed to be based on, not punishment."

Slater glared at Murphy. "Is that what they teach you in college now? Or did you come up with that laugh from the academy? In prison, even fellow inmates despise the chicken-hawk. God, how I hate their guts and don't give a damn if someone rousted them every day of the year."

"Well, it's pointless to argue with you," Murphy said. "Most of the men have alibis, some are leading normal appearing lives with new families. None of them have ever killed—at least not that anyone knew about. Nothing came close to matching the Shoe Man's M.O."

Slater stared up at the map on the wall. Blue headed tacks at the snatch sites, red for the drops. Still no pattern emerged.

Murphy cleared his throat to get Slater's attention. "Just talked with the M.E. He says the last one died by the same deal. Carbon monoxide. Didn't know what hit her."

"Let me guess. The stains on her blouse or sweater were from ice cream."

Murphy nodded. "We got to the others nearer the time of death. We almost missed this one."

"Did we? I doubt he'd have let us." Slater flipped his note book cover closed and put it in his pocket. "Did the M.E. say how long she'd been outside?"

Murphy nodded. "Twenty-five hours."

"What about the parents? You check on them personally?"

"Yeah. A big mess. They're divorced. The mother thought the father took the kid out of spite because she wouldn't let him have her after a big fight. She didn't want to make a lot of waves so she waited almost a half a day and when she didn't get a call from her ex, she panicked. He wasn't even in the city, and when she got his answering service, she called us."

Slater moved restlessly. "He snatched her around ten in the morning from her front lawn. Right?"

"That's right. Lots of bushes around the yard, neighbors all working, no one home. Perfect set-up. He had to case it well in advance."

"So from ten a.m. to when he killed her—that's roughly eight, ten hours. What did he do during that time? I need a transcript of the time between death and finding the bodies with the others."

Murphy made a delicate snorting noise. "If you'd let someone show you how to run it down on the computer, you'd save yourself and all of us a little time."

"Ah, hell, I hate those things. I've never been good with machinery, that's why I keep the same old car. If it ain't broke, don't mess with it," Slater said.

"Dinosaur, that's what you are. Your kind went out with John Wayne and—"

"Yeah, I hear you. You're probably right, but before mirandizing and ACLU and all that crap, we got things done, didn't we?"

"I guess you have a point in your own warped way. When the chief wants something done yesterday, he usually calls in the older officers."

"Damned straight. Chief Jackobson always says, 'The suits are so goddamned full of their own importance.'" Slater grinned, knowing Murphy was included.

"This isn't getting us anywhere. I'll order the print-out of what you want. Got any idea where this is leading?" Murphy asked.

Slater shrugged. "Maybe, maybe not. If he killed them right away it would be one thing, but keeping them alive for eight hours—without any signs of force or a struggle— that's off the wall. It could give us the break we need. Someone may have seen them together. Or something suspicious. Like you said, maybe the sonofabitch took them to an ice cream parlor."

"You know, don't you, that we have to release all the pictures of these kids to the news media so we can get the public to help us?"

Slater knew.

He also knew Murphy wanted to call in the FBI, if for nothing else but to soothe the mayor and councilmen who were on his back every hour, on the hour. They had special operators set up just to take the calls, dead-end time wasters so far. Calls from cranks who claimed to be the killer and people who thought they saw suspicious characters in their neighborhood. Problem was, every lead had to be checked out.

"I don't want the feds mucking around here," Slater argued. "They only muddy the water, and they don't share information. I'm tight with the case."

"The chief might insist on the government getting involved. Don't forget he's taking the heat from everyone above him, too."

Slater didn't need to look at the map again—every detail had burned into his memory. "Notice how he concentrates his grabs in the suburbs and unloads the bodies downtown? What do you make of that?"

"I don't think you can make any sense of a nutcase like this one. I know you're supposed to be good at putting yourself in the perp's shoes, but this guy is off the wall, you said so yourself. If you aren't making any headway, I've men who—"

Slater shook his head. "No. I got a feel for this one. So we can't psych him out like a normal person. We know he stalks his victim, the first abduction showed that with the scattering of scuffed stones on the pathway where he walked back and forth." Bastard was smart enough to stay on the path, no footprints there.

"Yeah," Murphy agreed.

Slater continued as if the captain hadn't spoken. "The other was probably watched as he sat in a parked car and at the park, he looked down from that knoll. At the convenience store and the daycare place, one more car on the street would never be noticed."

"And the last?" Murphy asked.

"Now with her, he had no place to park without being obvious, no empty lot with brush to hide behind. How did he get the kid from her front lawn?"

Slater flipped through his notebook. "Let's go over this again, make sure we haven't overlooked what little we've got. So far he's only chosen white kids, which means he's probably white," Slater said, talking mostly to himself.

"Sure. Stats show serial killers generally stay in their own race for their victims."

"He's fairly young—not old—and healthy probably, having to stay alert for hours while he's choosing his prey and waiting for his chance to pounce on her. He's ordinary looking, otherwise someone would have noticed someone like, say, a hippy type or a bum or a weird old geezer hanging around a kid's park and the playground."

"That's not much, but it's a start." Murphy sounded resentfully impressed. "I want you to tell this to the guys in the ready room this morning."

"I'm not finished. He's not a lightweight. The grass was squashed down one place he stepped while he watched his victim. Not a hard enough step to make an impression though. He knew what he was doing." Slater watched Murphy while the younger man toyed with a pen on his desk.

Slater began again just as the captain opened his mouth to speak. "He has to drive a car, even though we haven't isolated any particular treads. He knows what we look for." The bastard might be a weirdo, but Slater reluctantly began to respect his cunning.

"He doesn't want the bodies to go unnoticed, to lay and putrefy. He always puts them where they'll be found." Murphy managed to interject.

"It seems to me this killer is showing an inordinate amount of consideration for his victims—outside the fact that he executes them."

"You're right there. I've been thinking along those lines too. He somehow gets them to come with him—the bodies show no signs of force, not even a bruise on an arm like a child might have if he pulled her along with him."

"He gives them something all kids like to eat, ice cream and cake. Do you suppose he does weird things—like video tapes them naked or something during those eight hours?" Murphy asked.

Slater shook his head in vigorous denial. "No. I'd bet he never touches them after he brings them in—before he disposes of them. Something's yanking this guy's chain. It's like he *has* to do it. I'd lay odds, it's some kind of savior thing. Had a case like that a long time ago."

"Message from God?"

"Yeah, the worst scenario. You can't use logic to find him and speculating why he's doing it will get us zilch. It's a tough call."

"Well, your time as a loner is up. I had to call all the troops in on this, but you're still in charge. I checked with the chief again to make sure. Maybe you'll make Lieutenant if this works out." Murphy didn't bother to hide his annoyance at the idea. "We're doing the ready room tomorrow. Be here early."

"Okay. I'll be here." Slater knew he could've made lieutenant twice over in his career if he'd played ball with the right people. Murphy called it being hard-nosed. That wouldn't be hard to take, to finish out his work as lieutenant. Take a desk job, order the shifts out to duty...ah shit, who was he kidding—it'd be murder.

Why did he need the extra money? The house was paid for. Margaret's old man kept up the taxes with the stipulation that when Slater no longer wanted to live there, he give it back. It wasn't the first time he'd thought of the idea. That was the price for getting out of her life without a fuss. No need to keep a maid or gardener like when he was married, so what good was extra money?

He headed for home, hoping he wouldn't get any more calls.

ভ৩৩

The next morning, Slater, the captain, and a handful of plainclothes detectives sat in the ready room, staring up at the map on the wall. Slater had gone over the details so many times he no longer had to look at the map. It was imprinted on the inside of his closed eyelids and he knew the men felt the same. When he glanced at the map, it was as if the killer was out there, somewhere, laughing at them.

The public was angry. Neighborhood watches sprang up, which in itself was good, but the attitude was "act first, question after."

As if things weren't bad enough, Slater felt this nameless, intangible fear for Michelle. He was reminded of his daughter each time he looked into the face of another dead child.

Everyone stared at him, waiting for him to speak. He had to stop this woolgathering, it was very disconcerting to suddenly arrive in the present when he'd been daydreaming. The stress, the coffee nerves, something was getting to him.

Slater glanced at Murphy who motioned for him to begin. He cleared his throat to quiet the room. "Okay, it's pretty damned sketchy. What we've got here is *probably* a white male, reasonably young and strong, intelligent with some charm, some idea of how to administer a sedative and how to kill painlessly." At a raised hand, he shook his head impatiently.

"We'll have questions later," Murphy interjected.

"We got an invisible man who picks up little girls in front yards and parks in daylight, entertains them for eight hours, kills them, and drops them off so they'll be found. The last drop was more secluded than he bargained for. I'm convinced the anonymous caller knew more than we thought at first. In other words, we're fairly sure the killer wants the children found before they decompose. He could've hidden the bodies in places no one would ever find them."

None of the officers spoke when Slater finished. Several detectives snapped gum, one bounced a pencil eraser off his note pad a few times. It was easy to see they felt uncomfortable. "Okay, shoot with the questions. Anyone?"

"Well, sarge, there's the thing about where he dumps the bodies. It's mostly been downtown, not necessarily in slum areas, but vacant places. The sucker knows this city."

"Good observation. He could have thrown them away in fields, out in the suburbs. One example that comes to mind is construction sites. Or clean fill dumping areas. A small body might go undetected for months, years even. Especially if he didn't insist on wrapping them."

Murphy hit his fist on the desk. "Bottom line it. What does that tell us when all is said and done?"

"It says we're never going to find him. Not until he wants us to."

"Ah, for Chrissake, don't be so damned cheerful, Slater," Murphy objected. "You got a helluva sense of humor, anyone ever tell you that?"

That made Slater think of Margaret and Michelle. His wife always accused him of being humorless. Last time he'd talked to Michelle over the phone, she said Vincent was in France. The note of relief he heard beneath her words made him uneasy all over again, just when he thought he'd settled that issue in his head.

Sometime during this nightmare, he had to take a few hours off—sit with his daughter a while. He needed some island of sanity in the midst of all this.

෨෨෨

The next week a sleek BMW brought Michelle to the little cafe where Slater asked to meet her. The elderly driver got out of his side and opened the door for her as if she were an adult.

As soon as they sat down, she folded her hands primly and took a deep breath. "Daddy, can I come live with you?"

He looked at her across the table in the place where they served the hamburgers and fries she loved to eat— when her mother wasn't looking. Maybe that was most of the appeal, the food wasn't that good.

"Honey, we've been over this a million times. I can't take care of you."

"You could have a nanny too. Then you wouldn't have to always be there."

Is that how it was with Margaret now? What had happened to the devoted mother bit? Probably bored with the idea. Her attention span had never been the greatest. Originally, that had charmed him. Margaret had said Michelle was staying with her grandparents when she occasionally traveled with Vincent to Europe. How occasionally?

"Don't you like living with your grandma and grandpa?" He grinned, knowing Margaret hated those phrases, preferring the European Grandmama and Grandpapa.

Michelle turned away as if she hadn't heard his question. He wanted to hug her close, to protect her always. So pretty, with that blonde hair and wide, innocent eyes. He wished a little girl could stay like that, forever young and pure. He touched his fingers to his temples, feeling the beginning of a headache. Not now, not now.

"Does your head hurt, Daddy? Want me to rub it like Mommy does?"

Did—past tense. "No, thanks, sweetheart. It'll go away. Eat your fries. Like 'em?"

She grinned—his grin. "Yeah! You bet!"

His words too, Margaret must hate that. "How long will your—how long will Vincent be away?" He deliberately brought up the name, needing an opening to start the conversation in that direction.

She looked down at her plate, golden ringlets sweeping over the side of her face, hiding her expression. He took her chin in his hand and lifted it.

"Look at me. Why don't you like him? Is he mean to you?" His voice rose just a little, enough to make the patrons of the restaurant glance in their direction. He lowered his voice, cursing himself for not talking to her in the car or taking her home. Why didn't he want to take her to the house? Too many memories of the good times between the three of them—and the bad, he supposed.

It must be like Margaret said—he was with the underbelly of society so much that he didn't know how decent people acted. Nah, that was a load of crap. Of course he did. It was just that she was growing so fast, he didn't know how to talk to her now. He had missed so much of her childhood. Sometimes they were like polite strangers together.

"Daddy," she patted his hand awkwardly, as if she were the one who offered comfort. "Mommy says you're jealous. Don't be. I guess I like Vincent okay, but he's bossy and likes to hug and stuff. I don't like that."

Course you don't, poor kid. I never did any hugging with you much, did I? "Well, your mother should have told you what was acceptable behavior between you and grown-ups. Did you guys have talks?"

She squirmed in her seat. "In school the teacher tells us—things." She raised her shoulders as if to get the ordeal over. "Like we can't ever let anyone touch us, in private places. And not to go with a stranger, even if he tells us Mommy said it was okay. Stuff like that?"

He nodded, unable to speak. The subject was very personal, very painful for him, he didn't like it a bit. He had to ask. "And? Did anyone ever ah—touch you in those places?"

She folded her napkin primly and scowled at him in that grown-up way. "'Course not, Daddy."

He swallowed past a lump in his throat. He had a choice whether to believe her.

"Mommy says Vincent is coming back next week."

Slater gave in to the headache coming on.

CHAPTER 12

Kate had trouble sleeping for three nights in a row. The next night she took two prescription sleeping pills left from those the doctor had given her after Annie's death. She awoke with a feeling of cotton batting in her skull and a case of the guilts. Running away from responsibility, just like she hid from Mac's and Annie's deaths, wasn't helping.

She grieved for that missed time with her daughter. They had been together, but not together, since they both grieved for Mac. Instead of bringing them closer, it somehow separated them; each held inside her own grief. If only it were possible to live that part of her life over again.

This time the strong feeling of guilt wasn't enough to turn her numb. It was like dancing inside a barbed-wire hula hoop. Painful, but still playing a game. That's what she was doing. Playing at her life, pretending she was really living it.

The next child had been found by now. Could she have prevented the killing?

Little Bernie was the key. Over and over the details of that appalling scene with the father and the twins witnessed through the boy's eyes haunted her as she knew it haunted him. She felt his heart shrivel up inside his skinny little chest as though fear and guilt refused to let it beat.

Somehow she'd had a vision of the past—in the early 60s—she felt that plain enough. And there was that newspaper in the hallway, just delivered. Yet it didn't make sense. Why was the boy going through it now? It was impossible to guess from witnessing the ugliness, tasting the horror, feeling the suffering through the young boy— why she'd been dragged into this.

Bernie had something to say, and he wanted to tell her, but no one else. Somehow he connected with her mind, just as her daughter had, when she needed to tell her mother where the man dumped her so she could be buried next to her father.

Did that mean she'd met the boy somewhere, at sometime, and he clutched at her attention now? She didn't think so. The tie between them was too strong for a casual encounter. He *knew* her. She sensed that very strongly.

Kate walked to the bathroom and took out the sleeping pills. Without pausing, she opened the plastic container and flushed the contents. She lay down on the couch and left the computer on.

That night the sensation of heavy breathing, of feeling the air sucked out of the room, woke her. Heart tripping, she rushed to the desk. She sat in the chair and stared at the vision in the monitor. A man crouched at the side of a house, watching the window from behind a tall hedge. This was distanced, not like when, from behind Little Bernie's eyes, she traveled every step with him. The person she watched would never let anyone see through his eyes. Yet she understood his thoughts as if he'd spoken out loud. She concentrated hard, not wanting to miss a detail.

The home was in an affluent neighborhood, large and rambling. The back yard turf swelled upward gracefully to blend in with the forests behind. He had watched this home off and on for a week, mostly at night. He noted that the little girl's room was off to itself on the bottom floor while the parents slept upstairs. An elderly woman, most likely a housekeeper, stayed with her when the parents went out.

She could feel his heart thudding in his chest, hear his labored breathing. Even though she wasn't traveling in his shoes, she read him as if he'd spoken to her.

He had never taken one from inside a home before. He was beginning to take pride in the challenge of defeating the cops at every turn. Making them look like so much chicken shit.

But that wasn't right, was it? He did this for one reason and one only. Being prideful could get him caught. He saw the way the papers called him a monster. The cops had even given him a nickname, for God's sake. They called him The Shoe Man. That hurt. It degraded what he and the kid were trying to do here. Why did they talk about him that way, as if he enjoyed his work? He didn't have any feelings about it one way or another. It was just something he had to do, to help these little girls past a life of dishonor and pain. He couldn't stop yet, there was so much to do, so many little girls, so many like the twins, waiting to be rescued from their terror.

The man was still out there, doing his terrible things to the little girls.

Kate struggled to get a grip on her powers as electric shocks ran up and down her body. She was seeing the killer. This man standing before her was the killer. He mentioned the twins. He knew what Little Bernie knew.

"Turn around! Turn around!" She needed him to turn, to see his face. Her intense concentration and low whisper broke the thread between them and the screen went blank. Exhausted, Kate lay on the couch and fell into a deep sleep.

When she awoke hours later, it was dark outside. She'd slept without a dream. Pouring a glass of orange juice, she carried it back into the living room and sat at her computer. She had to link back up with that man, the predator who was even now, stalking his next victim.

As soon as Kate faced the computer she knew the connection would come again. Whether it was the children and their nursery rhyme or Little Bernie or this terrifying stranger, she was ready to face the vision head on.

She hadn't seen Sergeant Slater or heard from Captain Murphy for three days. The police must have found the body. Kate closed her eyes and prayed as she entered her bookkeeping program. Most times the visions didn't come to her until she was bored and almost asleep.

⁊⁊⁊

'I have to do it. I have to.'

The voice came strong, breaking into her nod, just as Kate began to doze at the keyboard. She rubbed her eyes, struggling to wake in a hurry.

'The kid didn't want no part of it from the first but I made him see it was right. We have a—a obligation to help these poor girls. He *wanted to help them too, but the little shit didn't have the guts. He never had the guts, he shoulda cold-cocked the old man when he caught him fooling with the twins that day, then it would've been over with. We wouldn't be having to set it all right. The little fucker set the fire to get attention, but he couldn't even do that right.'*

Kate wasn't inside this person's head, looking out his eyes as she had Little Bernie's. This one wasn't talking to her, hadn't acknowledged her presence. What if he knew she watched and listened? Was this the person Little Bernie referred to? The one who would kill her if he knew she watched? The thought was more than she wanted to ponder.

Kate was drawn into a wooded place, to the shrine of shoes.

The man, facing away from her, bent and picked up a red tennis shoe. It fit easily into his palm, so tiny, it barely reached the edge of his fingers. He rubbed some of the dust off, blowing on it gently. *He worried about them fading in the sun, although the sun never seemed to penetrate the gloom of the overgrown brush surrounding the place.*

He set the tennis shoe down carefully, just so, and picked up its neighbor, a tiny white patent leather pump with a blue bow. The strap had a button on one side. He closed his eyes, remembering how the white sock with the embroidered initial on the ruffled edge looked inside the shoe. So tidy, so neat. Should he have saved the socks too? No, too much clutter. It would just clutter up the beauty, the simplicity of his tribute.

From the back, Kate guessed this was a young man. He had broad shoulders but was slim and wiry-looking. He wore a dark blue turtle neck sweater and jeans, frayed and bleached out. Turn around. Turn around. She willed him to turn, needing, yet dreading to see his face. As if in answer to her command, he turned to face her. Shadowy, not clear, a haze surrounded his body. Even so, he looked familiar. He resembled Little Bernie, using some of the same mannerisms. The hair, the jawline, the eyes, seemed so familiar and yet different. It could be his older brother.

Kate recognized him as the man who'd watched the house so intently, stalking his next victim. She didn't like this person. He was street tough, maybe eighteen or so. His eyes were so old, so knowing.

In the background she heard sobs. Little Bernie had come, too. The two were together and yet apart. Neither acknowledged the other at first. Were they brothers then? She saw only Big Bernie and the younger boy stayed back in the shadows, out of sight but not out of sound.

'*I didn't want to do it, he made me,*' Little Bernie whimpered. '*I know what he's doing is right and we have to, but I'll be the one caught. They'll beat me and poke stuff up me and shut me in the closet like the man did.*'

Her throat dry, she reached for a glass of water nearby—carefully as if fearing to break the ties between them. It was hard for her to bear the pain emanating from this boy.

'*That's why we're doing this. Tell the little jerk. So the man can't harm the kids anymore. The little fucker won't get caught. I won't let him.*'

"What did you do?" She willed the big boy to turn and face her and he obeyed. Maybe they could communicate. He seemed more aware of her presence. He ignored her question, as if he didn't hear it. It was as if he spoke out loud to himself, not really speaking to her.

Little Bernie rubbed his eyes and stammered as he answered. *'He finds the girls, picks them out, then I bring them in. They like me, trust me. We gotta make it safe for them, they're better off that way.'*

"Better off dead?" Kate asked.

'Big Bernie says so and I believe him. His name's Bernie too. He's been to prison,' he added proudly.

'Aw, the dumb shit. I told him a thousand times, it wasn't prison, kinda like Boy's Town they called it. Soon's I left the home, I got picked up for shoplifting. Can you beat that? It was his fault.' He pointed derisively at the boy. *'He got scared the last minute.'*

"Tell me why you kill the children. I want to understand." She could feel her voice leave her thoughts but the sound never passed her lips.

The big boy looked thoughtful for a moment then set the shoe down in precisely the place it had rested, within the imprint on the grass. *'We have to.'* He finally directed his speech to her, staring at her through the screen, their eyes connecting.

She shivered. He'd known all along she watched. Remembering the heavy breathing, the air sucked out of the room as she slept, she knew he could reach her any time he chose to.

'The little girls are waiting to be hurt. They're helpless with the man walking around out there.'

"What man is walking around out there?" She spoke softly, fearful of breaking the tenuous thread between them.

'He is. The man. The father. Didn't the little shit tell you how the father got away? The little jerk had balls enough to set the couch on fire while the man slept, but it didn't work. Neighbors called the

cops when they saw smoke. By the time the cops came, the man was gone.'

"What happened to the twins?"

'Goddamn, you know about them? Did the little fucker tell you everything? They took the kids away. They got adopted. We never did, too old and too...ah, shit, who knows?'

"You've killed enough. Stop it. You're not helping."

'A lot you know, bitch. Who called you anyway, I sure as hell didn't. Someone's gotta stop the man. I don't know why people hate us for it. It don't bother me none, but it does Bernie, here. The cops call us The Shoe Man, you know. Isn't that the shits? Here we're doing the world a service and they call us stupid, ugly names, like the man did.'

Kate took a deep breath and let it out slowly. Good Lord, what did she do now? She was in the present with these boys—it was obvious they were doing these things now. She didn't know what to say next. If she spooked them, they might never come back. Obviously they wanted something from her, at least Little Bernie did.

"When will you stop—stop killing the children?"

Little Bernie began sniffling again. Big Bernie's mouth turned down in a grimace, his expression stony—unemotional.

'We can't stop. He didn't hurt the twins till they was five. After that, he never let 'em alone. When he couldn't do his dirty work at the house, he sneaked them out to the park at night. Can you beat that? The kid, here, screwed up royal. He let the bastard get away with it. If I'd a been there, I'd a stuck a shiv in his fat gut and walked all the way around him, bet me.'

Kate heard the younger boy throw himself down on the ground and sob into the earth, as if to become a part of it.

"Stop it! Don't use those ugly words on him! It wasn't his fault." This time she shouted out loud, her voice shrill in the quiet room.

'*Aw, go to hell, bitch. Watch how you talk to me. You and that cop, I know how to get to you. I won't let you stop me.*'

'*Don't make him mad,*' Little Bernie pleaded.

Kate wanted to hold him close, protect him. "I'm not afraid of him. How can he hurt me?"

The older boy's eyes narrowed, his lips turned down in an ugly grimace. '*Oh, hell yes, I can definitely hurt you. Don't think I can't. Lots of ways. I could stop him from talking to you, for one. I don't know how he got away from me long enough to find you. And I know where you live.*'

"You came to me for help too, didn't you?" she challenged.

'*Christ no. It's that little fucker there who wanted someone to hold his hand. He misses his mommy,*' Bernie's voice rose in a mocking falsetto that grated on her nerves.

"What happened to the twins? Did family take them?" She wanted to stall him, maybe something would slip as to where the boys were physically.

Big Bernie shrugged. '*In the orphanage I heard 'em say they got adopted. They didn't want the kid. Maybe it had something to do with the little shit trying to burn the house down with the old man in it.*' He snickered.

The young boy's voice sounded excited. '*I remember! Did he die?*'

Big Bernie didn't speak directly to Little Bernie. It was as if they weren't there at the same time, even though their images were. Big Bernie heard the boy, but addressed his talk to her.

'*Hell no, he botched that job too. But at least it got the welfare looking into us. Don't he remember they took him and the girls away to the orphanage? They didn't know what to do with the kid...thought he was dangerous.*' He laughed again, a deep throaty laugh that sent chills through Kate's body.

"What—what happened to your mother and father?"

Big Bernie turned away, looking back toward the shrine. '*Who cares? They just disappeared. We never went looking for 'em if that's what you mean. When the kid's time was up at the home, he was too scared to leave. Can you beat that? That's when I came along, to help him. First thing I did when we got out was steal a bottle from the corner liquor store and this creep got us caught. Never trusted him since.*'

"Are you his brother?"

'*Hell no, lady. You just don't get it, do you?*' He threw up his hands in resignation, as if he'd wanted her to understand.

She saw it as the first chink in his armor. Leaning back, digesting what she'd heard, so much was going on in her brain she was afraid her head might explode.

'*I don't know why the brat told you about us, but if you tell anyone else, we'll know. You'll pay for it. And I'll never let him out again.*'

His wild laughter blended away and before she could think of an answer, the energy leaked out of her body. Kate awoke to the sound of Rasputin meowing his complaint of hunger. She was hungry too for a change. Her head felt giddy, like it had emptied out during her sleep.

Kate poured a bowl of cereal and milk for herself and gave Rasputin some canned food. He was getting too fat, all this eating and sleeping and staying indoors.

"Maybe we can try the front yard today. What do you think, puss?"

She didn't turn on the television, which she usually did upon awakening. The sound of silence was healing somehow, the same sound she'd feared for so many years.

It was coming together. Would both boys keep their promise not to return if she told? What could she tell anyone? She thought of Captain Murphy. No, she couldn't tell him. Maybe Sergeant Slater—Richard. It would be good to tell him everything, but in the light of day, what she'd witnessed seemed so ethereal, so vague.

Kate accepted the responsibility of Little Bernie's trust and need, making a commitment to help him, and in doing so, end the killing of the little girls.

Otherwise the dying would go on and on.

CHAPTER 13

Hours later Kate sat up abruptly, hearing a loud knocking on the front door. No one ever visited. She'd forced herself to sit at her computer for hours, hoping Little Bernie would return. Her screen remained blank with only the sound of the fan inside the computer and the cat purring at her feet.

"Richard," she said when she opened the door. She wasn't sure if she was glad to see him at that moment. She needed time to digest what she'd seen and heard.

Neither Bernie really told her anything concrete to pass along—except the warning not to tell.

The sergeant looked so tired. Lines of worry had crept into his face, making him look older than his forty plus years. She took his coat and hung it up for him.

"Sit, please. How about some coffee?"

He slumped in Mac's recliner, unusual for him. He was usually marine-sergeant straight, sitting or standing.

"Fine. That'd be fine."

When she returned he had his head back against the chair, his eyes closed. She wanted to smooth the lock of hair away from his forehead, smooth the worry lines. How would it feel to touch her lips to his in a soft gesture of sympathy? He suddenly opened his eyes and she almost dropped the tray. His eyes were cold and implacable, his expression filled with hatred.

His next words, strung out like beads of sorrow with little chunks of hate joining them together, made her impulsive thought of a kiss seem frivolous. "I've got to get him, Kate. This is between me and you, but I'm going to catch that bastard and he's not going to prison. Some shyster lawyer or bleeding heart judge is not going to send him to some funny farm for a few years and let him out to do it all over again."

"Richard, what are you talking about?" She'd never seen this side of him—although in the beginning, she'd sensed an implacable toughness. He couldn't be a cop for twenty years without some frustrated hostility rubbing off on him.

"You should have seen her. Just five-years old, like the others. Blonde hair and..."

His daughter Michelle had blonde hair—she'd seen the picture in his wallet. This case must strike closer to home than he usually let it.

"You found the child I told you about?" She knew it already.

"Yeah. Same deal. You were right on the money about the housing project." He smacked his fist into his palm so that Rasputin jumped straight up, bumping his head on the bottom of the chair. For a moment no one spoke and then they erupted into laughter at the cat's astonished expression. Nerves, raw nerves.

He leaned back and took a swig of coffee. "Ah, Kate, that's good. You're good. Sorry I didn't call first, but I couldn't think of anywhere to go, anyone else I could talk to. I don't know how I'm going to do it, but when I catch up to that bastard, I won't even use my drop gun. I'll put these around his throat and—" He held out his hands and slowly compressed them together and then gave a vicious twist. "—wring his neck like a chicken."

"Richard." Kate sat across from him, close enough to put her hand on his knee, which she did this time with only a momentary reticence. "I feel as bad about these children as you do, but you're sworn to support the law, not to mete out justice. You can't be judge and jury."

"Why not? He is. Anyway, I've decided this is my swan song. I'm going to put in for a desk job the last couple years of my career. I've had it. I feel like a dead fish washed up with the tide. I should have solved this by now."

Emboldened by his cry of desperation, she sat by his side on the arm of the chair, taking hold of his fists, hugging them tight within her own hands. He pulled away for a moment, as if in surprise, then relaxed with a deep sigh, smoothing her hair with clumsy fingers.

"I—I've grown to care about you, Katie. You're important to me."

She smiled at his hesitant confession. "I know. I feel as if we've been friends for years."

"Friends?"

He bent and touched his cheek to her hands, she could feel the slight stubble of his five o'clock shadow scratching her skin and it thrilled her beyond words.

"That's good," he said. "Friends. I haven't had many of those in my life."

He pulled her toward him. Unprotesting, she sat almost in his lap, nestled into his broad shoulder. He smelled manly, with an indefinable combination of stale smoke and aftershave. Turning her chin with his hand, he kissed her, gently at first and then with impatient need. She felt his arousal beneath her legs and squirmed away.

The passion aroused from his kiss was more than she'd expected to feel from a man. She wasn't sure her husband had ever drawn such an extreme desire, such a fierce need out of her. Her heart pounded and her lips were dry, she moved away to stand next to the chair, still holding his hand.

"Richard...I...it's so sudden, this feeling. I don't know what to say."

He released her hand and instead of anger and impatience, his eyes showed only compassion and understanding. "Okay. Let's talk then. Friends'll do for now. I don't have so many that I want to take a chance of losing one." His grin was self-conscious. He leaned back, regarding her with that serious look that intrigued her. The look that said "you are important to me."

She changed the subject for a moment. The emotions inside the room crackled with intensity. "I can't picture you retired, puttering around in a garden or playing bridge at the local adult center."

"You're probably right. I've put in more than twenty years on the force, but me and my kind don't mix with the new breed of cop. The captain calls me a dinosaur."

"Have you thought of doing something else—sort of in the same line? You'd be a good private detective. It's a shame to waste your talents."

"Nah. We make fun of those jokers. Playing at being a real detective. Rent-a-cops."

"Not really. They do some good. Find missing loved ones, locate relatives, that kind of thing. Doesn't have to be sleazy."

"Maybe you and me, we should team up. We'd be unbeatable, me on the street, you on the crystal computer."

They laughed, but she could tell he rolled the idea on the tip of his tongue for a moment, savoring it.

When she had first seen who was at the door, she had been determined to tell him of her visions in spite of both Bernie's threats never to return. Now she hesitated. Something was definitely off-kilter here. What would Richard do about Little Bernie if he found him? She wouldn't care much if he wrung Big Bernie's neck but—no, that wasn't true—of course she'd care. It would mean the end of Richard Slater and all he'd worked for. So many years wasted. He'd be disgraced, put in prison.

And he wasn't just mouthing the words. He meant the threat and would carry the sentence out on this killer without a grain of emotion or compassion.

"Richard, listen to me a moment." She took a good, hard look at him, screwing up her courage. "What if—what if more than one person is involved in—in the killings?"

He pushed out of the chair to stand close, touching a finger under her chin, turning her face so he could look into her eyes. He wanted to kiss her again, and she wanted him to, but not now. Not with the situation that lay between them.

"That's not the way it works. Serial killers don't operate in packs or pairs."

"But what if this one does?"

"Once in a while a pair will go on a killing, and torture spree but that's rare. When that happens they pick victims of their own sex and the crimes usually involve sadism and sexual assault. Nothing like that here. Where'd you come up with such an idea?"

This was the turning point. If she didn't tell him now, how could she later? He'd guess she'd been holding out. It would mean the end of a relationship that was building into something fine, something she didn't want to give up. Yet she promised Little Bernie to keep his secret and the older one had warned her to keep her mouth shut.

Kate was sure the Bernies would know when she told about them. If they stopped coming to her, it would take away her shot at helping to catch them. Just one more vision, she promised herself, and then she would tell everything.

"Okay, say there's one killer then," she said. "If they catch them...if you catch him...what if the courts put him in prison for a very long time. Or a mental hospital. He could be cured of his...his obsession with killing, couldn't he?"

Slater shook his head in denial. "His character is set in a pattern. Pattern is everything to him. He can't change." He began pacing restlessly, looking out the front window, his hands in his pockets, jingling change.

"After the first victim it becomes like a drug—he can't stop. Probably the first one is the hardest, needing the most justification. It's easy to twist facts around to suit. If he goes to prison, he starts all over again when he gets out. And he does get out. No, once this bastard's caught he can't be allowed to live."

The sight of the twins' faces as their father abused them, the agony and helplessness of the watching Bernie had haunted her since she witnessed it. She could understand how the Bernies might come to the conclusion that every child that particular age was being molested by the father. It didn't make sense to a logical, adult mind, but both of the boys' emotions seemed petrified in time by that ugly scene. It was as if they'd never gone beyond that time emotionally.

Was she privileged to receive the visions because she was supposed to help Bernie or the victims, or both? There had to be some way the older boy, the actual killer, could be sacrificed without involving the younger. But then what would happen to Little Bernie without his big brother to watch over him?

Something else bothered her. The time element. It was as if she saw the sixties through Little Bernie's eyes. Flashes of recognition had come to her as he walked through the apartment house. Cars parked out in front in the narrow, trash littered street—big cars with fins and fancy trim. A radio playing in someone's apartment—some song by the Temptations, her favorite group when she was in high school.

Ah, Lord, it was so damned confusing. As much as Kate's pulse had quickened when Slater appeared, she wished now he would leave so she could sort it out.

❦❦❦

The next evening, when Kate sat down at the computer, she tuned in at once to Big Bernie skulking in the hedge again, watching the house. She tried to see a house number, a mailbox, but nothing zoomed into her vision but the crouched figure and the house a short distance away behind the dark hedge. She could tell by the weary set to his shoulders that he'd been there a while.

Suddenly his mind tuned with hers and she heard his thoughts as if he'd been thinking out loud.

'*Have to observe in snatches, that little shit Bernie won't let me come all the time. If I dared leave him alone for longer periods, we could get on with our work a lot faster.*

'*This was easy, so far. Every driveway had two or three new-looking cars. Rich bitches, he curled his lip in contempt. All I have to do is slide down into the seat of my car when anyone approaches and pretend to read the paper. They would take me for a worker, with the shovel and rake sticking out of the back window. He congratulated himself on the idea.*

'*It was a high income neighborhood with commuting fathers, mothers off to their pursuits, older kids at school and younger ones watched by maids or nannies.*

'*He really preferred to snatch the poorer kids. They didn't have anything to begin with and then to suffer abuse and rape on top of it all, well the injustice was too much to pass up. But something about this little girl intrigued him. She was so beautiful, so full of innocence. The first time he saw her, he followed her and her mother home from a shopping trip. One night he watched the father sit the little girl on his knee and talk to her. It looked very innocent, but Bernie knew better.*

'He *planned to snatch the girl at night; worked it out careful like, not to rush it. He'd never get caught, that didn't worry him. He felt invisible, like God must feel. He was doing God's work, after all. The work that God neglected. The papers and television were wrong. That was a load of crap to get more readers. He wasn't some awful monster creating suffering. He was saving those sweet, innocent little girls from a nightmare of abuse and pain.*'

Occasionally he moved his head with a restless twitch, as if feeling someone's presence. Kate held her breath, praying he wouldn't catch on that she was watching him. She had to find a way to stop him from killing this little girl, and that could only happen if she was smarter than him. He was streetwise, but his emotions drove him, which could give her a big advantage.

Bernie studied the people moving about the house for a few minutes and then looked at his watch. '*Time to go. He couldn't keep the little creep quiet for too long at a time. The kid wanted his time to go outside, too. If he had his way, he would shut the little bastard up forever. He was too much trouble to have to put up with.*

'*Anyway, the time wasn't right for this girl yet. Too soon after the last. He even had to get into that computer lady's head and tell her where he left the last one. The cops were so dumb.*

'*He didn't understand how or why the kid contacted her, but he could make it work to their advantage if he was careful. He put the precious one in plain sight so they would find her. He didn't want to think of her innocent little body all chewed up by rats and bugs.*

'*No, he wouldn't do anything yet. There was time to rescue this one later.*'

At the last moment, just before Kate sensed the screen was going blank, Bernie turned and looked straight at her.

Even though his features still were not clear like Little Bernie's, those dark eyes portrayed such a malignant regard. It was as if he knew she'd been watching him.

That's when Kate knew she wasn't safe either. He could come for her any time he wanted to, any time he felt threatened.

He knew where she was.

CHAPTER 14

When the call came from Murphy, Slater wasn't surprised.

"It's another one, sergeant. Meet the men at Fifth and Borden. I'm going out to talk to the parents myself this time."

"You know who they are? So soon?"

He could feel Murphy's sigh before he heard it.

"Yeah. The mother turned in a 207 but when the investigators went to the home, she reneged—said her daughter wasn't kidnapped after all. She saw her playing with a neighbor kid. The neighbor's place was a block away and she felt sure they went for cookies and milk. The officers waited while the mother checked. The girl had disappeared."

"God, we might've had a head start on him for once."

"Maybe. Maybe not."

Slater arrived on the scene in ten minutes, red light flashing, no siren. He had time to listen to the morning weather broadcast—a low of forty degrees so far. It would have a bearing on figuring the time of death.

No need to flash his ID. Everyone knew him. They hadn't had time to string the yellow tape around the site nor had the M. E.'s vehicle arrived yet.

Slater walked up to join the group of men looking down. One of them gently peeled away the covering. A flashing light to his left—police photographer.

Though the men looking on were prepared, the city-hardened officers turned away a moment. Slater swallowed through a dry throat. The little girl's angelic face was crimson from death by carbon monoxide.

As lead man in the investigative crew, it was Slater's duty to make a joint determination with the M.E. about manner of death and time. He was grateful that Sawed Off had only asked him to do that once. Slater knew, without removing the clothing, that her back, buttocks and the back of her legs would be the same color. Lividity. Somewhere in this city, the little girl had lain in death while her killer waited to put her outdoors. Her corduroy britches looked new, and her sweater had stains down the front. Slater knelt and held the little sock encased foot gently.

"Yep, sonofabitch took the shoe. Same as before," a gruff whisper, another flash of the camera.

"Take a soil scraping from the bottom of this shoe," Slater said. "Is this where the body was found?"

An officer pointed to a little dip that at one time might have been grass, beyond the sidewalk. "Just over there. The killer makes sure they aren't hidden."

The little girl had pale blonde hair, braided neatly with pink ties on the ends, eyes closed as if in sleep, mouth curled just a little as if the last thoughts had been pleasant.

"Do we know how long he kept her before..." someone asked.

At the shrugs and raised eyebrows, Slater knew the answer. Too many missing children were reported; most turned up at a neighbors or hiding under the bed asleep. They didn't have the manpower to check each one out at the first hysterical call from a parent.

Slater leaned backward, tilting his head until his neck popped, then grunted in satisfaction. That should keep his headache at bay a few more hours. "Okay, you guys know what to do. Comb the area, look for footprints—we might find some good ones behind that rubble of buildings. You know the drill, pieces of torn material on rough brick, hair—I don't have to tell you."

"This street isn't used much any more. The housing complex gave up the ghost years ago," someone commented.

There should have been tire tracks in the mushy earth. Slater looked at a vacant lot with empty buildings adjoining it. Wrecks of cars and graffiti on every available spot as far as the eye could see. It resembled a war zone. One pitiful tree struggled to live in the cracked sidewalk, twisted and malformed, it resembled an overgrown Bonsai. The place smelled like raw sewage. A broken pipe lay somewhere amidst the destruction, but the city employees hadn't had time or the inclination to check it out.

"Where's the witness who called it in?" Slater asked. Each time one person or several had discovered the bodies. Careful questioning had developed nothing more than innocent people who happened to come upon the grisly finds.

A uniformed officer shook his head. "Captain said this was anonymous. The person hung up."

A pulse quickened in Slater's temple. First break in routine noted. If this body proved to have been out here longer, and he would bet on it, maybe the killer watched and waited and when no one turned it in, did so himself. The taped conversation would be at headquarters, waiting.

Slater walked back to where the body lay. The county vehicle approached and Slater watched while the first assistant to the M.E. gave the required cursory examination.

The morgue assistants loaded the body onto a gurney. Even dead, the men were careful with the child. An officer made a small chalk tracing on the bumpy, uneven ground while others strung the barricade.

"He's not—it's not like he's throwing away garbage," Slater observed. "He places the bodies instead of, say, throwing them from a car. He probably carries them here. In his arms."

The men nodded politely and continued their work, knowing the sergeant was an odd duck who liked to talk out loud and wasn't embarrassed by the habit. When he wanted them to pay attention, they'd know it.

Something glinted near the curb, just at the edge of the ruined sidewalk. Slater knelt down to have a closer look. "Lambert—you with the gloves—put this in the evidence bag." The man with long pinchers carefully picked up a piece of candy, wrapped in cellophane and twisted on both ends. It could have been dropped any time, but since the wrapper was clean and the candy looked fresh, it could also be another tiny crack in an otherwise smooth surface.

Slater and the other detectives searched the perimeter of the drop site carefully. Sooner or later this guy would trip. But they didn't have the luxury of sooner or later, children were dying.

He thought of how he would feel if Michelle...no, he couldn't go down that road again. He had to give this a methodical concentration with no emotional ties interfering. Michelle was safe, she had to be. For one thing, she was on the other side of the city from where these children had been kidnapped. That was no consolation. By now Slater understood how psychos moved around inside their weird world of perverse reasoning.

This time the team came tantalizingly close to having a witness. A vagrant who slept in the basement of the subdivision had just surfaced for his usual morning meal at the Salvation Army about ten blocks away. "I always go to Sally for breakfast," the homeless man whined, as if Slater or the others cared about his daily schedule.

"Okay, go on." Slater had his note book out, the second one for this case. A first for him—he'd always solved his cases before filling half the pages.

"So I heard this peeling rubber. I runs out to the curb to have a look see, and..." He scratched himself under the arms, enjoying the limelight.

"Go on." Slater was having a hard time controlling his impatience.

"Where was I? Oh, well, I looks down the street and spies this car speeding off like the devils are after it. Know what I mean? All's I see is blue smoke coming out of the tail pipe. It's cold this morning, you know." His whine revved up to a little higher pitch, apparently hoping the cops might give him a buck for some coffee.

"How about the color of the car? Or a license plate? Did you see the color of the license plate?"

He shook his head. "Nope. I was just getting up, still groggy. You suppose a fellow sleeps sound while rats and roaches crawl over him at night? Know what I mean? I was half-asleep, half-awake when first I pokes my head out the door."

Captain Murphy walked toward them, glanced down at the mark on the broken pavement and looked at Slater who told him about the eye witness. "Could hypnotism work on him? Get him to remember more details?"

Slater shrugged. "What's with you and this hypnotism shit? That what they teach in the colleges now? Hell, it might work. You'd have to get him cleaned up just to talk to one though." The others had moved away when Murphy walked up, otherwise Slater wouldn't have been so outspoken. In spite of the captain's indignant front, Slater thought he relished the knife-sharp honesty between them.

Murphy sighed; Slater knew he was thinking of the paperwork it would take to get the witness ready and then it didn't look good. The guy was a wino, a couple of bottles short of the DTs.

"Show us where you saw the car. Exactly." Slater led the man down the street, motioning for the forensic team to follow. If they got tire prints this time, it would be a help when they nailed the bastard.

They tried hard, but nothing had left a recent impression on the paper-littered street.

ᚼᚼᚼ

Back at the precinct, Murphy called Slater into his office. Even with the doors closed, everyone heard the captain. "I'm not asking the impossible, sergeant. Somewhere there's the key to this killer and we have to find it. Did you clean up that street guy and get him to the hypnotist?"

Slater nodded. "Yeah. Big fat zero. Bad luck, our only witness and he's almost blind. Cataracts. He heard the car speed away, smelled the exhaust, could tell where it sat, but that's all. He did say it sounded like a faulty muffler. You know, barroom—barroom, that kinda sound."

"The mayor and the chief, they're on my case day and night." Murphy walked to the window and rubbed some dust from the glass with his spread fingers. He swerved around to stare at Slater "How about the psychic? Mrs. Macklin. Anything more to go on there?"

Slater considered. "I don't want to push her. She knows he's got to be caught and soon. She's trying hard to get a fix on a location, something we can track down."

Murphy shrugged. "Oh God, our best hope—a wino with cataracts, a woman who sees things in her computer and an officer in charge who thinks ACLU is a ball club. Why me, Lord, why me?"

He wanted to laugh at Murphy's litany of doom, but refrained for once, sensing the captain wasn't exactly kidding. "That piece of candy at the scene, it was fresh, not hard."

"It could have fallen from the vic's pocket, she was wearing corduroy pants, wasn't she?"

"Yeah, but she was packaged in that plastic sheet. He brought her that way, there wasn't any sign of wrapping going on in the street."

At Murphy's raised eyebrow, Slater tried to hide his disgust. Didn't they teach them anything at the academy anymore?

"Of yeah, of course. There would be displaced stones and swept dirt on the sidewalk if he'd done it there."

"Right." Slater was this close to saying "Right, asshole" and caught himself in time. There was a certain limit to how far he could antagonize his captain. He tried to maintain a modest threshold. "He brought her to the scene, like all the others, laid her in place and then waited for us to find her."

Murphy leaned back in his chair and closed his eyes.

"I've been thinking. Kate—Mrs. Macklin—mentioned several ways psychics see and feel things." Slater pulled out his notebook and flipped through a few pages while Murphy waited. "Oh, yeah. Here it is. Psychometrics. She hasn't tried that yet. It's when a psychic holds an object belonging to someone and uncovers certain information about that person."

"Sounds like a long shot, but what the hell, ask her to try it. Check out some of the kid's clothes from Property."

"I think the killer's getting too cocky," Slater said. "He almost had a witness this time and he's dropping bodies closer to the inner city. It's about time he screws up bad."

"Maybe. He almost goofed this time with an eye witness—well, sort of one, and if that kid hadn't called in—"

"The kid. Now that strikes me as strange. Where did he come from?" Something about the call made Slater edgy.

"What do you mean? The youngster was walking through on his way to the drug store or so he said."

"Hell, no one hangs around that neighborhood in the daytime even. It's a known haunt for gangs. Besides, the boy sounded cherry. Not like a street punk."

"Yes, but—"

Slater got a perverse satisfaction from cutting Murphy off and watching his cheeks puff up in impotent resentment. He let himself out of the captain's office quietly, not wanting to interfere with Murphy's continuing inventory of bad breaks.

Next, Slater went into the ready room alone and listened to the telephone tape over and over. A male voice, high pitched, sounded like a teenager or younger, had made the call. Brief, scared, stuttering in his haste to get it said, he told about passing by and seeing something funny near the sidewalk. He said he thought it might be a dead animal wrapped in plastic.

So much for that lead. The kid had to have been cutting through the old neighborhood on his way somewhere. Too scared to leave his name and stay put, he'd just left the message with 911. Funny though, if he'd thought it was an animal, what was he afraid of? He could have just clipped something from a nearby store and had a guilty conscience. Any kid with street smarts wasn't going to deliberately set out to talk to cops. It just didn't work that way.

They had to catch this guy and catch him fast. Whatever his reason for killing, the act would become easier and easier with each child. Their best hope was that he would get careless. But the key had to be hidden in Kate Macklin's computer.

CHAPTER 15

Slater felt restless that evening on his way home from work. Margaret had taken Michelle along with the grandparents to Vermont for the weekend. At least Vincent wasn't with them, but still in France.

He didn't want to think along those lines.

Without conscious thought, he stopped his car, not at his own house but at Kate's. It pleased him when she opened the front door wide and stepped outside as if it was nothing to her. He knew better.

Her "Hi, sergeant," was like a gentle caress. He wanted to crush her slight frame against his body, to hold her and protect her. He had to tell her they'd found the body, but not yet.

He stood two steps below, their eyes on the same level. "How've you been? That a new outfit?"

Kate laughed. "No, but I guess it's one of the few times you've seen me out of my old cotton muumuu. I walked to the edge of the curb yesterday and half a block down the street." She looked as proud as if she'd gone to the moon and back.

Slater put a hand on her shoulder, startled at how fragile it felt. "Great! How come you backslid from Richard to sergeant?"

Kate smiled. Her lips were not full and pouty like Margaret's, yet her mouth was generous, going well with her somewhat square jawline and her long, graceful neck.

"I'll see if I can manage. Sergeant suits you, though."

They went inside, the cat tangling in their legs making them laugh at his antics.

"I stopped on the way home from work, to see if you'd go to a hamburger joint with me. Ah-ah—before you say a word." He touched a finger gently to her lips. "It's a quiet place, hardly any customers this time of day. You'd think you were sitting right here in your own kitchen."

Kate felt a familiar quickening of her pulses at his touch. Splendid. Hot pants for the first man who talks to you in years, she chided herself. That wasn't it exactly, though, and she well knew it. This man, behind his tough veneer, hid a vulnerability that shocked and dismayed her. How did he manage to function over the years against the dregs of the city he came in contact with every day of his life?

She knew it was impossible to ask about or even let him know she realized the sensitive core he hid so well. Probably few people even had an inkling. It was only through her intuitive nature that she felt it.

"We'd have to ride through the streets. A week ago I couldn't have done it."

"You can do it, or I wouldn't ask it of you. You'd be doing me a big favor. I've got the blues tonight and I don't want to eat alone."

"I can fix you something here."

"Nope. My mind's made up. I want a big, juicy hamburger, covered with cheese and mushrooms, loaded with fat and cholesterol and all kinds of stuff you're not supposed to eat if you want to live past forty."

"Oh, my, aren't we rebellious? Well, I guess I could try."

"Hey, pretty lady, I'll be with you all the way."

She went in to brush her hair and add a little eye shadow, something she hadn't used in ages. The jeans and tee shirt looked okay, setting off her slight frame to good advantage. Kate looked in the mirror, hating what she saw. Her face was so thin with bruised areas under her eyes from lack of sleep. She was trying so hard to help the police and yet she couldn't let Richard loose on Little Bernie. The killings weren't his fault. The boy was weak, used by his big brother or whoever that boy was.

That was something else troubling. Kate was so tuned in to the younger boy, so much a part of him, that she sensed a larger problem. Was Big Bernie his brother? She had seen them both, but now that she thought of it, they had never come within her vision at the same time. They spoke about each other, but had they ever really talked directly to each other? Like the parade of little girls, both boys had been on different levels or planes of reality—of time.

That's what bothered her. Were they real? Was someone deliberately filling her mind with the Bernies to keep her off the real killer's tracks? The chilling thought came to her, that the killer could be someone entirely different and he was toying with her mind and emotions. Putting what he wanted to put there.

Who? Why?

The idea made her shiver and she pulled her sweater closer over her shoulders. What a crazy notion—that her mind was vulnerable to someone out there, a cold-blooded killer, who could enter her thoughts and leave anytime he chose. No, it couldn't be. She hurriedly discarded the idea.

If it was true—her only salvation and that of future victims lay in catching the killer before he had the chance for more destruction.

"Hey, what's taking so long? You're already beautiful and I'm starving," Slater called from the kitchen.

His voice chased away the shadows that had descended upon her. She would work on the computer tonight, but until then...

Kate looked at her image in the mirror again, seeing a rebellious, challenging expression on her face. She lifted her shoulders eliminating that little habitual droop. Suddenly she *felt* beautiful.

It was very flattering, the way Slater watched her on route to the restaurant, as if checking out her stress level. Not much of a talker, he painstakingly led her into conversation about her work. If she showed the first sign of panic, she figured he'd decide to turn around and take her back home. It was a big step for her.

Inside the restaurant, Kate noticed there weren't many customers and she was glad. She felt comforted by the clatter of dishes and the jukebox wailing out a country-western song. The large room smelled like apple pie and meatloaf. It was nice, sitting next to Richard. Almost like a real date.

"Ah, hell, maybe this is a bad choice of eating places," he said, as a waitress came to wait on them.

"Hi, how you been?" The waitress offered a careful smile, no hint of familiarity, but Kate knew at once they were acquainted.

Slater introduced them.

"You two know each other." Kate spoke when they'd turned in their orders and Thelma walked away.

He shrugged. "Yeah. She's a—a friend."

Kate wasn't sure why this should bother her. It was obvious they had some kind of relationship now or in the past, even though the waitress tried to be nonchalant.

"We go out once in a while for beers. Nothing heavy. Never mind about that. You doing okay?"

They carefully skirted his job or her visions. This was clearly a night off for both of them.

Slater told her about Michelle and a little of his marriage. He accepted his part in its disintegration without pointing a finger at Margaret. Kate liked that in him.

She told him about her husband, Mac, and what a good life the three of them had until his accident on the job when the building collapsed on top of him and two other workers. She couldn't talk about her daughter yet. Not even with him.

They finished eating, continuing to sit and talk until suddenly she yawned. "Oh, excuse me. It's not the company. I've enjoyed every minute, but I had better go home, get to work on my bookkeeping."

"You still work all night and sleep all day? I would've thought—"

"Not so much anymore. It's hard to break a habit though. I did it for so long. It seems funny now that I was so afraid to go to sleep at night—a grown woman and afraid of shadows."

"Nothing unusual in that. Enough shadows out there for everyone."

"Come on, now sergeant—Richard. I bet you've never been afraid of anything in your life."

Slater wanted to tell her of the first time he'd shot a man in the line of duty. How he went home and puked his guts out. Or when he first made love to Margaret, beautiful, aloof Margaret. He had been scared shitless even to put the move on her in the beginning. There was the first time he held his baby daughter in his hands and weighed her helpless fragility against the mean streets, the ugliness of the city.

"Don't kid yourself. Everyone runs scared. Some of us just learn to hide it early in life." He didn't want to spoil the evening by telling her about finding the body. But he didn't want her to see it in the morning paper.

They left the restaurant, and on the way home neither wanted to talk. When they reached the front door, Slater held her tight, her head pressed into the curve of his shoulder and chest, until he bent his head to kiss her.

"We found her, Kate. Just like you'd said we would."

His voice was so soft, she almost didn't hear him. Kate pulled away and looked up at him. "Oh God. Each time I hope and pray it's the last one."

"I know." He bent and touched his lips again to hers before he released her and turned toward his car.

Kate suddenly realized he'd taken valuable time and energy to help her crawl up out of her dismal cellar of despair. What she was feeling for him was far more than gratitude. She wanted him to make love to her. The thought came slamming into her with the force of a hundred freight trains. She was willing to trust him, to ask for nothing beyond whatever he had left in him to offer her. Weakly, legs trembling, she went inside and sat down at her computer. She had to help him and those little girls.

That night and the next, Kate sat at her computer until her head nodded and jerked, but the accounting figures remained. Nothing else came. Normally she would have been grateful except for one thing.

In seeing the last victim at the end of the row, she had no idea if it was one they had just found or a preview of what was inevitable. It was taking the police a long time to find a next one. Kate had never seriously considered the idea that she was seeing beyond what the killer had done. If that was so, then the next little girl didn't have to die. Somehow she should be able to stop the process. Yet the picture of the wrapped body in the abandoned row of houses would not go away.

Tears came to her eyes and she rubbed them in angry frustration. No, it didn't have to happen, but who could have prevented it?

കരുക

At the station, Slater juggled his schedule. He had an appointment with the M.E. and Murphy wanted him to confer with the police psychiatrist this morning, hoping to get a line on the killer's motives. He didn't want anything to do with the shrink and told Murphy so in no uncertain words. They gave him the willies.

Michelle's call came unexpectedly. "Daddy. We're home."

Margaret had never called him at work. He was surprised she would permit Michelle to do it.

"Have a good time, honey?" He absentmindedly scribbled some questions to ask at his meeting.

"Daddy, can I come stay with you?" He could see her make that little face when she tried so hard to be a big girl and not cry.

Slater's heart tripped over a few beats and the pencil snapped between his fingers as he gripped the receiver. "Is your mother there? I want to talk to her."

"No! It's our secret. She'll get mad."

"Then what's bothering you? Talk to Daddy." He paused a moment, hating to say the name. "Is Vincent back?"

"Yes." He heard the soft hiccup behind her whisper.

Margaret's voice came over the wire, sharp and clear. "Michelle! Naughty girl, who are you talking to? You mustn't talk to strangers on the telephone. Last week you dialed someone in California."

"Don't hang up!"

"Hello. Who is this?"

He sighed. "Me. Richard. The kid got lonesome I guess. No harm in calling me. After all, I am..." He almost said "her father" but didn't want to open that can of worms again.

"At work? I thought that was the cardinal sin of all sins." Her laugh was brittle and he knew how her long, graceful neck would bend back and her lips part. The thought of that fluid movement didn't stir him anymore which surprised the hell out of him.

"I got time. Put Michelle back on. She wanted to talk to me."

"Oh, she's getting to be such a little brat. She's jealous of Vincent, thinks he takes too much of my time. She's even jealous because her grandpapa enjoys Vincent's company too. Can you imagine that? I'm really sorry she bothered you, Richard. Perhaps I'll get back with you this week."

He listened to the hum of a disconnected line. Damn her to hell! But she was probably on the money. Michelle might feel a threat of losing both her parents. Especially since each time Vincent came back from Europe it must be like having a honeymoon all over again for Margaret.

Slater waited for the resentment at his ex-wife's new sex life to pour over him but it didn't. He only felt angry frustration because he still wasn't sure about Michelle. Damn, it was no time to get one of his headaches.

When Captain Murphy pushed through the door, Slater welcomed the interruption. "In the ready room. Now."

Murphy had never talked to him in that tone of voice. Slater followed without question.

"The investigation is going too slow, I know that, you know that." He looked pointedly at Slater. "Got anything for us?"

Slater looked at the men seated in the small room. He couldn't be taken from the case now, he felt close to the killer, felt as if he was finally getting inside his head. Slater turned back to the map and pointed. "We may be honing in on some kind of pattern here. As you can see, the pickup areas are scattered. He has to find the kids where he can. But the drop sights are narrowing down to this area." He stabbed his finger into the center of the pins.

"So far we haven't noted a particular time element—when he moves in on the kids, have we?" one of the officers asked.

Slater shook his head. "No, and that's unusual. Something sets him off. It isn't the moon, we've checked that out. It isn't a certain day of the month. The victims are all killed at different times. I'd say random only my guess is this predator doesn't kill haphazardly. He has his own timetable. We have got to find the key. The key to why he does it. Only then can we get closer to who."

"He doesn't do it for kicks. Otherwise he wouldn't dose 'em with a sleeping pill before he offed them," one of the men said.

"Yeah, he wants someone to find them. Maybe that's where he gets his jollies. Outsmarting us."

"Right you are," Slater said to the two officers. "I thought of that, and so far it's his one weakness, wanting us to find the bodies right away. But I'm not sure that's his motive, to rub our noses in it."

"What then?"

Slater scratched his head. He started to refer to Kate as the computer lady. He knew the men did. "Mrs. Macklin agrees with our assessment. She thinks he wants us to find the body because he doesn't want the victims to be ravaged by rats and bugs. I think so too."

Several men laughed nervously while more made rude noises of disbelief. Slater waited until the noise subsided. He'd had a hard time swallowing that one too, but Kate assured him it was so, and it did make sense in a weird kind of way. If he learned anything from his years on the force it was that a serial killer didn't think in straight lines of logical progression like a normal person, so maybe that idea wasn't so strange.

He thought of Kate and wished she hadn't become involved. She was probably better off staying indoors as a recluse the rest of her life, at least she would be safe. He knew Kate enough to know part of what she wasn't talking about. Did the killer know she watched him? Kate always avoided talking about that. What if the killer decided she knew too much? So far Kate had seen the dead children, but why had she asked if there could be two killers?

That was what bothered him. He was certain Kate had looked into the killer's face.

ଏଓଏଓ

That afternoon Slater left the station with a definite urgency to see Kate.

She seemed strangely hesitant to let him in.

"God, you look like hell," he said.

"Thanks for your kind words, sergeant, but I know what you mean and I'll take it as a gesture of sympathy. Besides, you don't look too great yourself."

They gathered up the tray of coffee and cups to go outside in her backyard.

"Ah, Katie, I wish you hadn't got yourself mixed up in all this."

"Then we'd never have gotten together again, would we?" She touched his hand tentatively.

"I hate to see you so strung out. I don't know..." He rubbed his thumb lightly against her cheek.

She leaned into his warm palm and they stayed close for a moment. "You get the 'sick headaches' don't you?"

He moved away to see her face. "Reading my mind? That's not kosher."

She smiled. "No. I don't read minds—not often, anyway. I only go where I'm invited, I guess that's the idea. My mother had those awful migraines. I recognize the pain behind your eyes. Have you seen a doctor?"

"Nah. They just started in the past month or so. I might have a brain tumor and then I'd be canned. What's the point of kicking off with a rotten brain and no job?"

"It's nothing to joke about, Richard."

"Who's joking? Kate...you've been holding something back from us. I need to know everything that you're thinking and seeing. Leave it to me to sort it out."

His abrupt change of subject startled her. She broke away and paced the small yard. "Yes. I couldn't tell you before. I'm not sure it's right to tell you now. I've seen the killer—killers, but I can't let you hurt him—them."

He was at her side in a flash, spinning her around to face him. She cried out in fear and pain as his hand gripped her shoulder. "I didn't mean to scare you. But we've got to get this guy."

"My thoughts are in a jumble. You said there would never be two killers working together, but there are. A young boy about eleven and an older boy about eighteen. I think they're brothers."

He eased her into the chair and knelt on the grass in front of her. "Your signals are mixed in with something else. The pattern—"

"To hell with your lousy patterns!" she exploded.

Her unusual outburst stunned him. She was normally so controlled.

"I don't care about your patterns and profiles and all that police jargon. You've been wrong about him—them."

"How long have you known this?" Anger replaced his astonishment. He glared down at her.

"Not long. I had to put it all together before I could tell you. It didn't make any sense otherwise."

"Still doesn't. I don't see how two youngsters could pull off these killings. It's taken a lot of methodical planning, stalking the victims, getting away with them. Do you know why yet? How much more are you holding back?"

"That's it."

"How about describing what you saw to the police artist. She can draw what you tell her."

Kate rubbed her temples. "Not yet. I—I haven't got it clear in my head yet. Their faces are shadowy, I just see forms and hear voices."

"A responsibility comes with your helping us, whether you like it or not. There'll be others until we stop this maniac."

She stared into his angry eyes. "Don't you think I know that?" Her voice was jagged. "It's ripping me apart, Richard! I'm trying to help the best I can." She paused and then sat back and rubbed her eyes. "He told me if I said anything to anyone about this, he wouldn't come back. He isn't clear enough to picture completely anyway, and he's our only chance. You have to trust me."

He knelt again and pulled her to his chest while she sobbed, patting her back with a clumsy hand, as he would have consoled Michelle. "I know you're trying. When you get it together, tell me." She'd gone through a lot. This could send her around the bend. He hated to see that happen, but getting the murders stopped had to be top priority. That was when the job took over and left your personal life to fend for itself.

Kate pulled herself together and Slater made her drink some coffee. He smiled at the soft hiccups she made around the sips. Like Michelle. He couldn't imagine Margaret making that sweet, vulnerable sound.

"Maybe there's another way you can help. Come inside a minute." In the living room, he reached down next to the recliner and put a brown paper bag up on the coffee table. "Here's clothing from three of the kids. You mentioned something about—ah—psychometrics."

She reached for the bag and then leaned back without touching it. "I tried this once before and it didn't work. Maybe it will this time."

"Do you want me to leave?"

Kate considered a moment and then shook her head. "I don't think so. Just let me concentrate without any sounds for a bit." She closed her eyes. Without hesitating any longer, she pulled the crisp paper bag closer and reached in, her hand fumbling toward the bottom and grabbing onto a shoe.

When she pulled it out, Slater thought he caught a flash of recognition in her eyes, but it was gone immediately.

Closing her eyes again, Kate held the shoe to her cheek several minutes. "I'm sorry. It doesn't work for me. I think it's that I can only see through the computer. Why this is, I have no idea. Probably something to do with wave lengths or magnetic fields—something of that sort."

Slater took the bag from her and rolled the top closed. "Never mind. We took a shot at it. I hate to leave when you feel so wiped out." He pulled her closer and rubbed the tears from her cheeks with his thumbs. "For some reason you were chosen to communicate with the killer and so far that's all we have to go on, Katie. "Could he stand by and watch her sacrifice her sanity to catch this killer?

He had no choice.

CHAPTER 16

Oh, please, someone help me. I don't want to do this anymore. He can't make me do it.' The boy's sob echoed inside Kate's head.

Kate struggled to her feet, tangled in the blanket thrown across the couch. She had been catching little naps off and on during the day and night to be near the computer, afraid of missing something.

She wheeled the office chair in closer, staring into the screen. Rasputin came out of nowhere to land in her lap. He hadn't been around the computer lately, but seemed to deliberately want to be near her now.

When she touched a key, the usual golden outline of her word processor page disintegrated into fog sifting up into the screen as if propelled by the soft purring of the fan in the base of the computer. She put her elbows on the desk, her chin in her palms and waited.

Little Bernie stood out in the street, in front of the rundown apartment house she'd seen before. Through his eyes, she saw the overgrown park behind the building. Wrapped in his skin, she felt his body shiver and knew he feared the park. His father had taken the twins to the park to do his terrible things when he couldn't find privacy in the apartment. Not knowing what he was doing was almost worse than having seen it happen.

The evening smells of cooked cabbage, stale beer and baby vomit spread over them like a suffocating blanket when someone opened the door.

'*You good for nothing little shit, I know you're down there. Come up here. I wanna talk to you,*' a heavy male voice yelled from upstairs.

It was *him*. Drunk again. Bernie's thin body flinched as if the blows had already been struck. He tilted his chin and shrugged his bony shoulders, walking slowly inside.

"I'm not going up there with you! I won't go!"

Kate closed her eyes, trying to break free of the horror she felt from behind Bernie's face. It was her first deliberate attempt to break contact, but she couldn't stand any more of what Bernie was going through.

For a long moment the struggle continued, as if the boy didn't want to let her go.

Suddenly Kate felt something different in front of her eyelids and slowly opened her eyes. She was in the wooded area, the quiet peace such a contrast from where Bernie had just taken her. She knew it wasn't behind his apartment house. These woods were unkempt but not in the way the park was. Was Little Bernie with her here?

Kate's gaze traveled to the mound with the tiny shoes. She heard the clear, sweet voices trilling the nursery rhyme from somewhere in the background, but didn't see the girls. Without wanting to, she began to count. One, two, three, four, five...Oh sweet Jesus, what was he doing?

She could barely see beyond the man's wide shoulders as he knelt down and gently placed another just so—in line with the others. A fuzzy little bedroom slipper. Pale blue. Kate clenched her eyes tight, thinking of the living child who had lost her tomorrows.

"You bastard!" She hadn't realized she shouted at the computer screen until Rasputin leaped off her lap in terror, digging his claws into her legs.

Big Bernie turned and stared straight into her eyes. The realization came as a shock. He'd known she watched.

Kate stared at the shrine of little shoes, unable to turn away. The children's voices gradually receded and Little Bernie's whimpering sounded closer and closer. Keep your thoughts on him, her inner voice counseled. You're distracted, mixed up. It was the boy who called out for help. He was the one who needed her. He was the key to stopping the older one.

"I'm listening, child. I'm listening," she whispered.

'*He didn't—we didn't do it yet.*'

"You mean the little girl with the blue slippers isn't dead?"

Little Bernie shook his head and the words came out in a stammer which he tried to control. '*N—no. He's ob— observing her now, he calls it.*'

Stalking, not observing.

"Yes, go on."

'*He stole the shoe ahead of time, he never done that before. He watches a long time, to be sure the girl is the one, otherwise it's not the righteous thing to do.*'

"Righteous? Did *he* say that?"

The boy nodded, a shaft of pale brown hair fell over his forehead and he brushed it back impatiently.

'He knows which ones.'

"Do you help him?"

Bernie hesitated a moment, then nodded again. *'Yeah. The little kids, they like me a lot.'* His eyes lit with pride.

"But your brother, he kills them. You know that."

Bernie looked hurt, as if she had struck him across the face.

'He's not my brother. Anyway, he doesn't hurt them. He promised me. That's the whole idea of this, so they won't have to suffer.'

"No. Maybe he doesn't hurt them, he told the truth about that." Unless you want to count stealing away their lives as hurting them. So many questions, but she had to be careful. He could shut down any moment. Kate sensed his fragility.

"Why does he do it? Do you know?"

Bernie dried his tears and looked pained. *'Sure I know. You should, too. I took you there to see. He does it—we do it—to save them.'*

"Save them?"

'Yeah, save them. When they get to be five, he will...will...' the boy was unable to finish.

"You mean Big Bernie?"

'No! Him! The man, the father! He does terrible, ugly things to little girls. You saw what he did to the twins. Fathers do that to daughters. Big Bernie, he says we got to rescue them. It's better if they go to sleep where no one can touch or hurt them ever again. God takes them then. He says God won't take them if they're impure.'

How to get through to him? She prayed for the right words. "All fathers don't do that to their daughters, Bernie."

The boy looked unconvinced, as if he'd stopped listening to her.

"Son, don't go away. I must talk to you. Where is this little girl with the bedroom slipper?"

'Oh no. You're trying to trick us. I let you in because you helped your daughter. I thought you could help us, but you can't. No one can.'

"Yes I can! Trust me, baby, I can help you if you let me."

Poor kid, he was torn between knowing in his heart that this was wrong and trusting Big Bernie that it was right. Kate felt his image fading as desperation caused sweat to trickle down her armpits.

'Her name's Jennifer.' The boy whispered hoarsely, as if he didn't want to speak but had to. *'He likes that name. She has blonde hair, like the twins.'*

"Do you know the last name? Of the little girl?"

Bernie wrinkled up his face in an effort to remember. He resembled a dried up little old man, already dying.

Kate turned away for a moment, afraid of absorbing his appalling torment. When she turned back, the computer was blank.

"Damn!" She booted it up again and entered her word processor. Only the amber words of the program menu stared mockingly back at her.

Kate laid her head on her arms and sobbed. She screwed up. So close to getting the last name of the little girl.

The little blonde girl with soft blue bedroom slippers who wasn't dead yet.

For two days and nights, Kate sat close to her computer. She left off her one pleasure, drinking coffee, to stay on the verge of sleep—when the Bernies were most likely to appear.

Jennifer. The unremarkable name reminded her of Jane Doe. Only this was a name without a body. Yet. The next victim. She should have called Richard, but her inner voice warned her to wait. Wait for what?

Sometime in the early hours of morning Kate felt the hairs raise on her arms. Shrugging out of her doze, she sat up, rubbing her eyes. The computer screen lit up with a golden haze that surrounded the screen. She heard the crying before Bernie appeared.

"Here I am, son. Here I am. Why did you stay away so long?"

He stammered, a sure sign of his distress. *'The little girl, the one we showed you...oh, I hope you won't tell Bernie that I told you...stuff. He'll be mad. He won't let me out again.'*

"No, I won't tell him." His continued trust was all she had going between her and a host of dead children.

'Johnson. I saw the name on the mailbox.'

Her heart threatened to swell up into her throat. Calm, move slowly. "Jennifer Johnson? Is that her name? Did you see anything else?"

Little Bernie shook his head. *'He knows about you watching him. And he knows about that cop. He doesn't like it.'*

Was Richard in danger? How could a figment from her computer reach out to hurt anyone? He killed the children, she answered her own question.

Kate gently prodded the boy to say more. "What could Bernie do to harm the sergeant? Detective Slater is a very unforgiving man. He would like to hurt Bernie."

'*Big Bernie knows that. Only difference is, Bernie can get to him. And—and he can get to you, too. He didn't call on you, I did. He doesn't care about me, he doesn't care about anything but saving the girls. I gotta go now. I didn't mean for the cops to catch him, they'll hurt him—us...*'

His voice trailed off and Kate sat staring into a dark screen. He didn't want Big Bernie caught, he wanted the little girl not to be killed. On top of all the boy had gone through with his father, he now was torn between the older boy's belief that he was saving the children and the idea that it was wrong to kill them and the fear of his protector being caught or hurt.

She gritted her teeth in anger. The father is the one who should be caught and punished. He started this nightmare. Little Bernie was only eleven, he said so himself. The background in the tenement house was off-center, something left over from the Sixties. Now that she thought about it, music playing on someone's radio was definitely Sixties and the furnishings in Bernie's apartment would be considered collection pieces today if they hadn't been so beat-up and falling apart.

Next time she moved through the scene in Bernie's head, she was determined not to back away. She would keep her mind clear and remember everything she saw.

Something was strange here. Something she didn't understand. Part of her needed to talk to Richard, part of her didn't want to.

The imperative knocking on the door roused her from her thoughts.

Slater stood in the doorway and she blinked, for a moment thinking she'd conjured him up. Kate beckoned for him to come in. "I was just thinking of you."

He grinned. "Good. Sorry I pounded so loud, I knew you had to be home. Maybe you ought to spring for a doorbell."

It was her turn to smile. "I had one once. Darn thing played some song. I had a repairman disconnect it."

"Yeah. I hate those things too." Small talk, they always began that way, slowly as if feeling out the water temperature and the depth.

She brewed a fresh pot of coffee, reveling in the aroma. The veins in her temples throbbed, a sure sign of caffeine withdrawal.

When they settled on the couch with the cat curled between them, Kate continued to agonize over what to say and then chided herself for being so suspicious and mistrustful. Why wouldn't he believe her? She took a deep breath. She could no longer trust her visions. Big Bernie might be toying with her, confusing her.

"I know the next victim's name."

Slater looked stunned.

"Jennifer Johnson. I'm sure she lives somewhere in the city."

"Well, that narrows it down. There are probably 4 pages of Johnsons listed in the phone book. Just in the metro area."

"You don't have to be testy. At least it's a beginning. Somewhere to look."

"Sorry. Anything else you can think of?"

Kate looked down at the cat, stalling. No place to go, nowhere to hide. "You might say that. I had to marshal my facts before—"

"That isn't your job. It's ours. All we asked you to do was tell us what you see. We can sort it out."

"Don't you suppose this is hard on me, too? I haven't had a good night sleep in—I don't know how long."

"Ah, Kate. I can see it in your eyes, those lines around your mouth. I know it's hard. We—I wouldn't ask you to do it if so much wasn't at stake. You listened to the parents of those little kids—"

She held up her hand in protest, wanting to stop him. Enough torment slogged through her head without visualizing the anguish of the families of the dead children. She couldn't bear that too.

If they found Jennifer in time, they might catch Big Bernie. Neither boy could keep from doing what they saw as their mission. Big Bernie would never turn himself in. He had to be stopped.

From some of the things they both said, the Bernies lived together. The older one spoke of an orphanage once and the younger one mentioned living in an orphanage. Maybe they weren't brothers after all, but she was sure they were related. The resemblance was there in the mannerisms and speech patterns. That was yet another puzzle. And what a bizarre idea for a parent to call both sons by the same name. Yet she knew it happened, even with celebrities.

It was frustrating, eking out tiny bits and pieces at a time, fearful of scaring the Bernies away forever. Her memory and powers of observation had diminished over the years, unused. Now she tried to hone them so as not to miss anything important. She had already screwed up on the displacement of time when she walked within the boy to his home. She just now grasped that puzzle. Were the past and present connected inside the boy's thoughts and transferring to hers?

Slater had been speaking and looked as if he expected a response.

"Oh, I'm sorry. Woolgathering. What did you say?"

"I said we'll get everyone on this Johnson situation, but meanwhile I'm asking you to think about it. What else can you tell me, even something you don't think is important?"

She studied his face for a moment, liking what she saw. A strong, honest, what-you-see-is-what-you-get kind of face. Brown eyes crinkled at the corner from the sun and a big grin that could spill over when you least expected it. She felt sorry for his wife. Sorry that the good qualities in this man hadn't meant enough for her to overcome the obstacles in their marriage.

"Sometimes there's just this amber fog and I don't really see anything, just voices coming at me. He did take her slipper ahead of time. According to...She almost said Little Bernie. "I don't think he's done that before."

"You're right. It may be a break in his concentration. You locked into the Shoe Man and the plastic wrapping and the single shoes." He took her hand. "Ah, Kate, this is an important step. You're really tuned in to him now. I got to confess, I had a hard time believing, but you came up with your daughter's...ah, well." He fumbled, apparently not wanting to add to her troubles by bringing up a sore subject.

"It's all right. You haven't said anything wrong. The memory of Annie is finally glazing over so that I can live with it."

She knew he hadn't wanted to believe in her powers. That was understandable. Neither did she.

"Anything else?"

Stall, she had to stall. Wasn't it enough she gave them the name of the next victim and maybe the life of Big Bernie, if the police were clever enough to lay a trap for him? She still felt an overwhelming need to protect the boy, at least for the time being.

Kate pushed away the vision of Richard's strong fingers wrapped around Little Bernie's slender throat.

৩৩৩

Slater called Murphy, who woke up short tempered at first until he told him about Jennifer Johnson as a possible next victim. After that, Slater sat at his desk, feeling strung out like a mile of dirty sidewalk, his nerves twanged on the edge of snapping. He had noticed over the passing weeks that his fellow officers kept their distance more than usual. It was always like this when he couldn't get a handle on something. Margaret had hated it when he was in one of his moods, as she called it. God knows, she had told him often enough.

Michelle would be five soon. That fact loomed ominous in his mind. Why did it bother him? Why now when he had so many other concerns, did he think about

Michelle's birthday? Her mother hadn't let her call again. He called, leaving messages on the phone and hating it, knowing Margaret's father listened to every word he said. Gloating. Did Vincent listen too?

Vincent. Did he really think Margaret's new husband was mistreating his daughter? What if he was the killer? He'd been here in the States each time a victim appeared. Part of Slater felt justified in thinking this way. No one was above suspicion. But deep inside his gut instincts told him he was jealous. It was too much of a coincidence. Yet something wasn't right with Michelle. He couldn't still the small voice inside his head that worried over his daughter's strange attitude toward her new step-father, and the fact that she kept asking to come live with him. It didn't help to question whether he should have shared his suspicions, right or wrong, right from the start.

Slater looked at the map on the wall. He'd memorized the whereabouts of each of the six tack heads. He'd memorized where the children were picked up and where they'd been dropped. Where was that creepy bastard? What was the killer doing this very minute? He felt his hands twitch every time he thought of the monster. He wanted to wrap his hands around that bastard's neck so bad. Maybe it was wrong to have confided in Kate. Hell, it was her word against his if it ever came down to that.

If? He meant when.

Captain Murphy walked by and stopped to talk, his voice and expression almost apologetic, as if sorry that Slater was as powerless as the rest of them. The captain was probably planning to relieve him and felt ill at ease about it.

God, he hoped not. Not when he was getting close. He felt it in his bones.

"We're dancing with shadows on this one, sergeant," Murphy said.

"There's something we're missing."

The captain shook his head. "Don't beat yourself up, man. We went over every damn detail a hundred times. We've got all the manpower available, but he's left nothing for us to check out. We just have to wait until he makes a mistake."

"K-ee-rist! How many more kids have to die until he gets bored with what he's doing? What if he never does?"

"Hell, Slater, we all feel rough about this. Every precinct in town is plagued with calls from worried parents or the press. Our switchboard is loaded twenty-four hours a day. We had to hire an extra person to take the calls. Did you catch the midnight talk show last night?"

"Yeah, I was up. Everyone had something to say. The next thing they'll find out is what we call him—the Shoe Man. God how I hate nicknames for criminals. It makes them sound so—so—human."

Murphy swallowed, the sound loud in the quiet room. "I know I hold a different set of values from you. My training was from the state university with a degree in criminology while you walked the beat with your stick and gun. But the days when you can separate issues where black is black and white is white with no grays to muddy your vision have passed. Sometimes I almost envy your tunnel vision but that's become a luxury on the way out with the last of the 'old timers.'"

Slater nodded, accepting Murphy's words. The captain was right on all counts.

"He *is* human, sergeant. And don't forget it. Don't even think about committing 'punishment with extreme prejudice'. That's nothing more than vengeance and it's not our job."

"In other words, a righteous bust even for a maniac." Slater groaned.

"You're almost at the end of your career now. You can retire with full honors. You could earn a little more pension, extra time to be with your daughter...or you could screw up so Brown and Jimenez can take over."

"Hell, they haven't got the experience to find a drowning skunk in a pail of water. You can't let them head this. It'll set the investigation back months."

Slater stared at the map on the wall, knowing it creeped Murphy out. The captain turned away to his own office.

The race to find Jennifer Johnson before the killer consumed Slater's every thought. Second came his lust to do it alone, so that he had time with the Shoe Man before the other officers came on the scene. He flexed his hands as if measuring his strength.

Then he felt ashamed. The important thing was to find Jennifer in time. Period. The killer seemed to outguess them at every turn. He was probably watching the Johnson house even now, picking the right time to strike.

Slater forced his thoughts away from that area. Murphy had officers go to daycare centers, kindergartens and nursery schools in the areas that Slater had described. He only had so much manpower at his disposal but the desk staff stayed on the phones too, asking questions.

His plan was to find Jennifer—remove her family to safety and then set the trap. If that didn't work, if they didn't catch him, maybe it would break into this guy's killing pattern, and make him stop.

But Slater didn't think so. It could drive him to desperation, to work faster, do more, grow more cautious. Another worry ate at him and he tried to dislodge the nagging warning but couldn't. Kate was in danger.

The waiting sucked Slater's nerves to the surface of his skin. He stood looking at the map in the ready room. All through this, he tried to believe in Kate and even though he could see for himself that she was on the money about many things that she shouldn't have known, it still eluded him, the faith. The faith to believe that she could actually look inside that computer and pull out people who talked to her.

It was the only thing holding the case together right now.

CHAPTER 17

As soon as Kate told Slater the intended victim's name, every available person including volunteers worked on the Johnson angle. Murphy had them using city directories but it wasn't a perfect solution. Not everyone chose to be listed. Also those in the outlying areas were not included in this directory.

Slater knew Murphy hated the idea of calling every Johnson in the book to see if they had a child named Jennifer. Not only did it make the force look like it didn't know what it was doing, but it alarmed many parents. Murphy had to caution the callers not to fully explain why they asked, to avoid a panic. The idea was to let the people know they inquired about a missing child.

The map could be a little help. The killer normally wouldn't go too far outside his comfort zone. That could eliminate some of the Johnsons.

The newspapers were having a field day at the expense of the entire police force. It would be like adding gasoline to a bonfire if they found out Jennifer's name and the police couldn't locate her in time.

Many people wouldn't talk and hung up. He didn't blame them, but there wasn't enough manpower to check out each address in person.

"How much time you suppose we have?" Murphy asked.

Slater considered the captain for a long moment, as if he looked right through him. Murphy shivered.

"It's hard to say. I asked Kate—Mrs. Macklin—to work on it. She knows something else, but—"

"Oh? Like what? You mentioned that idea before. Any notion what she's leaving out? And why?"

Slater shook his head. "Not a glimmer. She might not even be doing it on purpose. She isn't trained in investigation and observation, so things could get by her." He felt reasonably sure Kate wouldn't hide anything to screw up the case. Not deliberately. She had come a long way since he first saw her. She could go forward or backward if she bounced against too much at one time and couldn't cope.

He'd grown very fond of Kate, maybe fond was too mild, but the kids—the little dead children and those who would surely follow were the important elements here. Everything else, even his own problems and Kate's hangups were incidental to that.

They had finally located two Jennifer Johnsons, but neither qualified. One was a black teenager and the other eight years old. A serial killer might break out of the mold occasionally, but not to that extreme. Two down and hundreds to go. He worried about the families who might not be home to answer the phone or those who hung up on the callers.

Word had to get around, there was no help for it. Nearly all the city employees volunteered to make calls on their lunch hours or before and after their shifts. Slater wanted to save the kids but he also wanted the killer. God how he wanted that slimy bastard! Talking to the wounded parents, listening to the heartbreak, marriages cracking apart with the strain, one mother already committing suicide over her daughter's death. The killings were like an avalanche, gaining strength as it plummeted heedlessly downward, to destroy everything in its path.

He flexed his fingers, feeling their strength. Just let him have two minutes alone with the killer, that's all he needed.

ⴲⴲⴲ

Across town, Kate sat at the computer, doodling on a notepad, wishing she could draw. Her fingers itched to make a sketch of the Bernies and the little shrine. She had the strong feeling that if she let the young one confide in her enough, he would finally tell her everything, like where they lived, their full names—everything.

Big Bernie's threats against her and Richard put her visions in a different perspective, though. It had become personal, not just a video she watched passively on screen. Until now, some part of her had to hold back from describing the Bernies. Since he'd made threats, it was becoming foolhardy to leave anything out. The boy said Bernie was angry at the cop. That he knew how to get at him. The punk would be no match for an angry and vengeful cop. Richard could take care of himself.

Ignoring her aversion to deliberately using her psychic abilities, Kate put her head down on her arms to concentrate on the name of Jennifer Johnson. She didn't want this so-called gift, hadn't asked for it, but now she was determined to use it.

Jennifer...Jennifer...Jennifer Johnson. All of the slain children were pale and blonde. She concentrated on that. After a little time passed, she received the sensation of cool tiles—an entry way. Then thick carpet as her feet moved into a large room with vaulted ceiling and a winding staircase. Kate kept her eyes closed, afraid to move.

A voice came to her, a soft whine like little girls are prone to when they want something badly. "Mommy. Don't want to play with Mrs. Garrett today. I'm almost a big girl. Stay home with me."

Chills skated up and down Kate's arms, raising the fine hairs. She knew she was in the home of Jennifer Johnson.

Mrs. Johnson was a tall, slender woman, dressed in an expensive power suit, like one of those mannequins in the best department store windows. She had a briefcase tucked under her arm and Kate felt her distraction.

Listen to her. Please listen to your daughter. The woman didn't hear Kate's prayer.

"Mrs. Garrett will take care of you today as always. I thought you liked being with her."

"I do, Mommy. I like you better. When's Daddy coming home?"

"He's staying in the city." The mother knelt and hugged her daughter briefly. "Your daddy and I are going to take a few days off—stay in a hotel—see a play and meet friends. We haven't done this since you were a baby. You wouldn't begrudge us that, would you? Your mommy and daddy work so hard."

Jennifer leaned away and looked up at the middle aged woman standing a little to the side. Kate felt Mrs. Garrett's warmth and love for the little girl. But it wasn't enough!

Don't go. Stay with Jennifer. Stay to protect her.

The mother gave some last minute instructions. Jennifer had already disappeared into the next room and the sound of television came through the closed door.

Kate knew this was what Bernie waited for.

As soon as her energy returned, she dialed Richard's precinct. He wasn't in, but Captain Murphy answered immediately. She could almost see his frown, the shake of his head when she asked him if they'd found Jennifer.

"No. Not yet, Mrs. Macklin. I've got a lot of people working on it. I thought perhaps you had heard something."

"I think he's going to move on Jennifer tonight."

"Tonight?"

"I'm afraid so."

Captain Murphy didn't question how she knew but just accepted it. There was something satisfying as well as spooky about that. These men were city-hardened cops and she wouldn't have blamed them for labeling her a kook.

"Jennifer's parents have gone to the city and only her nanny, Mrs. Garrett, will be there to take care of her. I've got to talk to Sergeant Slater," Kate said

"Of course, I'll get someone right on it. He doesn't always check in with us. He makes his own hours. Refuses to wear a pager."

The sarcasm in his voice was wasted on her. "I'll be waiting."

☙❧

Kate worried and fretted, waiting to hear from Slater. She could describe the inside of the house now and she couldn't wait to tell him, but she didn't want to give it to Murphy. The captain was just waiting to replace Richard as head of the investigation and she didn't want that. But if she told what she knew it could speed things up by an hour, maybe that was all they needed. What should she do?

When the imperative knock sounded at her door, she ran to let him in.

This time they didn't bother with small talk. Slater followed her into the kitchen, the place he enjoyed most in her house.

"We've found three Jennifers who might fit the bill," he pulled out a chair and sank wearily down as if he'd continue on through the floor.

She poured them coffee and put four spoonfuls of sugar in his the way he liked it.

"Maybe I can help. I saw the inside of the house. The mother called the baby sitter Mrs. Garrett."

He stopped stirring the coffee and stared at her. She wanted to touch her palm to his face, smooth away the frown across his forehead. He put so much of himself into this, she didn't see how he had lasted so long on the force without burning out.

"That's the good news. The bad news—I think he might move tonight."

"How—"

"I...I travel through the young boy's mind, see through his eyes just as he does. Remember what I told you about astral projection and distant viewing? I think the boy took me to Jennifer's house."

"You're in the killer's mind?"

She sighed. "No. Not the killer's, although I can see things through—I don't know, following his footsteps. It's hard to explain. The boy's not the killer, I'd bet my life on that. He's only eleven, a small, delicate little boy. But I saw the killer, I told you that. I don't travel in his mind, he wouldn't allow me there, but I do move sort of with it." She cupped her hand around Richard's which still held the spoon. "You're right, I haven't leveled with you all the way. It—it's so complicated, I still haven't sorted it out yet."

All anyone needed to know right now was about Jennifer's home, she must concentrate on that. She had to keep her promise to the boy as long as possible. A strong feeling came to her that she and she alone had the best chance of stopping them. Stopping them a lot faster than the entire city police department, if she didn't lose the communication.

She feared to tell about that awful scene with Bernie, the father and the twins. Instinct warned her that going against that particular promise would shut it all down, all the communication she was building on. If she was wrong—if it came out in the end that she should have told everything, she'd have to carry that responsibility the rest of her life.

Kate took up the pencil and a piece of computer paper to make a clumsy drawing of the outside and inside of the house as she'd seen it. Her powers of observation were still nothing to brag about but she was getting better. "The mother seemed to be some kind of a professional person. She wore a power suit and looked as if she was used to being in charge."

"That could be a lead down the line. While you're at it, can you draw or give me a description of the—the person you did your—whatever you call it, astral..."

"Astral projection?" Her heart beat faster in her breast. She was tempted to try and draw Big Bernie. She looked into Richard's eyes and felt a strange chill. Fingers trembling, she laid the pencil on the table. "I'm sorry, Richard. I am not good at this, never have been. I can't even describe the older boy. It's kind of a fog I see him."

"You're so sure the young one's not the killer?"

Kate knew he was thinking that she was still a recovering basket case. The fear of leaving the safety of her house had not left her completely. He probably supposed these visions wouldn't come to her if she was in complete control, emotionally. She also sensed he wanted to trust her but his long years of police work made him a skeptical cynic. He had learned the hard way over the years, not to depend on anyone but himself.

"Yes, I'm sure he's not the killer. The boy is sort of a watcher, an innocent witness." *A victim himself.* If the police found the house in time, if they laid a trap for Bernie, with the older one out of the picture, the killings would stop and the young boy could get help. Little Bernie had called out to her, wanting someone to stop them, finally willing to sacrifice his protector and thereby his own self to prevent the killings.

"Oh, something else. While I went up the walkway, I heard water. It came from in back of the house. Remember I told you about a creek? It was closer than I'd first thought, judging from the sounds."

"In the city?"

"Yes, well, I know it sounds weird, but the area was full of trees—big trees that the builder left as a kind of a strip park behind the houses. My husband was a contractor and used to try to salvage trees in a new subdivision, if the money people—the investors let him."

Kate could no longer ignore the vexing puzzle, the suspicion that the two Bernies did not operate on the same plane of time or place. But that was impossible. The whole Bernie thing was like a ravel on the end of a sleeve hem, annoying and continuous. Yet she was afraid to pull too hard for fear of it all coming apart. At times her mind was like that.

Slater took hold of her hands and held them in a grip that made her flinch. "Have you thought of your own danger? You've got to be at risk. If the killer knows how to find you through your mind, he knows where your body is."

He knows about you, too, she wanted to tell him. Maybe she should. "Yes, that makes sense and I've thought of it. I...I think he knows about you, Richard, that you're hunting him."

"What?"

"Well, you understand this is all coming through a kind of a hazy fog, nothing's completely clear. But I heard this voice...he knows your name."

"That wouldn't be such a feat. My name's in the newspapers or on television in connection with this case. Murphy insisted I talk to reporters a couple of times. What exactly did he say?"

"Something like—oh—that you'd be sorry you messed with him, something like that. He said he knew how to get to you. That's the words he used."

Slater grinned, the look in his eyes hard. "I've been threatened by the best and worst, don't expect me to get shook up over your computer ghost's warning."

Kate watched the emotions fighting beneath the calm exterior of Richard's surface expression. The only outward sign was the working of his jaw muscles, just a slight tightening which she sensed more than saw.

There were times when she understood his need to punish this murderer. She often thought of how she'd like to see the destruction of the father who ruined his family— destroyed them all with his perverse lust. She felt sure that wherever the twins were, they hadn't fared any better than the Bernies. You don't crawl up out of a sewer without some of the slime sticking to you.

Kate thought back to the days of blessed oblivion after the passing of her husband and then Annie. She slept a lot, took sedatives and stayed inside her home, thinking of it as a healing process. But she realized it was merely hiding. No way to hide now. Everyone looked to her for help and all she had was the turmoil of her mind, the intrusive Bernies taking over her life, and the pathetic little parade of victims that kept growing and growing.

❧❧

Back at the station, Slater waited for Murphy. This latest kick, that the killer had threatened him, served to energize. He had to be getting too close for comfort, to annoy the killer so much. How could the Shoe Man hurt him? Killers with a pattern seldom deviated from an objective, known only to them. Suddenly the hairs on his arms stood up and he picked up a tack from the board.

He poked it into the section where his daughter and ex-wife lived. He sucked in his breath, his legs felt weak, and he leaned against one of the chairs behind him. If he pulled back toward the old part of the city, the neighborhood coming up had homes like Kate described. Top drawer but not extravagant, not old money—young corporate robots, on their way to the top of the heap. It was the only section he knew of with a small creek running past the backs of the homes. Five years ago it was swampland.

Was the killer heading in Michelle's direction?

He dropped the sheaf of notes he was holding and hurried to Murphy's office.

CHAPTER 18

Kate sat in the backyard, notepad and pen in hand, trying to marshal her thoughts. Something was wrong here, some part of the puzzle was missing. She bent and began writing on the long yellow pad. Rasputin purred loudly, tail switching as he watched a mockingbird light on the edge of the bird bath to take a drink of water. Kate refused to be distracted.

She listed all the observations about the boy and on another page, information gleaned from watching and listening to the older Bernie. It still didn't make sense. They never talked directly to each other on her screen, yet they knew the other existed. Little Bernie said the big boy was not his brother. Did he mean that literally or did he say it because he was afraid of him? Or didn't like him?

If they weren't brothers, what then? They had too many mannerisms in common to be unrelated. They obviously shared the same experience with the father, else why would the older boy turn into a relentless killing machine to save the five-year-olds? The older boy knew of

Little Bernie's pathetic attempt to set the father on fire as he slept on the couch.

Thinking back to their mannerisms and speech patterns, it was as if they were one person. One person with two minds. That didn't make sense, they had different bodies too. She threw down the pad and rose to her feet, startling the cat and birds. She barely noticed.

The computer. All this began with the computer. She had to talk to the Bernies. She would make them tell her what she wanted to know.

Kate sat in her office chair, blinds and drapes pulled, the room twilight-dark. Only the blank screen of the computer glowed, reflecting against her face as she stared to no avail.

"Son, I need to talk to you." First she said it out loud and then thought it. Hard. "You came to me for help. I want to help. I'm ready to help you." Little Bernie had the key to the puzzle. It was time he gave it up. Every passing day brought the threat of another Jennifer disappearing from life.

"Bernie, if you don't talk to me, I'm going to the police. I'm sorry to break my promise, but I must tell them everything. About the father, about the twins...maybe the authorities can help you, if I can't."

"*No!*"

The word exploded from her monitor, causing her heart to flutter up in her throat for a moment.

'*What do you want to know?*' The child stood in front of her, staring back from the screen. For the first time, he wasn't crying. His eyes looked so old in his almost-pretty face. It was in his eyes that she saw the most resemblance to Big Bernie.

"You came to me for help, disrupted my life. I want to help you. I've kept my promise about not telling what you begged me not to. But there are some things I must know. Are you alive? Now?"

The boy looked down at his scuffed tennis shoes for a long time until she thought he wasn't going to answer. When he looked up, he straightened his skinny shoulders and stood as if in obedience to an adult. *'Course I'm alive. How else could we be talking?'* The illogical logic of a child made her smile.

Kate waited, afraid of breaking the tenuous link between them.

'I'm alive but not alive, it's kinda hard to explain.'

Scratch that question for a while. "Are you and the other one brothers?"

Another explosive *'No!'*

"Then what?"

'Two minds, one body.'

Could he have heard her talking to herself on the back steps a few minutes ago? She didn't think so. "I don't understand."

'I don't neither, but Bernie says it's something we gotta live with. He says we're like a...a family. We all gotta stay together or die together.'

"All?"

The boy shrugged. *'You got me. But he ain't my brother. Sometimes I hate him. Most times I do. He's so bossy, always wanting things his way. He's trying to help the twins—I mean the other girls—it's too late to help the twins. Bernie says the old man ruined them. He says they'll never see Jesus.'*

"Do you—do you have anyone else with you—in your family?"

'I don't think so, but I'm not sure.'

"Where..." Kate started to ask where they lived but he would think it a trick. She had to be careful, envision each question in advance. "Do you live together?"

He laughed at that question, a pitiful, mirthless giggle that grated on her raw nerves. *'Yeah. We live together all right. He never lets me out unless he wants something from me. I had to trick him to get out and find you the first time. I wanted you to help us like you did your daughter.'*

How did he know about Annie? A chill settled over her body so that she pulled her sweater closed in front. She didn't ask the question about Annie. She didn't want to know. Not yet. "You mean he keeps you a prisoner? You can't leave when you want?"

Bernie shrugged, raising his palms in a gesture of hopelessness. *'Where would I go? He protects me. We have to stay together. We have to.'*

"I'm trying to understand. But I don't," she admitted.

'I'm sorry. Bernie never tells me stuff and I don't wanna know neither.' He began to cry, tears running out of his open eyes.

Her throat tightened with the fierce desire to hold and comfort him. "Bernie. Son. Don't carry on so. I won't ask any more questions just now if it upsets you."

He rubbed his fists into his eyes as if to shut off his tears. *'I want you to help me—us. But if Bernie finds out, he'd be awful mad. Like he is at that cop. And you. I wanna protect you, I swear to God I do, but I wasn't much help with the twins, was I?'*

She struggled to slow her speeding heartbeat.

"Did Bernie tell you he knew about the sergeant? That he was angry with him?"

'Nah. We don't talk, but it's like I know what he's thinking and he knows what I'm thinking. Most times.'

"I wonder why he wants to harm the detective. There are others on the case too."

'Yeah, but they can't hurt us like he can. Bernie thinks he wants to kill us. Why would he want to do that?'

"Bernie, you're only a child yourself, but you must know that what you're doing is wrong. You're robbing little girls of their lives. Robbing parents of their babies."

He shook his head in fierce denial, his bottom lip pushed out. *'No! We're helping. We're taking the kids away from their fathers. They hurt the little girls.'*

"But what about their mothers? What do you suppose they feel when they lose their daughters?"

He looked away, finally breaking eye contact. *'I gotta go.'*

"Don't go. Please. I do want to help you but I don't know where to begin. There's so much I don't know, don't understand. Things I must know if I'm to help you."

'Maybe so. Only I can't tell you. Bernie can, but he won't. I wanna stop. I don't wanna do this no more. You can't help us, no one can.' He began fading, until all she could see was the swirl of amber and hear the faint echo of his sobs.

Now what? None of it made sense. What did he mean, two minds with one body? Schizophrenic? That would explain some of it, but not all. Split personalities? A zing of recognition struck a nerve. She had read about multiple personality disorders in her quest to understand her psychic abilities. *Sybil, The Three Faces of Eve*, the television movies that had fascinated her years ago came back to memory.

What Little Bernie saw that day with his father and the twins, coupled with the hatred, shame and frustration of helplessness that might have continued for years after the family broke up—that could have split his personality or identity.

If that was so, then the young boy was from the past. That would explain the 'sixties music and the newspaper when she walked in his shoes, the dated cars and furniture in his home. Was he the first personality to split away? The older boy had to be in the present, actually doing the killing. Which one had really called to her for help? She felt blown apart by the thoughts leaping about in her head.

Kate turned away from the computer and left it on in case one of the Bernies wanted to contact her. Pulling open the drapes and the blinds, she looked out the window but didn't see the street. Her shoulders slumped in weariness. What should she do? The police would never go for this idea.

The library. She must go to the library. Not the little one she could get to on her bike. She gathered up her glasses, pen, and notepad, stuffed them into her purse, and reached to pick up the phone to dial for a taxi.

She jumped when the phone rang just before she touched it. Richard wanted to see her right away. He needed her to help them look for Jennifer Johnson's house.

Kate felt troubled by the odd mixture of sadness and elation that coursed through her mind and body. Close to finding out the answers, she alone was coming into a position of stopping this reign of terror. It was too much, too heavy.

Had Big Bernie found out that she knew more and more of the puzzle? Then she would be a threat to them. He wouldn't hesitate to kill her although she still wasn't convinced he knew how to physically find her. What if other personalities were loose out there on the streets?

The thought made her want to crawl back into bed and pull the covers over her head. That was the old Kate.

She reached deep inside herself to find the courage to help Richard and the others search out the house—to keep Jennifer alive.

CHAPTER 19

Kate and Slater sat in a car at the end of the first in a succession of streets with cul-d-sacs. Each home site encompassed a quarter acre of land, most bordering the meandering creek. Behind the development came a little rise of ground with woods overlooking the homes. Just as she'd seen it on the computer.

Slater ordered a check with the corporation in charge but no Johnsons were on record as buying property here. He looked at her anxiously. "You okay? Lots of people around. Couldn't be helped."

Kate managed a grin. "You remind me of a mamma bird worrying about her chick leaving the nest too soon. I'm fine. At first I wanted to turn tail and run, but you know I need to help."

"For starters, we've checked out the city tax records in this area. No Johnsons so far. No deeds recorded in the court house. We may be in the wrong area. That scares the hell out of me. He's tracking this kid, and I don't think there's a very long time span between his stalking and grabbing. Couldn't be, or he'd have been spotted."

"How about the mailboxes? He...the voice said the mailbox had Johnson on it. Maybe the Johnsons are new owners. Could have bought privately from the original owners and there's no deed recorded."

"Good thinking. And I've ordered a canvas of the mailboxes." Slater pointed toward the two people casually walking down the street.

"To speed up the investigation, I had to think of a cover that probably wouldn't fool the Shoe Man if he's watching us. I hope to Christ he isn't."

Kate didn't agree with his pessimism. "That's brilliant! That pair going from mailbox to mailbox are police officers posing as either Jehovah Witnesses or Mormon missionaries. Judging from the dark pants, white shirts, ties and brief cases, I'd say the latter." She hadn't intended to make a pun, but they both smiled, getting it.

"It was the best I could come up with. If we find anything here I want you inside the house. See if you recognize it. We haven't got much time—maybe only a few hours before he makes the grab. There's another subdivision a few miles over the valley, almost like this one. We don't have enough manpower to cover both in a few hours."

"I wish I could have helped more. This—this gift—if you want to call it that, doesn't work just when or how I'd like it to. I guess I should have experimented with it more, but I never liked using it. It's an eerie feeling, you've no idea how eerie, to have no control over your own thoughts and mind."

"I sure as hell wouldn't want any part of it. It took a while to make a believer out of me, that's for sure."

"Do you think he's up there in the woods? Watching us? I haven't felt a presence yet. I think I might have felt him if he were close by."

"It's hard to tell." Slater looked out toward the trees. "Where are you, you bastard?" He clenched his fists.

Richard's fierce anger made her uneasy. It smacked of a lack of control that was unlike the man she'd begun to know. "This is the area, all right, I feel that strongly. Only which one is the house?"

"If he is watching and we stop him from taking the Johnson girl, he might come after you." Slater touched her knee. She put her hand over his.

"I don't think he's watching," Kate answered. "No." She spoke more positively. "He isn't here now. I'd tune in on him if he were close by."

"Maybe we'll be in time." Slater didn't sound as if he believed it.

The younger boy had explained how painstakingly Big Bernie went about selecting his targets. He would be enraged to have his plans thwarted.

"Why does he do it, Kate? Sure you don't have any clue as to what's going on with this guy? It's got me. Usually I can get a handle on what motivates them, but not this time."

She tried not to squirm in her seat. Her decision not to tell about the scene with the twins was a promise Little Bernie extracted from her early on. This promise came at a high price. She was gambling that Slater's team would find Jennifer in time and Big Bernie would become so frustrated as to get careless. She didn't see how the twins could be a factor—it must have happened long ago. If Little Bernie knew she told the sergeant, it would all be over for them and they might never connect with Big Bernie.

"Is it so important to know why a killer kills? I mean, if you don't have anything to go along with it, is knowing why so important?"

If she told him about Little Bernie, about the father, what immense upheaval could it trigger in the Bernies? It wouldn't stop the rein of terror they were perpetrating on the city, and it would surely sever her link with the boy. This one point was crucial to him. She understood that.

The squawk of the radio interrupted their conversation. "I think we got something here, sarge. In the next street, second from the end, north side, Johnson is on the mailbox."

"Disperse the men so that it doesn't look suspicious. Continue your canvass of the residents. We may fool him yet."

Slater put the car into gear and made a slow U-turn. "We'll go in as church people." He took a Bible from his jacket pocket and held it in his hand.

As they walked up the sidewalk to the house, he whispered to Kate. "I feel the skin on the back of my neck crawl, as if a pair of binoculars focused in on us, close range. Don't you feel it?" He squeezed her arm tight. "No! Don't look around!"

Her throat tightened at his note of anger mixed with apprehension. How odd that he would feel it, and she didn't sense anyone looking at them.

When the door opened, she knew they were in the right place. A little girl peeped shyly from behind the skirt of the woman she'd seen in the hallway. The child's fine blonde hair was tousled from playing. Slater extended an open Bible, his shield lying on top.

When the puzzled housekeeper invited them inside, Kate looked around. Everything was exactly as she had seen it on her computer screen.

"Kate, take the girl into another room, I want to explain to the housekeeper why we're here." He waited until the two walked out of hearing range. Without any preliminaries, he began to speak. "You've read the papers and watched television—about the killer of the little girls?"

The housekeeper nodded, not yet touched by any inkling of Jennifer's danger.

"We have reason to believe Jennifer Johnson is—is his next victim."

"Oh, my Lord! How can you be sure? I'd better call Mr. and Mrs. They'll want to come home."

"No. We'll take care of that."

In the other room, Kate watched Jennifer for a moment and then walked to the large window. Trees and bushes surrounded the wide lawn, plenty of places for a stalker to hide and watch. She closed her eyes for a moment and relived the identical scene as Bernie studied Jennifer from out there.

"Have you ever seen anyone walking outside?" She pointed to the yard. "Someone you don't know?"

The little girl stood at her side, looking out the window. "No, only the man with a rake."

"Man with a rake?" Of course. A cold chill ran up her backbone. What an excellent disguise—a gardener. Few people would question his presence. Workers were invisible to most people.

"Did you tell Mrs. Garrett? Or your Mommy?"

The child shook her head. "Nope."

The dead children had never been so real as when Kate looked down into the face of the little girl. Delicate, blonde hair and pink skin—the child was precious. Kate sighed, hating both of the Bernies. That they would snuff out an innocent life like Jennifer's for some twisted idea of rescue was inconceivable, even though she knew the whole sordid story behind their motives.

"Wait here and play with your dollhouse a minute, will you, sweetie? The grown-ups want to talk."

Obediently, the girl sat on a cushion near her dolls and tuned Kate out.

"I think I know how he does it—at least this time." Kate said the words that caused a vacuum of silence to descend into the room as she entered.

Mrs. Garrett and Slater looked at her. Months ago Kate would have cringed at their curious stares. She didn't have time for that now. She told them about Jennifer seeing the gardener working outside her window.

Slater put a call in code to the waiting officers, in the event the killer had a portable scanner. They sat down in the living room, waiting to listen to his plan.

"I'm against a wall, Katie. If we take the girl out of the house now, and if he's watching, he'll know why. You're right. He'll be mad as hell and probably search out the next victim without wasting any time. He'll become more guarded, more unstable."

The chilling idea came to her at that moment. Bernie would make good his threat against Richard, but he would get to him through Michelle. Slater must realize that too by now. That was the only way Bernie could hurt him.

"We don't know his timetable, but these methodical killers usually have one. I'll call in two partners, male and female, as undercover police. They'll show up with suitcases, stay here, maybe it will fool him. So far he hasn't had the balls to take a kid from inside her home, but someone could get careless with an unlocked door or he could cut the glass in the sliding door to her bedroom."

"I don't think he's watching us now. I'd feel him out there," Kate said.

"I hope you're right." Slater turned back to the housekeeper. "Keep Jennifer indoors at all times. This is a must, no exceptions. It only takes seconds for him to grab her. We don't want to notify the Johnsons yet. If they come home together unexpectedly and he's watching, that won't be good. The important thing is, we have to keep things appearing as normal as possible. We can't spook the killer away now that we're so close."

Kate took a deep breath. Richard's plan sounded logical, but the Bernies were so dedicated to destruction.

"Would you bring Jennifer back in here?" Slater asked Mrs. Garrett.

The housekeeper went to get her.

What now, Kate wondered.

When the little girl entered the room, Kate watched Slater kneel on one knee, as he probably had done with

Michelle many times. At the child's level, he took her hand, and Kate's heart wrenched at the trust coming from the little girl's eyes.

"Jennifer, your mommy and daddy and Mrs. Garrett don't want you to talk to anyone outside. Not a man with a rake, not the mailman. Don't talk to anyone. Can you do that for us?"

"'Cept you?" She looked around at the other strangers in her living room.

Slater nodded. "Yeah, excepting me. Of course, you can talk to me." The strain broke as everyone smiled at Jennifer's serious expression.

Later, in the car, they sat quietly.

'Christ! If we lose it now, he could go to hiding for months— years—and surface again when the city least expects it. Or unleash a reign of terror that the city would regret forever.'

It wasn't until halfway home that Kate realized Slater hadn't spoken his last words out loud.

CHAPTER 20

Kate and Slater rode back into the city, each absorbed in their own thoughts. Kate hoped he'd left behind enough to guard Jennifer, but it had been squeaky at best bringing two strangers in at the last moment. Carrying Bibles helped if someone had watched. Yet the two undercover cops inside the house did not seem like much. Bernie was so coldly clever.

Richard had explained that he couldn't stake out officers in cars on the street. When Kate closed her eyes, she could visualize the area. Street parking was forbidden. The yards were neat, orderly and identical with no toys or bikes lying about on the clipped grass. One neat tree stood in self-conscious solitude in each front yard, as if stamped out with a cookie cutter. No doubt the contractor counted each branch before buying them.

Slater echoed her thoughts as he spoke. "This is a tough one. No way I can order a patrol in the streets here. I could place a stakeout at the closest neighbor's, connected with radios, except the houses are so far apart. Not only that, but if he's watching or listening..."

She nodded, deep in thought. "Richard, what if B— what if the killer is using the same type of disguise to get to the children, to become invisible, sort of?"

"We've thought of that. He could wear an animal control officer's uniform, with a small dog or a cat in a cage, as if he had just caught it. An adult would never give the scenario a second glance, a child would be entranced. Just think of how many disguises he could use that might get by a watchful guardian's eye, but call out to a child."

The Bernies never mentioned wearing a uniform or she'd have passed that information on right away.

"You said you didn't think he was watching us. We may have an edge here, but not for long."

"I can't explain it, but no, I'm sure he wasn't anywhere near there or I'd have sensed his presence."

"He could have gotten wind of our looking for Jennifer. There's no way to keep it a secret with the volunteers and all the outside help we had to call in. It's a miracle the news media have stayed out of it as much as it has. The chief held a long conference with the press the other day—that helped."

"Why don't I get a cab from the station? Save you time taking me home. I know you've got a lot to go over with the captain."

"Thanks, Kate. Think you can handle it?"

"I went with you today, didn't I? Besides, two days ago I practiced by calling a taxi and going ten blocks to a little Italian market where I used to shop and stopped at a library."

"Great! I'm proud of you. Like they say, you've come a long way, baby."

After Kate left the police station in a cab, she decided to stay in the city to check out some books at the library. By now she felt certain the Bernies involved multiple personalities, but how many and who were they? She needed to understand them better, try to decide how to break the news to someone. Who could she tell? Richard or Captain Murphy? She was sure either one would explode.

She looked at her watch. Several hours had passed checking through books. The library had an amazing assortment of articles and books on the subject of multiple personalities. She called a cab from the front desk. Time to get home.

When Kate opened the front door, Rasputin leaped against her legs, causing her to nearly drop her load of books. "Good lord, you crazy cat. What's the matter with you?" Rasputin acted nervous, not exactly frightened, more like when she brushed or played with him. She set the books down on the coffee table and tilted her head, sniffing the air as an animal might in strange territory.

Someone had been inside her home.

Grabbing the wrought iron fireplace shovel, she made her way cautiously through the rooms. No one in the kitchen. She crept down the hallway, heart pumping in her throat. This was crazy. She should call 911 and stay outside. In the bedrooms, she was tempted to raise the coverlets to look underneath the beds. Movies where a hand reached out and grabbed the unsuspecting ankle came back to her and she shivered, even though she hadn't sensed a presence back here. Yet.

Satisfied that no one had come into the bedrooms, she tiptoed to the front again, stopped at the archway and scrutinized the room. It was amazing how her powers of observation had become sharp and clear since all this began.

"Who was here, Rasputin? You are really getting weird in your old age. You'd think if an intruder came inside, you'd be all a-twitter." He hated strangers, ran and hid for hours if the mailman knocked on the door with a special delivery or the meterman read the meter in the basement, even though the man used the outside entrance. She looked down at the cat. He was edgy, nervous, but not frightened.

Suddenly Kate focused on the computer, feeling the presence centered there. Setting aside the shovel, she approached, heart tripping fast, skin cold and clammy.

Her printer cover was off. She bent to look at the typing she hadn't left there.

> *Get off my back or you'll regret it. Tell that*
> *cop to leave me alone, or someone he loves will die.*

Big Bernie didn't have to sign it. She knew he had found her. Her body trembled so that it was impossible for her legs to stay upright. She collapsed on the couch.

How long ago was he here? Was he still out there, perhaps in the back yard—waiting? How did he find her? It wasn't as if he had merely sent a message to her over the computer. He had been here. In her house—her one refuge from the world.

She wanted to wipe the cryptic message from her memory, but didn't have that luxury. Did it imply that Bernie would harm Richard's daughter? Did "someone he loves" refer to herself? Had Bernie discovered her growing attachment to Richard? A wave of pain and despair washed over her. It was the first time in so long she had begun to let down her reserve, to care for another human being. It could cost Richard dearly if the killer saw any vulnerability there.

Kate closed her eyes, willing calm to fall around her like a blanket. When she felt soothed, she thought about the situation. If the older boy knew how to reach her mind, he knew where her physical body was. Richard had pointed that out to her days ago. What the little one knew, the big one also knew.

She had no fear of the young boy, but the other one— he was capable of anything. Apparently the two personalities, if that's what it amounted to, knew about each other and struggled for separate existence.

Her first instinct was to call Richard and show him the note, but when she called, he was out. She left a message for him to come to her house. The next objective would be to read the books from the library. That could help her decide what to do or how to tell Richard and the captain.

$$\sim \infty \sim$$

At headquarters, the shift was almost over, the chaos of the night had evened out, the big room was reasonably peaceful, as it always was just before dawn and the onset of the new day's business. Beyond an occasional raised eyebrow or tentative show of interest, everyone sitting at a desk ignored Slater. He was always popping in and out at unusual times.

He could tell by the closed door and the dark office that Murphy hadn't come in yet. Slater looked in the ready room. It was empty, the large map still hanging from the blackboard. He sat down in a desk in front of it and stared, concentrating so hard that after a minute, he felt as if all the tack heads glared down at him accusingly, each shouting, "Help us! Help us!" The map grew fuzzy and then sharp, fuzzy and sharp like a camera zooming in and out. The tacks began to ooze red liquid like round drops of blood.

Slater broke out in waves of sweat. His shirt stuck to his back as he fought for control.

Not the headache. Not now, he had too many things to do. He couldn't become incapacitated now. He concentrated on Jennifer Johnson, knowing what would happen to her if he didn't do this right. Willing his head to clear, he managed to close his eyes, to break the spell of the grid of streets intersected by markers which only served to point out his failure.

He took a deep breath and wiped the stinging sweat from his eyes, afraid to open them again. The map had receded to its proper place. He felt such a stunning relief that he didn't notice the change at first and then he rushed to the wall where it hung.

The circle around the Johnson's house had disappeared.

"What the hell? Am I losing it?" His voice violated the silence. He was about to turn away when something made him look to the north, in the direction where Margaret and Michelle lived.

Their street was circled in blood-red.

While Slater waited for Murphy he called Margaret. She sounded crabby when she answered.

"Is Michelle there?" Oh God, if she was off somewhere unsupervised—

"Of course she is. But she's taking a nap. I let her stay up late to watch a special television program."

Slater felt the sigh of relief well up from his toes. "Keep a special eye on her, will you? It's important, but I can't give you the details yet." It would be a long drawn out conversation to explain everything that was happening and he couldn't cope with that just now.

"Well, of course, I watch her. You're an idiot, Richard."

As he'd thought, it wouldn't have done any good to give her the details. He'd just have to trust her. By the time he hung up, the captain had come in.

Not in a good mood, which didn't improve as Slater told him about the map.

"You've done okay so far, sergeant, but it's way past time to take you off this case. It's getting to you. You're losing control." Murphy sat behind his desk while Slater paced.

"I'm not losing it! Like hell I'm quitting either. I just told you this bastard is dropping the Johnson girl for now to zero in on my daughter. What don't you understand?"

"I said nothing about your quitting," Murphy interrupted with all the authority he could muster. "You're getting too emotionally involved to lead this investigation. I've already assigned two men to take your place."

"I'll see about that. The chief will back me."

Murphy shook his head, not bothering to hide his smug grin. "Not this time. I'm waiting to get in touch with him, but he's behind the eight-ball on this one. The governor on down to the mayor and all the city council—

they're riding the hell out of him and that comes down to me."

"I know. You've shunted the parents and relative calls off to my line," Slater accused.

"The papers are raking us over the coals for not stopping this guy," Murphy continued as if Slater hadn't interrupted. "You've gone paranoid on me with this ridiculous idea. We've got the killer boxed in with Jennifer Johnson. We found footprints outside the window to back up Kate's ah—vision. And here you go off on some goddammed personal tangent. It's time for a change."

Slater knew he'd seen the circle disappearing at Jennifer Johnson's and re-appearing at his daughter's house. It sounded 'round the bend even to him in the stark light of day.

But when he dragged Murphy back to show him the street grids, the circle was back in place, drawn neatly in dark ink around the Johnson house as if it had never moved.

"By God, I swear, Murphy! I saw it!" Slater felt as if a hand gripped him by the throat. He couldn't breathe and turned away so Murphy wouldn't see the weakness.

The captain looked unimpressed by Slater's outburst.

"You're going to put some snot-nosed college suits on this just to prove a point, aren't you?"

"That's out of line, sergeant. I don't have to justify my decisions to you. Take a few days off. We can set a trap for this slime, and it'll be over before you can say Shoe Man. We got him now."

"Not in a million years," Slater said under his breath as he walked away. Murphy couldn't do anything until he heard from the chief, and unless Slater missed his guess, he would be incommunicado for a while.

He still had a few hours to work on it, but he needed to talk to Kate first.

 భచ

"Kate, I don't understand it. What the hell happened to me back there at headquarters? I know I saw the blood dripping from those markers and the red circle around Margaret's street. I know he's not going after Jennifer first."

She sat on the sofa next to him, needing the warmth of his solid body, needing to feel him close. "I don't think so either. There's nothing wrong with your powers of observation, although you might have had a momentary breakdown. You've been through a lot."

The yellow legal pad on her desk was filled with notes from her library research. How could she pile her new idea on top of everything else he had to think about, when she wasn't sure she believed it herself? She should wait until it became more clear to her.

Slater looked down at the stark white sheet of printer paper Kate handed him. Reading it again as if he might wrest some little piece of importance out of the few simple typed lines.

"Shouldn't you have tested the paper for fingerprints or whatever you do?" she asked.

"Nah. He's too smart for that. He's never left a print yet, probably uses gloves. Was anything else touched or moved?"

She shook her head. "No. I guess you noticed that I'm—I'm organized. I've always been 'a place for everything and everything in its place' kind of person." She spoke apologetically, guessing most people had little patience with that sort.

"God, Murphy is so stupid. The killer's not going after Jennifer. Not now. This is the clincher. He's stalking Michelle. To punish me."

It was hard for her to understand what had happened to this stalwart, rock-hard man. He looked so shaken, but he had every right to be rattled. Big Bernie was capable of anything. He was on a crusade and whoever stood in his way was perpetuating the injustice that he was trying to correct.

Slater took Kate's hands in his. She felt the tension under his skin, pulsing into her flesh, felt the pressure of his strong fingers.

"It's not only Michelle I'm worried about. The psycho would kill her to get back at me and then still go after Jennifer. But first he might go for you. You see more than you're telling me. He knows it too. Katie, for God's sake, level with me."

She swallowed and pried her fingers out of his grip. He didn't even notice, he was staring into her eyes so hard.

When she didn't—couldn't—answer, he continued to talk. "It's not a closed deal like Murphy thinks it is and it isn't just my worry about Michelle. I know I can catch this bastard. Stop him dead in his tracks, if they let me alone."

Unfortunate choice of words, dead in his tracks.

"I don't think he'll harm Michelle. You said she's out of his—what did you call it?—his comfort zone. Yet he does know where she lives. He's trying to scare you off. Maybe he wants you to think he's going after your daughter so you'll let up just enough on the Johnsons."

Slater's jaw tightened in uncompromising stubbornness. "I've seen how these killers operate, they don't think in straight lines, like we do. Come on, Katie." He took her hands between his big ones and looked into her eyes. "What else have you got to tell me?"

Should she show him her notes on the split personality idea? It was only a guess on her part, a feeling. If she told him this much, she'd have to tell him about the Bernies. He'd know she'd been protecting Little Bernie. That would infuriate him.

She had to be certain first. She had no choice but to hold off until she talked to Bernie again.

"I've told you everything I can, Richard. As soon as I get something concrete, you know I'll tell you," she hedged.

He released her hands, as if embarrassed by holding on so tight. "Okay. That's good enough for me."

He bent and taking her chin in his hand, kissed her. When they parted, he moved his fingers lightly through her hair and brought her close to his chest with his hand on the back of her neck. She trembled at the feelings rushing through her. His voice sounded muffled but she heard every word.

"I care for you, Kate. A lot. It's bad timing, but it doesn't change my feelings. When this is all over—"

"I know, Richard. I care for you, too."

They stayed close for a long moment. She reveled in his strength and warmth. Neither of them could say the L word, but caring was good, too. It might come to them later, when they both learned to trust fully again. When this terrible time was over.

He released her and touched two fingers to his lips, then gently to hers. A special kind of troubled kiss that moved her beyond anything he could have said.

"What will you do about work? Can the captain take you off the investigation?"

"I'm still the detective in charge. He'd have to suspend me first to get rid of me." Slater smacked his fist into his palm. "I've got to stay on this case. I want this guy bad."

෴෴෴

The next morning, Slater knocked on Kate's door. It was like having a beloved old friend for breakfast, the first time she'd had such company in years. Only his worried look diminished her enjoyment.

"Have you been to the station yet?"

"No. Stopped by to see you first. Needed a day-brightener." He kissed her lightly on the lips.

"Did you call Margaret?"

Slater looked worried, unsure of himself. "No. I tried, but all I got was the answering thing and I couldn't leave a message. She wouldn't bother calling me back."

"Did the captain tell you to go home?"

"No. He said he had the replacements lined up, but he admitted he had to get the chief to okay it. The chief knows what's going on, and he'll lay low for a while, incommunicado."

"I guess you have some borrowed time then."

"Yeah. Got to work damned fast. I think I figured a way to trap this guy or at least needle him enough so he might get careless. Here's what I have in mind, but it won't be easy for you."

When Slater finished explaining, Kate sat back, moving her tongue across the fine line of perspiration above her upper lip. "No way, Richard. I'm sorry."

Kate could never go across town to a stranger's home, uninvited, posing as his date for Michelle's birthday celebration. Her flesh cringed at the thought of meeting all those people in Margaret's parent's home, talking to Richard's ex-wife who would surely be hostile, his ex-father-in-law who obviously detested him, the new husband. No matter how badly he needed this from her, it was asking too much. She couldn't do it.

Not for him, not even for the children. Kate saw how her answer affected him. His shoulders slumped, he suddenly looked old and worn. Was she going to lose him over this aberration of hers? He really thought Michelle was in danger. Maybe she was. Bernie said he could hurt the sergeant. That would be the only way. She saw him to the door and spent the balance of the day working on her books, but neither of the Bernies intruded.

'One...two...buckle my shoe' echoed over and over in her mind as she tried to sleep through the night.

In the morning she called Richard to say she would go.

CHAPTER 21

When Slater picked up Kate for the trip across town they didn't have much to say at first. Finally he said, "You look swell, Kate. I like your hair loose on your shoulders. It shines. You look so...different—" He broke off, plainly embarrassed at what he nearly said.

Kate delighted in his admiration for a second before she laughed. "I'm not insulted. Not too long ago I was never out of my duster and fuzzy shoes, was I? Guess it was part of my security thing. Anyway, thanks."

"I've always been partial to long dresses, real feminine. The color suits you too. You should wear blue all the time."

She wanted to tell him how handsome he looked, too, slicked up like a little boy dressed for a party, his cowlick tamed from damp combing. Only he wasn't a little boy. Sitting next to him in the intimate enclosure of the car, a light rain, almost like a fog, insulating them even more, she felt his strength, the controlled energy of the man. Had Margaret ever had regrets? Kate would lay odds on it.

"Do you—are you angry because Margaret remarried? I get the idea that you don't think much of her new husband."

Richard made a noise through his nose. "I don't give a damn what Margaret chooses to do with the rest of her life. I worry about Michelle though. Is this guy going to be a good father to her? I've serious doubts about that."

His doubts were palpable, strong in the close confines of the car. He was afraid. She felt his fear, filling the inside of the car like dirt covering a grave.

They rode the balance of the way in silence.

When they pulled into the circular drive the size of her front street, Kate's hands trembled, her legs threatened to give way.

"Oh, no! You didn't say—it's a mansion. I can't go in there. Why do I have to? They must have tons of security. They don't need you." How embarrassing if Richard had to pick her up and carry her inside. She wouldn't put it past him. Kate longed for the comfort and safety of home, behind her safely closed doors.

Slater tightened his grip on her elbow, offering support, forcing her to move ahead. "This is her father's place. You're right. There are plenty of hidden cameras around the perimeter, security galore. I counted on Margaret listening to me when I told her about my hunch, that he'll be here today. She hit the roof, going on about me endangering them, bringing the ugliness here with me. She figures if I'm right, her father's place is tight with security. She warned me not to blab my suspicions to her father or spoil the party."

At Kate's look of shock, he tilted his chin in a defensive gesture of stubbornness that she was coming to recognize. "Margaret has a way of grabbing the conversation and slapping on the sarcasm to where you wished you'd never brought up the subject. No, matter how important you think it is."

"But Michelle could be in danger."

"Ah, but we don't *know* that for sure, do we? I got to thinking about the red circle. If he set his sights on Jennifer, I don't think he'll be distracted. Not until he finishes what he started. Michelle is a bluff. I'd stake my life on it. But I can't stake hers. He wants us to run scared. He'll be here. Keep your eyes peeled for extra men around, like gardeners or pool men that don't have to be here today."

Was he putting Michelle's life on the line? How could he be that certain Bernie wasn't going to make a grab for her? Kate's thoughts were invaded by guilt. Should she have told Richard everything about the Bernies? It was too late to tell him at this point.

"Murphy's determined to pull me off the case tomorrow—or the next day. I don't have many options."

"What if the killer isn't bluffing? Aren't you afraid for your daughter?"

"Damn straight I am, but like you said, the old man has security better than any bank in the world. And I'm here."

"I still think you should have insisted on the captain or Margaret—someone to believe you. It wouldn't hurt to have backup available."

"God knows, I tried. There are some things I want to see to first, anyway. I need to talk to Vincent. Without Margaret listening."

They waited at the door. Huge pots of real trees lined the walkway and cascades of florist flowers dotted the porch. Little sparkling fairy lights surrounded the area.

Richard looked into her face to check if she was okay. Kate knew he felt her arm tremble beneath his fingers. He bent to lift the leg of his trousers to adjust a gun strapped in a holster.

Kate looked away. She hated Bernie, hated what he was doing, but she couldn't condone Richard murdering him in cold blood. Bernie should go to trial and get justice handed out to him.

"I decided against strangling the killer when I catch him. Don't want to touch the slimy bastard."

She had read about some cops keeping an unregistered drop gun and thought it a fiction ploy of mystery writers. Obviously not.

"The killer never uses any kind of weapon, does he?" Little Bernie said the older boy hated guns and knives.

"Too bad for him. I don't want fingers pointing toward me later, or chance I.A.D. raking me over the coals. They might suspect I did it, but they'd never know for sure."

"I.A.D.?"

"Internal Affairs. The suits have to investigate any kills, righteous or not. That's what they're supposed to determine."

"I wish you wouldn't tell me these things, Richard. I don't like to think of you in that light."

He changed the subject. "Don't let Margaret bulldoze you. Her jabs can cut to the bone and you're so defenseless."

He kissed the top of her head. Just then the butler opened the door to a crowded room filled with people, all talking at once.

"Oh, Lord, I can't do this. It sounds like a swarm of bees ready to attack," she whispered.

He held her arm tightly, supporting her. Finally, blessedly, when she strained to invoke the blanket of tranquility to surround her, she felt calmer, concentrating on the job at hand. She touched the small microphone hidden beneath her waistband. The mike was hooked directly to a police car somewhere in the vicinity.

Kate thought back to yesterday when Captain Murphy and one of his officers turned up at her door. She had invited them in and offered them coffee, but they declined. The captain got right to the point.

"Ma'am, I know Sergeant Slater is obsessed with the safety of his daughter. It's no secret that I think he's out of line. In this city of millions, it's just too much of a coincidence the killer would be after Michelle."

"Not so much as you think. You saw the note. He warned him to stay away from the case." Now was an opportunity to tell them about her theories on the multiples. She hesitated. Murphy's stolid expression of smug pomposity told her he would ignore her politely, as though embarrassed at her deficiency of judgment.

"I know. Slater told me. Showed me the note. We should have had a tap on your phone line, but so far all this stuff's been in your..."

"In my head?" she finished the sentence for him.

"Yes, well, you know what I mean. We're going a lot on your say-so. Of course, you came up with certain classified information like the single missing shoes and our tag of The Shoe Man and where some of the victims were dropped off, so no one is taking you lightly, ma'am."

She wished he would quit with the ma'am business. The captain was probably only a few years younger.

"The chief hasn't called with the orders to transfer Slater back to robbery. Until he does, I'd like to help him, if I can."

"Help him?" She had her doubts.

"Yes, well, if he's determined to go to his daughter's birthday party thinking the killer will be there, then we need someone inside to let us know if he needs backup, isn't that so?"

"I—I guess."

"I'd like you to wear a wire. A hidden one. I'll spare one team of officers who'll be within a couple of miles from you. If the Shoe Man does turn up."

"You want me to wear a bug? Without Richard knowing?"

"Ah, Mrs. Macklin, they don't call them bugs anymore, but yes. A bug, if you will. For the sergeant's own protection, if you get my drift. It can be our little secret, he need never know about it."

In spite of being pompous, the captain was no fool. He undoubtedly suspected Richard was out for blood and wanted to stop it. She did too. But at what risk? Richard was just learning to trust her.

That had been yesterday and at the time, the captain's idea had made sense to her. But now, in the middle of all these people, she wasn't sure. She wondered if Murphy didn't have an ulterior purpose in using her. He didn't think Richard had any grounds for believing the killer was dropping Jennifer and moving on to Michelle. He might be out to prove it and in so doing, get Richard off the case permanently. Maybe even bust him down to a desk job, a transfer Richard insisted Murphy wanted badly.

Bringing her thoughts back to the present, Kate tried not to feel the room vibrate with animated conversation. Outside on the back lawn, children played with loud enthusiasm. The rain had stopped, leaving only wisps of light fog against the background of dark trees.

Richard frowned. She knew he was thinking that Michelle shouldn't be out there.

"I really can't believe your wife didn't take your warning seriously."

"Ex," he reminded her. "I told you, she wouldn't listen. This is Margaret's idea of a kid's birthday party, can you believe it? We wouldn't want to spoil it on the off-chance that someone might be waiting in the bushes to kidnap and kill her daughter."

"Save the sarcasm, Richard," Kate said. "It doesn't suit you."

"Richie! How lovely of you to come. Vincent, look who's here for Michelle's birthday. Imagine taking time from his busy schedule." Margaret stretched to give Slater a peck on his cheek, but her stare—cool, appraising, haughty—rested on Kate.

Through the flurry of introductions and handshaking, Margaret asked. "Do you want me to introduce you to the others here?" Her voice said she would rather not.

Richard shook his head. "Nah. They probably figured out who I am. Anyway, Kate isn't too keen on crowds. She came because I asked it as a favor. This is Kate Macklin—Margaret and Vincent."

"Such a lovely dress...Katharine, is it?" Margaret's voice lapped like silken milk poured into the sudden silence that surrounded their little group. "Naughty Richie, he never tells me anything. I didn't know you had a girlfriend."

Close to Richard, Kate felt his effort not to squirm. From what he said, Margaret always put him on the defensive. She made "girlfriend" sound like a one nighter in a two-bit motel room. And the Richie bit. Richard would never permit anyone, not even a wife, to call him that on a permanent basis. She was just showing off.

Richard's jaw tightened. He looked as if he could have bitten nails in two.

Kate hated his sudden vulnerability, because of his caring for her. She could take care of herself. She stretched as tall as she could manage, several inches taller than Margaret, which gave her an edge.

"We've been ah—friends for a long time. Richard keeps his own counsel, doesn't he? Unlike most people who sometimes babble, he only talks when he has something to say," Kate answered quietly.

Margaret's eyes narrowed at the implied criticism. "How long have you two—how long have you known him?" Her voice was deceptively soft.

Kate smiled broadly and took hold of his arm in a possessive gesture. "Ages and ages. We met at one of those support groups, you know, where everyone tries to get over a negative relationship?"

Richard turned his head, but not before Kate caught his grin. Margaret must have seen it, too and mumbling an excuse, pulled Vincent away.

"You got stones, honey. You blew her out of the water."

Kate smiled at his conspiratorial whisper, sensing that he would've liked to lift her off the floor in a bear hug.

"I need to go outside and check on Michelle. Can I leave you for a while?"

"Sure," Kate smiled. "I think I've got the hang of this now. Nothing to it."

His eyes told her everything.

She walked around the room, able to tune out the roar of conversation knowing she had a task to do. She clutched a glass of club soda with a slice of lime.

Buzz, buzz, giggle, giggle. She felt guilty judging them. They were probably very nice people, most of them. She just felt uncomfortably out of their league. Trying to be as casual as possible, she looked at each person in the crowded room, hoping to get a sense of danger or evil— she wasn't sure what.

Over near the stairs, Margaret stood alone for a moment. This might be a chance to warn her. Before Kate had the time to retreat, to wonder what she would say, she hurried over to Richard's ex-wife.

"Nice party. Sounds like the kids are enjoying it too."

Margaret raised a well-plucked eyebrow. "Yes. I understand you don't like festivities. You and Richard are alike there."

"Margaret—may I call you that?" Kate didn't wait for an answer. "Richard told you that Michelle may be in danger today. I believe he's right."

The woman stepped back, her mouth grim. "I think he's gone crackers. He refused to tell me how he reached that conclusion. Wouldn't it be a very large coincidence that in a city of this size, the detective in charge's daughter is an intended victim? He's paranoid, the job is too much. He should have never returned to homicide. I warned him."

It was harder than she'd imagined. How to break through the barrier without sounding like a total nut herself. "It's the five year thing. The killers—killer—strikes when he discovers a blonde child who is five." She treaded carefully now, afraid of saying too much or chasing Margaret away altogether.

She had the woman's interest. "Really? How bizarre. I haven't paid all that much attention to the papers, actually. But I still don't see—"

"Richard has had a death threat sent to him by the killer. But not against him, against his daughter. The police don't take it seriously, but Richard and I do."

"Jesusmaryandjoseph! Why didn't he say something? No, it's too far-fetched." Margaret shook her head and immediately pushed her hair back in place.

Before Kate could say anything else, Margaret took hold of her arms, looking deep into her eyes. "I'm not accepting this absurd idea of Richard's. Understand? He just wants to spoil this evening—this party—for me and my parents. I won't let him. Play his silly game if you wish, but don't count on us to support it."

Vincent walked up to them and Margaret reached for his hand. "Darling man, do be a gem and show our guest around. This is a party, in case you hadn't noticed," she said pointedly to Kate. "For God's sake, lighten up."

Kate watched Margaret sashay away, her slim hips moving beneath the soft folds of expensive fabric.

She should go out to find Richard, but first she needed to talk to Vincent.

"So. You are—ah—you are Richard's little friend who seems to upset Margaret."

His accent was charming, but Kate didn't have time to be charmed. "Margaret isn't angry at me because of Richard. I told her Michelle was in danger. She refused to hear me out or Richard either when he tried to warn her."

Vincent pulled Kate toward a corner of the room, where the noise smoothed out and softened. "What do you mean? Tell me about it. I assure you of my undivided attention."

Kate told him all she dared of the case and then told him why Richard thought Michelle was in danger.

Vincent rattled off a barrage of French, until Kate touched him on the arm, shaking her head.

"Oh, my apologies, Madam. I forget myself. You do look rather French, if I may say so."

She tipped her head in answer to what he must perceive as a compliment and then did something she had never done before. She reached to take the Frenchman's hand in hers. He looked surprised, but allowed her to hold it. She closed her eyes a moment and concentrated, then opened them to stare into his. She was startled at what she saw.

"You love Michelle and Margaret, don't you?" she asked, still holding his hand.

"But of course! Long have I been without a family." He reached toward a picture on the nearby end table and held it out for her.

Kate studied the portrait of Michelle and Margaret.

"My parents were killed in a plane crash nearly twenty years ago. I could not let anyone close, until Margaret. Michelle is like the daughter I never thought to have. We hope to have more sons and daughters so she won't have to be alone."

Kate let go of his hand gently. She felt it through his skin, saw it in his eyes. He was telling the truth. Richard was jealous, that was why he hated this man so. Not jealous of Margaret, that was truly over. It was more like he was jealous of Michelle. That wasn't healthy. She'd have to talk to him, try to convince him that Vincent would be a good father too.

"Lovely picture," she murmured politely, handing it back to him. "Do you stay here in the States a lot?"

He set the photograph in place, exactly as it was. "Ah, no. My work keeps me in Paris all but a few weeks of the year. Soon, I think, Margaret will cut her ties here and my family will move to France permanently."

My family. That would really tick Richard off to hear that. "I thought you were going to stay here."

He shook his head vehemently. "Impossible. I cannot work in the embassy here, it is so different. I prefer the

European atmosphere and I'm certain Margaret feels the same. Michelle will have the best of schools."

Looking at her watch, Kate saw that too much time had gone by. Richard should have brought Michelle in, wasn't that what he had in mind when he went outside? She'd kept her eye on the wide glass doors and he hadn't reappeared.

Suddenly she stiffened in alarm, the hair on her arms stood at attention, the back of her neck felt warm, as if someone blew on it.

Bernie had come.

She set her drink down clumsily on an end table. Mumbling an excuse, pushing past Vincent, she hurried toward the sliding doors. She had to intervene. Richard mustn't be allowed to confront Bernie alone.

Kate pushed her way through the doors to the outside. Children played on the lawn, shoes damp from the misty spring shower. There wasn't an adult supervising—but then who would suspect danger at a birthday party?

"Richard!" She called out. The sudden hush of the children as they turned to stare at her in curiosity, struck her with the impact of a slap. The habit of wanting to be invisible made even the stares of children hard to take. Dusk moved in through clouds and the yard lights just flickered on. Lightning bugs flitted through the background of the dense woods beyond the manicured lawn.

"Have any of you seen Michelle or her father?" Kate forced her voice to sound calm, a smile pasted on her lips. Only her eyes betrayed her anxiety and she hoped the children wouldn't pick up on it.

The children looked toward a large bush and one pointed.

"Michelle?" Kate called out.

A girl peeked from behind the bush but didn't come out. It looked like the Michelle in the photo.

"We're playing hide and seek," a child said resentfully.

"Go inside, Michelle. Your mother wants you. Now!" For a long moment the little girl hesitated. Kate moved away when she finally turned to go inside with some of the girls. Several remained outside and one child spoke, her voice raised in irritation at an adult spoiling their games. "I saw Michelle's father walking that way." She pointed toward the woods.

"Thank you," Kate cried over her shoulder as she grabbed up a flashlight on the picnic table. No point in alarming anyone or making a fuss. Not yet.

As the woods closed in on her, she remembered the wire. Kate paused and carefully removed it. It was doubtful Richard would need any help against the Bernies. They were good at killing children, but neither boy could outmaneuver Richard, could they?

Captain Murphy wanted any excuse to go for Richard's scalp and she wouldn't be a party to it. Not until she sorted this whole mess out. Finding a niche in a partially rotten tree, Kate left the mike there. Belatedly she thought of her own jeopardy. Bernie had threatened her too. Was she exposing herself to danger?

It depended on which personality was present. Maybe her premonition of Big Bernie's presence was a false alarm, raw nerves. Little Bernie would never harm her.

"Richard. Where are you? I need to talk to you." She spoke in a normal voice which sounded like a shout in the earthy stillness of the woods. It would be dark soon. She didn't want to be in the woods after dark. Suddenly her back felt exposed. Big Bernie wouldn't give her life a second thought.

She wanted to turn back so badly, regretting her impulse to leave the wire behind. The gloom of evening settled overhead, sifting down into the thick branches of the trees. When the light drizzle had stopped, the humidity felt smothering. The leaves on the ground slipped beneath her feet. She jumped when she heard an owl in the distance. Above her in the leaves of the tall trees, birds twittered and moved around restlessly, settling in for the night.

Had Bernie overtaken Richard in a surprise move?

"Richard! You shouldn't be out here. Michelle is at the party. She was hiding from the children." This time she spoke louder, hating the trembling of fear in her voice. When she spoke, the birds stopped their fidgety movements for a second and then began all over again.

A twig snapped behind her. Sweet Jesus, it was him. The woods grew hushed again, the birds still. Kate felt Bernie's implacable rage rising up, reaching forward—a thick, dark shadow overtaking her. She felt his heavy breathing, his hoarsely whispered words brush against her ear, puffing the hair along the side of her cheek.

She couldn't see him without her computer, but she heard him—felt him.

'Interfering bitch! I'll get you now.'

She couldn't tell if the obscene whisper was in her head or she actually heard it.

Should she hide like a rabbit or run for her life? Kate struggled for calm, needing to tune in on his thoughts. It didn't work. She was too distraught to feel anything but his anger and her own terror.

Not daring to call out Richard's name again, she crept through the woods, trying to step on leaves and not fallen branches. If she'd held on to the mike, Murphy would never make it in time to help her, but he might save Michelle if Bernie went back to the party for the little girl.

Kate paused, wondering if he heard her thumping heartbeats. What were the chances of turning back toward the house? The faint sounds of music and occasional shrill laughter came to her—as if from miles away. It was hard to estimate how far behind he was. She might pass right by him if she turned back.

She called out for Little Bernie. He wouldn't hurt her. A waste of breath. Big Bernie was the stronger. He wouldn't let the boy out unless he wanted to. The boy told her that before she understood what he meant.

Gathering up her full skirt to lessen the drag against her legs, she cursed her high-heeled sandals. Her heart fluttered out of control at the snap of another twig behind. This time she heard the muttered curse out loud.

He was close. He could have caught up with her. He was stalking her. Like he did the children.

Richard? She feared whispering his name out loud for fear Bernie could find her. *Where are you? I need you, Richard. Help me. Please help me.*" She concentrated on sending the message through her mind, knowing full well that he wasn't the kind to be receptive. Yet, it was her only hope. Maybe Bernie didn't know Richard was in the woods, too.

Kate conjured up Richard's face, thought his name with every pulse of blood through her veins. Pleading with him to come to her.

Her throat was dry. Her lungs threatened to burst in her chest at the heavy humidity and the strain of crouching down and walking as fast as she could in the dark. She was so out of shape from staying in the house. A light drizzle started again, sifting down through the thick trees.

She stopped in confusion. Had she started to go in circles? She couldn't afford that. It would be easy to walk into the enemy in the dark. Thunder rumbled in the distance. Several bolts of lightning flashed close together, low overhead, flinging ghostly shadows that mixed with slashes of light.

Kate didn't hear the noise of crunching footsteps from behind until too late. A hard hand grabbed hold of her shoulder and she screamed, trying to pry off the hurtful fingers gouging into her flesh.

For years she hadn't wanted to live. Now survival had become a desperate need. Instead of giving in to her terror and collapsing, she struck back with her fists and the flashlight, aiming for an unseen face.

"Kate! Stop it! It's me, Richard."

It took a moment for his voice and words to work past her panic. "Richard?" She let her body sag against his broad chest, unable to hold herself upright any longer.

It could be a trick, she didn't trust Bernie. She pulled away far enough to flash the light in his eyes. Yes! Richard had come to help her.

He lifted her easily, carrying her to a sheltered overhang of rocks, holding her close. She put her arms around his neck and kissed him on the lips, so glad she was to see him.

"Where's Michelle?" he asked.

"She never came into the woods. She was playing hide and seek with the kids."

"I thought for sure she went into the woods. I started tracking and couldn't find a damn thing. Yet I know the killer was here."

"He was here, in the woods, stalking me. I felt his anger. It's amazing you didn't run into him. How long were you following me?"

He groaned and held her hands, rubbing the chill away. "I just picked up on your trail only minutes ago. If you heard something before that, it was the Shoe Man. Oh Christ, Katie, do you know how close you came to being killed?"

She did. Oh, but she did.

"How did you know it was me?" she asked.

"I didn't. Thought I was tailing the killer at first and then you called out for me. I followed your voice until you showed up in the lightning flash."

"No, I never spoke out loud. I was afraid to let him know where I was."

"I definitely heard you."

"I called out, but only in my thoughts. I concentrated on my need for you."

"Hell, I don't believe in that stuff. Your voice was so clear and close. You probably didn't realize you spoke."

He didn't have to believe it. She knew better. The important thing was, Bernie had gone. She could no longer sense his presence. They were all safe. For now.

CHAPTER 22

Kate didn't feel Bernie's presence any longer in the woods. He'd left the premises completely. When she and Slater emerged from the forest and entered the clearing of the yard, Michelle was playing with the children on the brightly lit patio. How strange to see such a normal scene of tables covered with pink tablecloths, laden with cake, ice cream and lemonade. It felt as if hours had passed while she was out in those woods, running for her life.

"Goddamn it! I told Margaret to keep her indoors."

"Relax. You admitted this sounded far-fetched. You can't blame her for not listening to you." Has she ever really listened to you, Kate wanted to ask.

"Here, let me get that leaf out of your hair. God knows, Margaret will raise those eyebrows as it is. Not that I give a flying f—er—tinker's damn, but I don't want you to be uncomfortable." He stopped her and picked out the offending leaf. "Are you okay?"

She nodded. "I am now. But you were right, Richard. He was here. For Michelle."

"Maybe for both of you. Christ, you could be lying out there dead if I hadn't caught up with you. He could have snapped your neck like a twig, or stuck a knife in your back."

Kate felt his tremor beneath her hand resting on top of his arm.

"Shh. He didn't, and he's gone. That's the important thing right now. Maybe when Captain Murphy finds out, he'll stop trying to get you off the case."

"I don't think it'd do any good to tell him. It's just our word. Neither of us actually saw him."

She waited in the background as Richard stepped onto the patio and over to Michelle. He knelt and took her hand, while Kate's heart lurched at the unconcealed tenderness in his expression. They hugged and he stood to face a grim Margaret, her eyes narrowed in suppressed anger. Kate hesitated only a fraction of a heartbeat before she walked up to stand at his side.

"Where've you been? This is a lousy way to celebrate your daughter's—" Margaret stopped abruptly at Kate's appearance.

"Thank you very much for a lovely evening," Kate said innocently. She turned to Richard and took hold of his arm. "Guess we'd better go now, dear."

Margaret swirled away in a flurry of gauzy silk.

In the car, heading back toward the city, Kate hoped Captain Murphy's men weren't sitting out there somewhere waiting for her call. She felt guilty for letting them hang. She could always tell them the wire fell off when she ran through the woods.

"You aren't going to tell the captain the killer was there tonight, are you?" Kate asked.

"No one knows he was there but you and me. And we didn't see him, did we? It wouldn't help my cause with Murphy. He'd still think I've gone paranoid on him."

"But I felt him. I heard him talk to me. He called me a bitch."

"Ah, Kate. It's bad for you. I'm sorry as hell you got involved."

She wondered if she should tell him about her secret conversation with the captain. Now that it was past, she saw how misguided it was to go behind Richard's back. Captain Murphy said he wouldn't tell, but if Richard learned of it, his trust in her could be irrevocably damaged.

How was she to tell him about letting Murphy talk her into the bug so he would hear it from her first?

Before she had a chance to decide, a call crackled through the radio. It sounded like a lot of gobble-de-gook to her, but Richard hit the steering wheel with his open palm and swore. Her head jerked back on her neck as he tromped down on the accelerator.

For a moment it was as if a stranger sat beside her in the car. She was terrified, afraid to speak. They went for miles until his white knuckles on the steering wheel went back to normal. He turned toward her, a grim smile on his face.

"Sorry, kiddo. Reflex. Did I scare you?"

She nodded. "For a minute. Was it the police call?"

"Yeah. The bastard hit the Johnson house."

"Oh, my God! How is that possible? Did he..."

Richard shook his head. "No. The captain had a stakeout, remember? But they didn't catch him either."

She touched his arm. "Richard, I *know* he was out there in those woods. He couldn't have been in two places."

"I know that too. He must have stayed long enough to needle us and then slipped away to Jennifer. Or could be he was at Jennifer's before coming here, got screwed out of that move and wanted to get back at us. The two places aren't so far apart, what with the back roads he might know. Sonofabitch is crafty."

"Does that mean both children are still in danger?"

"I'd bet on it. He probably doesn't care which one he does first now, but he's targeted both of them. And you."

"Maybe when he discovers both girls are being watched, he'll quit."

"I wouldn't count on it. The heat will only egg him on. So far, it's like he has a job to do, but outsmarting us is becoming an extra perk. A bonus he hadn't counted on until now. Besides, the last thing we hope for is him switching targets. Not now. Not another unknown victim. At least this way, we have a little edge on him."

"Want to drop me off in the city? I can take a taxi home."

"Hell no. It's late. I'll check this out—it's on our way. Then I'll take you home. That okay with you?"

What if the captain and Richard got together about the wire? She didn't want to be there when that happened. Kate sat still, worrying. She had no choice. She'd passed the point of confiding in Richard. It was out of her hands.

Squad cars lined the street in front of the Johnson home. Strong lights cut yellow swaths up into the woods behind. A group of officers came down off the knoll, crossed the stream, heading their way. They cradled shotguns in their arms and big flashlights.

"Captain, I heard the call on the radio."

"Slater. Where the hell were you? You're still the whip on this investigation. You know the rules, always within reach of a phone." Murphy slanted a stony look in Kate's direction, but didn't acknowledge her.

She leaned back into the seat with relief. He wasn't going to talk about her role in this. He had kept his promise, after all.

"I told you I was going to my daughter's birthday party. Even I take some time off, once in a while."

"Yeah, well, I don't remember you telling me anything. This won't look good on my report."

Kate sucked in her breath. Murphy knew where Richard was going. She was witness to that. The sneaky, underhanded creep! The captain stared at her, as if challenging her to speak, guessing she decided not to use the wire behind Richard's back. This was blackmail.

She watched Richard shrug off Murphy's obvious lie as if to say, if the captain wanted to nail him, he'd find an excuse.

"Okay, so what's the skinny? Anyone see him? Did he get inside?"

"He's a goddamned spook if you ask me. Slipped in here as easy as you please, past the stakeout, past the locked door. How in the hell did he do it?"

"How'd you stop him from making the grab?"

"We didn't. Not exactly. The little girl heard a noise and woke up. Her bedroom's downstairs, next to the housekeeper's room. Jennifer says she heard the garage door open into the kitchen and thought it was Mrs. Garrett. She called out to her, and when Mrs. Garrett came to investigate, the door was open and no one was here."

"Then how do you know..."

The captain held up a small plastic evidence bag with two pieces of what looked like taffy inside. The kind that had the paper twisted on both ends.

"We're going to have these tested. I think he loads these with dope. He could talk the kid into going with him a ways and by then the tranquilizer or whatever he used would start to work and he could just pick up the kid and go."

"We checked the other candy found at the scene," Slater reminded him. "It didn't turn up any additives."

"Yeah, but things change. The guy's under pressure. He knows we're onto him."

"How the hell would a man, scary and threatening to a little girl, especially at night, how would he expect to get her to calmly eat candy?"

The captain smoothed the top of his head as he did when agitated. "That's where we draw a blank. Somehow or other he manages to get these kids to trust him. How?"

As Kate listened, she knew exactly how they did it. Little Bernie. He would bring them a toy to touch, to hold, he would know how to talk to them—child to child, on their level. A child wouldn't see the incongruity of a young boy in an older boy's body. They'd probably only listen to the voice of Little Bernie.

What was she going to do with her knowledge? Who could she tell? Richard? He'd never believe it. Captain Murphy? No way he'd believe such a story.

She rested her aching head back against the seat, waiting while the police satisfied themselves that the killer was no longer in the vicinity and there were no more clues to find.

When Richard came back to drive away, she let him get down the highway before she could speak in anything near a normal voice.

"Is he going to take you off the case?" Kate asked.

"Not yet. He's bluffing. Pretending to be mad at my not being there, but I told him where I was going. Chief Jacobson hasn't given him the word yet to yank me off the case. Jake's holding off, unless I screw up royally."

"You didn't tell him the killer was at the party?"

"I will. It wasn't the time. I'll drop you at your house and then go back to the station. I'll see Murphy there."

"Don't you ever sleep?"

He shook his head. "Not much. Sleeping tires me out more than not sleeping. I doze in my chair a lot."

"When you finish with the captain, I need to talk to you. It's important. I've got some ideas that might help, some details I've gleaned from my visions."

"Good girl. I'll try to make it early tomorrow afternoon."

"Are you keeping a watch on your daughter?"

He looked worried, trying to hide it behind the macho image he had perfected over the years. "No. In my off hours I could watch her, only I don't keep off hours. You know that. The killer won't come back in the next few days.

He'll lay low, licking his wounds. Until he builds up a fresh head of steam. By then I hope to convince Murphy that Michelle needs round the clock surveillance, the same as Jennifer."

"If you need me to verify anything—"

"You did good, honey. I know how much it cost you to go to that party. You'd better keep a low profile for a while. The killer has enough on his mind, divided between Jennifer and Michelle. But if he's mad enough, he could still come for you."

"You may be right."

He was right. She hadn't forgotten his voice in the woods. '*Bitch! I'll get you!*' Bernie would be enraged and unforgiving.

CHAPTER 23

S later didn't make it to Kate's that afternoon. She waited until the street lights popped on—for some reason choosing that as a deadline, and then she called him at the precinct.

His answering machine came on. She pictured him listening, deliberately not picking up the phone. When the signal came for her to speak, she chickened out and set down the receiver.

Why wouldn't he have come by? What was the worst scenario imaginable? He had to return to watch Michelle because the captain wouldn't supply any manpower? He could have called her. Did the captain ream him out for not being handy and he went home to sulk? Possible.

Something told her it was worse than that. Richard and Murphy probably argued. Words flew back and forth, and the captain told him about asking her to wear the wire and her agreeing. That had to be it. Richard thought she'd betrayed his trust.

᜶᜶᜶

Three days went by with no word from Richard. After the second day she called the station repeatedly, leaving messages, but he never returned any. Even through her despondency Kate continued to keep the computer running. Bernie might try to contact her. Still basking in Richard's praise before, during, and after the party, Kate hadn't realized until now that she was not completely well, emotionally. Indecisive, she hid from a confrontation until finally she could stand it no longer and took a cab to see Captain Murphy.

Without preamble, she drew a deep breath and asked him point blank if he'd told Slater about the wire. "The subject came up, I believe." The captain sat staring at her, elbows on the desk, his fingertips together like a pious praying mantis. "I know I gave my word not to tell him, but it was unavoidable."

"That's why I haven't seen him. We had an appointment three days ago. I need to talk to him."

"Sergeant Slater has been known to withdraw, especially when he's on a case, but he's a professional. He'll come around. He's been avoiding me, too."

"He's worried about his daughter. Did he tell you the killer was at the party?"

Murphy fiddled with his papers, plainly uncomfortable with the conversation. "So Slater claims. Neither of you actually *saw* him, right?"

Instead of cringing at his impatient skepticism and slinking away, Kate straightened her shoulders and tilted her chin, ready for battle. "He was at the birthday party. I heard his footsteps right behind me in the woods and felt his evil presence. Richard—Sergeant Slater—intervened just in time."

"Why did you get rid of the wire?"

"I ran through the brush and it fell off. I went back to look, but couldn't find it."

"Yes, well, I had already decided to order a stakeout for Slater's daughter. Under normal circumstances, I'd be inclined to believe you. Your visions, as you call them, have been on the money so far. But the fact is, the killer was at the Johnson's, too. Don't you think that's a little hard to explain? I can't stretch my manpower all over the city."

Kate gritted her teeth and mentally counted to fifteen, just to be on the safe side. "You don't know when he was at Jennifer's home. You can guess, but you don't know. Children have no concept of time. Was Mrs. Garrett sure of the time? He must have gone there first and then to Michelle's."

"That's a distinct possibility, of course. Is there something you could tell me, since you can't reach the sergeant? I'll pass it on to him." His mouth pursed into a forced smile.

Pompous ass. She could see why he set Richard's teeth on edge. "No, I'll wait for him. He is still heading the investigation, isn't he?" She was hoping the jibe might force the captain to tell if he'd taken Richard off the case, but he turned away, dismissing her.

The police thought they didn't need her any more. They had the Johnson stakeout and Slater's daughter as an alternative. Richard had told her that serial killers are obsessed to complete what they start. Chances were Bernie wouldn't move on until he tried again. Either with Michelle or Jennifer.

That evening Kate sat in front of her computer, staring at the profit and loss statement for Maria's Gift Shop. She would lose her jobs if she wasn't careful, neglecting them like this. She had enough of the insurance money to live on, but it wouldn't last forever.

She decided to try Richard's phone one more time. This time braced to leave a message if he didn't answer. He didn't. "Richard, I have to talk to you. There are things you must know, and I won't tell anyone else. Please, I'd like the chance to explain everything." She hated the sound of desperation in her voice as she hung up.

Going back to the computer, she worked several hours, trying to catch up on her book work. Rasputin lay nearby, his purr gently overlaying the Mozart Violin Concerto on her stereo.

Her neck jerked when she gazed off into space. The spreadsheet on her monitor scrambled and she felt a presence along with the familiar sobbing. For the first time, Kate lost patience with the boy and felt ashamed. As she'd read through the stack of books on the subject of multiple disorder, it was clear the boy had been doomed since he was eleven, poor kid. Trapped in a time warp.

'*You almost caught Bernie. He told me.*' The sobs quieted and she waited for the hiccups to subside.

'We have to talk to him.'

'*No you don't. That cop wants to kill us. Bernie hates his guts. I'm afraid of him.*'

"Afraid of who? The detective or Bernie?"

'*Both of them!*' he sobbed. '*No one ever wanted me around.*'

Kate took a deep breath and leaped over the edge of the yawning abyss. "I found out why you are so lost. You aren't real. You're not a real little boy."

He looked down at his body in an almost comical expression of bewilderment.

"What I mean is..." she hurried on, knowing his attention span was short. "You became stuck in time when you witnessed your father—when you saw the man abuse your little sisters."

Bernie tossed his hair back from his forehead in that endearing gesture that tugged at her heart. He waited for her to go on.

"It's what's called a multiple personality disorder. There are several of you inside one body."

'Aw, gowan, we don't believe in that stuff.'

"You told me that before, remember? Two minds, one body? That's how I got the idea to look it up at the library."

'Well, if I did, I don't remember nothin' about it.' His mouth turned down, his expression sullen.

She could see the older boy in him now, how had she ever missed the signs in the beginning?

"You're not alone, there are other people who have your same problem. My guess is—and it's only a guess— when you saw what happened to the twins it stopped you at eleven years. When you left the orphanage, you were so scared, Big Bernie came to help you. He was the one who thought of kill—taking the little girls from their homes."

Bernie nodded. *'I guess so. If I'm not real, is Big Bernie?'*

Smart little kid. Kate swallowed, delaying her answer until she gathered the courage to leap over the next chasm. "I'm pretty sure Bernie's real. Someone is taking the little girls. I'd like permission to share your secret with someone."

'You wanna tell that cop about—about that time the man took the twins and—' Bernie shook his head, unbelieving. *'No! You promised! It was my fault, I shoulda stopped him. I don't want strangers to know about it.'*

"Son, someone is killing these children. Big Bernie must be alive. He's the one we have to stop." In doing so, they would probably integrate into one person, the strongest personality, which would be Bernie. Little Bernie would be lost forever.

As if he heard her thoughts, the boy started to cry again, great wrenching sobs that wracked his puny body.

Kate looked down at her chewed fingernails, but knew she couldn't save him. All she could offer was temporary solace.

When he subsided, she plunged on. "You have to understand that you couldn't have stopped the father from doing those bad things to your sisters. No way you could have stopped him. You were—are a little boy yourself. If you'd confronted him, he would have beaten you and maybe the twins too and done it anyway in the park like you said he did."

'Maybe I coulda told someone.'

"You know better. Who would have listened? Who would have believed? I want to help. You called out to me. You somehow knew I'd found my daughter so I could bury her in peace and love. You needed help and had no one to turn to but me, looks like."

'Aw, I don't think Bernie'll go along with this stuff about the...the...'

"The multiple personality disorder?" The boy was so old for his years and yet so pitifully young in some ways. "I think deep inside you know what you're doing is wrong, don't you? You want to stop this. You don't want to help take children away from their homes. These are happy little girls, they don't have bad fathers and think of the poor mothers without their babies."

'M—*maybe, but our mother didn't care,*' the boy conceded at long last. '*Big Bernie says the man's out there. The father didn't die in the fire and the cops didn't find him. So he's out there doing...*'

"I don't have all the answers, but I don't think he's here anymore. These little girls have a right to their lives. Their parents have a right to watch them grow up. I think you know that."

More sobs, no answer.

"I have to tell the sergeant what I know. I don't know how to do it, but it must be done. He can help us figure out how to stop Bernie. I can't help you by myself. I can't. You have to help, too."

The boy's face crumpled but the tears were gone, as if he'd emptied out. '*The cop—he has to kill us.*' His passive acceptance of doom fell on her like a heavy weight.

The words of comfort on the tip of her tongue stayed there. She couldn't lie. Richard did want to kill Bernie, and in so doing, the boy would die, too. He must have known the truth in that. She'd stop Richard if she could, but he didn't *have* to kill and might not after he thought about it.

'*I don't care if I die. But Bernie has work to do. He has to help these children. We can't let them be hurt.*'

Kate chewed her last remaining decent nail, stalling for time. She hadn't gotten through to him about leaving the children alone. Most of what she said went over the boy's head. He heard only what he wanted to hear. Big Bernie believed in what he was doing and it followed that the little boy would too. How to get through to them? The multiples who recovered—in all the books she read—had a lot of help. Help from professionals, trained in psychiatry and it took years, ending in something called integration. All the personalities had to go but one. The thought niggled at her, demanding attention. Were there more than these two personalities?

Something important perched on the edge of her brain, wanting to drop off into her thoughts, but stuck— just out of reach. She couldn't get help for the Bernies unless someone else could see or hear them. How could she expect the captain to accept this at face value? Richard believed in her—had believed in her.

He was all she had left and he no longer trusted her.

ぐろぐろ

Slater sat in front of the iron gates of the estate. He'd finally convinced Margaret to stay with her father, since the old man had the closed circuit burglar alarms and that fancy electronic gadgetry. Maybe after all these years her father's paranoia was paying off.

Even that wasn't foolproof. The killer got in the other night, hadn't he? Of course that was easy, in such a crowd. He'd probably just mingled with the birthday party guests.

Now that Margaret's old man was tipped off, it would be almost impossible for the killer to get inside, but once in, he could do what he wanted. Murphy had refused to assign a watch, stubbornly concentrating the team at the Johnsons. Slater knew it was the captain's slick way of getting rid of him. If he didn't obey orders to lead the investigation at the Johnsons, the captain could throw him off the case, chief or no chief.

Slater thought back to the night of the party. Kate double-crossed him by agreeing to wear a wire for Murphy. Slater had come to trust her. He wouldn't have approved of a bug, just on the principal that Murphy thought of it, but she could have told him—not let Murphy hit him with it.

Maybe he was being too hard on her. He started the car. The killer wouldn't be out here again within days and Jennifer Johnson was covered. Kate said she had something to talk to him about. It was time she leveled with him.

CHAPTER 24

When Slater knocked on the door, Kate was ready. She had all her notes laid out, the books on multiple personality disorder stacked near the computer. She was amazed at her composure, her heart was sealed off so that her chest felt heavy and numb. This wasn't going to be easy.

She let him in, noticing the tired lines around his eyes and the grim set to his mouth. She braced herself against the feeling of pity that rushed through her. He was part of the problem if he was determined to execute the killer.

Killing the Bernies wouldn't bring back the little girls. Bernie had to be caught and put away in a safe place where he could never do harm again. There was no way to justify Richard's lust for vengeance.

They went into the kitchen and after the usual routine of pouring coffee and setting out the sugar bowl, she sat across from him, wanting so badly to touch him.

"Richard, before we begin, let me explain. I shouldn't have gone behind your back with Captain Murphy, but I was desperate to stop you from doing something you'd regret the rest of your life. You're so transparent, everyone knows you want this guy dead."

To her delight, he cupped her hands inside his own. "It's okay, Katie. I've had time to think. I know you'd never do a number on anyone."

"No, I wouldn't. Not intentionally. When the captain learned we were going to Michelle's birthday party, I guess he had second thoughts about not providing backup for you. So he came out to the house and asked me to wear the thing. After I thought it over, I decided we could handle the situation. Together. Without Murphy's troops. So I left that bug somewhere out in the woods with the real bugs."

He smiled and for the first time, his eyes lost that haunted look. "We almost didn't handle it. The killer could have terminated you, while you were tramping around out there alone. He could have sneaked back in and grabbed Michelle, too. I thought about that. Later."

"Richard, I need to talk to you about that." She moved around the counter, keeping her back to him. "I baked a cake last night. How about a slice to go with your coffee?" She turned away, hoping he'd glance at her pile of notes and books, but he didn't even look at them. He sat, eyes closed, the hard planes of his face relaxed and disarmed.

"What makes you think he wasn't after *you*?" She threw the question into the silence. It landed like a bomb.

He opened his eyes, looking directly into hers. "Why?"

"I told you before, he knows you're looking for him. He knows you want to kill him, too."

"What?"

"That's right. Don't ask me how, but he knows that and it's provoking him."

"That's too damn bad, wouldn't you say?"

Kate sighed. "Maybe. But it could push him over the edge."

"He's already over the edge. He could've taken us both in the woods, or seriously tried. I think he's bluffing, trying to scare us off."

"I don't agree. He's enraged at our interference."

"I didn't hear him in the woods, the way you said you did. But then I didn't spend a whole lot of time out there. I don't like woods." His lips curled in distaste. "I hate trees."

She laughed. "What a thing to say. No one hates trees."

"I do. It's sort of like with people. One at a time they're okay, but in groups—they squeeze out the air."

Kate felt unsure how to proceed. She didn't underestimate his reluctance to learn something new. "Hold on a minute, I want to show you some of my notes."

She began telling him about the Bernies. When she reached the part of the appalling scene with the twins that she'd witnessed with Little Bernie, her voice faltered and she couldn't continue. Some sixth sense warned her to stop.

"Christ! That's a lot of stuff to lay on me at one time. I know you believe everything you're telling me, but—"

"Now do you understand why I held back? I didn't see how you or the captain or the police department could back me on this. It's so far out, even I had trouble at first. But it's the only explanation. They have to be split personalities."

"You saw the—what did you call it—the shrine with the shoes?"

She nodded. "Big Bernie's the killer. The young boy's personality is an innocent victim, but then if you want to get technical, they are both victims. The older one's got the boy believing that they're doing the world and the little girls a favor by removing them from harm's way."

"But why? It doesn't make sense to kill the kids to save them."

"No, I agree, it doesn't make sense. To us. But these boys—this boy—was traumatized dreadfully at an early age. It warped his emotions, freezing him as an eleven-year-old. When he could no longer cope as a boy, he had to have help. Since no one outside could or would help him, he turned within himself. That's when Big Bernie came to life."

Slater pointed to the stack of books she'd brought to the table. "You got that out of there?"

"Yes. There are documented cases of this disorder. It happens more than you'd imagine. The idea seems to be that all the personalities have to integrate into one, the least harmful or self-destructive. In this case, there doesn't seem to be much alternative. Big Bernie's a killer and Little Bernie's emotionally incapacitated—beyond repair."

Slater scraped the chair away and stood. "No matter who the killer is, he has to be stopped. He has to accept punishment for what he's done."

"I'm afraid it's not that simple. Everything can't be black and white, yes or no. There are gray areas—"

"Try telling that to the parents."

"I know. I understand your frustration."

"Have you told any of this to Murphy?"

She shook her head. "No. I wanted you to hear it first."

"Do you have any idea where he—they live? You know what he looks like, don't you?"

"No and yes. I'm not good at drawing but I could describe him."

"We could get a police artist to make a composite if we can get Murphy to buy this. He'll love it, multiple personalities, Jesus, that ought to scuttle my command forever, but that's not important. It's the kids we have to worry about."

"Does that mean you won't—won't hurt him when you catch him? He's a very sick young man." She still wanted to protect the boy and the only way to do it was to protect the big one too.

"Haven't you listened to anything I've said, Kate? All these bastards that rob and rape and kill—they all have their stories. None of them are ever guilty, according to them."

"Surely some are punished appropriately. You couldn't have gone on for twenty years if you don't have some faith left in our system."

"I know what you're saying, but truth is, I don't have any faith left. I'm wrung dry." He sat down again and leaned his elbows on his knees, pressing fingers against his temples in that now familiar gesture of despair.

"Headache again?"

He either didn't hear, or ignored, her concerned question. She leaned forward to hear his hoarse whisper. "Some shyster plea bargains the ones we catch—down to a nickel or dime. That's five or ten years and time off for good behavior. Hell, they're claiming now that they aren't responsible for a crime committed while on drugs. This guy will probably claim to have been abused as a child. Half of them get sent to a rubber room for a few years and then they're back out again, no space to keep them all."

She had to ask. "Then you still want to kill Bernie?"

"I'm not making any promises I can't keep. Have to let it play out, that's the only way."

It wasn't a satisfactory answer, but she knew he wouldn't be pushed into a corner. "Is the captain making good his threat to take you off this case?"

"He's breathing down the back of my neck. He wants to get rid of me. Real bad. It's only a matter of time."

"Then let someone else handle the command."

"I can't! Michelle's involved. You may have scruples about harming your precious Bernie, but stop and think what he's done, how many lives he's fu—screwed up."

"I know."

"Do you? Do you really dare think of them as anything besides dolls standing there on your computer screen? Dolls singing their little scrap of nursery rhyme."

He ignored her stricken look and continued, as if needing to shock her out of her calm belief that everything would turn out fine sooner or later. "All those dead little girls—one mother committed suicide, one marriage broke up, the parents are in therapy. Now the bastard's picking on my daughter. And you want me to show mercy? Good Jesus Christ, woman, you try my patience."

"I promise to come by the station and talk to the police artist about Bernie. I will, Richard."

As soon as he was out the door, she made sure the computer was off. She didn't want to be disturbed. It was time to think about all the loose ends, to think how to capture a multiple personality killer when she didn't know which one was real. She and Rasputin went outside to sit in the back yard.

༄༅༄

At the station house, Slater sat at his desk, staring into space. Several detectives standing nearby walked toward him. "Sarge, anything new on the case?"

They all knew which case and he was grateful they hadn't said the Shoe Man or he might have come undone. Slater shook his head and the men moved away.

The more he thought of the nerve of the sonofabitch, invading his daughter's life, threatening the only soul he held dear, the angrier he became, the more outraged. How dare he? This business of multiple disorder shit, it still boiled down to some weird psycho offing little kids. The bastard was still accountable, wasn't he, no matter what his problem was? He had to be stopped. Permanently.

Then there was Murphy, smugly disbelieving, unconvinced that the killer was a threat to Michelle. How to make him understand? If the captain pulled him off the case now, there wasn't any other way to save Michelle except to quit the force and watch her day and night. That would put him completely without authority, but at least if he caught the sonofabitch, he wouldn't have to worry about the consequences swamping the department. Every do-gooder in the country would probably be after his badge anyway.

What was he going to do about this new wrinkle in the case? Multiple personalities—damn what a crazy twist. He trusted Kate's instinct, he had to by now. But what would Murphy and the others think, especially after this incident at Michelle's party?

Kate had given him her notes, scribbled on the yellow legal pad, page after page.

As he began to read them, the sick headache wormed its way into the base of his skull. Home, he had to get home before it really set in with a vengeance.

CHAPTER 25

The phone rang and woke Kate out of a sound sleep, the first she'd had in months. Hours ago she had turned off the computer, put a cover over the whole works and gone to bed. A real bed, with sheets and a pillow, instead of the couch that had claimed her tired body for so long.

"Damn! I should have pulled the cord so it wouldn't ring," she told the cat curled in a ball at her feet. She sat up and scratched him a moment, hoping the ringing would stop. It sounded long distance, not like a normal local when people hang up after five or six times.

Only she didn't know anyone out of town who would call. She climbed out of bed and walked slowly towards the phone. Something inside her cried out, *Don't answer it. Don't answer it.* But it would just be postponing the inevitable. Sooner or later she'd have to.

"Yes?" Her instincts were not alert, she had no warning.

The hoarse whispered voice of Bernie hit her like a fist. Kate knew it was him, even though she didn't think she had ever heard him out loud, but through thought transfer.

'I warned you, bitch. You didn't listen. Now you'll both have to pay for screwing up our work. He's no better than the father who ruined the kids. He's no better than the mother, who knew it was going on.'

"Who is no better than the father? Who are you talking about?" She tried to placate him, although he sounded stony-calm.

'You dumb broad. You're just like the mother, looking the wrong way too. You know who I mean. The cop is screwing with us. Fucking up the works. Condoning what the fathers do.'

She closed her eyes, willing Little Bernie to talk to her. She felt the struggle, as if it might burn up the line between them.

He finally laughed, a short, burst of rude mockery, an ugly satire of humor. *'You're trying to bring out that little fuck, but he ain't coming out anymore. I don't need him, he's a liability now. It's just me, lady. You gotta deal with me. I'm gonna off you first, then the cop.'*

"You can't harm me. The sergeant will protect me. And you can't hurt him. He's too strong for you. Too smart." Could she scare him off or was she adding fuel to the fire?

'She—ee—t. You're thinking I need to go after his daughter to get to him. That could work, serve him right, but I don't have to do it that way. I don't work that way.' His whisper rose a notch in self-righteous indignation. *'You think I do this for kicks? I thought you knew better. But after Jennifer, then comes Michelle. Like*

night follows day. I gotta finish what I start. That part's got nothin' to do with the cop.'

"You have to stop killing, Bernie. It's not helping the girls. Not all fathers do terrible things like yours." Keep him talking. While he talked he wasn't doing anything.

'People do things in secret. Think anyone knew about my old man? What he did behind the bedroom door or out there in that park at night? Anyways, the cop's daughter has a step-father. He could be a weirdo, far as anyone knows. You can't trust anyone.'

"Why are you telling me this? You know I'm going to warn Richard."

''Course you are. That's what makes it cool. He'll know I'm coming after him. He's gotta die. No other way. But you go first. As long as the man's out there, I gotta be left alone to finish my work.'

"Maybe I won't warn the sergeant I'll just let him find you. He'll squash you like a bug."

That harsh laugh again. *'You got sand, lady, I'll say that. No wonder that little fucker Bernie thought you could help him. No way Jose. I'm stronger, I'm the strongest.'*

Kate paused, wondering what to say to keep him talking. "Did you follow me the night of Michelle's party?"

'Damn straight. I just about caught up with you, too, until you called out to the cop. He was too close. I had to leave it alone.'

"They're on to you, Bernie. They know how you got close to Jennifer. You pretended to be a gardener, didn't you?"

For a long moment the voice was silent, as if considering what she said.

'First I do you, then him. Got it? You're beginning to bore me.'

"You and the boy, are what they call multiple personalities. It's a mental illness. Someone can help you." She pumped out the words, hoping he would listen.

'Aw, that's nuts. The kid told me what kind of crap you been filling him with. Me and the little guy, we're together, a family. Everyone else is trying to hurt us. That's why I ain't letting him out no more.' He sounded ready to hang up.

"Wait! It won't do you any good to kill the sergeant They'll only put someone else on your case. You'll still be caught and—"

'Tell him he's gotta die because he's too much trouble. Tell him he shoulda left me alone. Tell him to look in his own back yard.' The loud shriek of laughter hurt her ears and she held the phone away for an instant. When she came back, the buzzing of the empty line was loud in her ear.

Kate put down the phone and laid her head on her arms on the table. Her head might burst apart any moment with all she was trying to understand. She had to call Richard. Warn him. She dialed his direct line at the police station but no one answered. She continued the ringing until the switchboard operator cut in.

"I need to talk to Detective Sergeant Richard Slater. It's an emergency."

The line was still for a moment and the operator came back. "That number doesn't answer."

"I know that! I have to find out where he is." Another long pause.

"I'm sorry, but he left no message."

"Connect me with Captain Murphy. Please." She said it as an afterthought, choking down her impatience.

Ring, ring. Answer, please answer, she pleaded.

"Sorry. The captain doesn't answer his phone."

You stupid moron, I can hear that, she wanted to yell. "Would you locate him and give him a message? It is very important. A matter of life or death. He really needs to get this message."

"Of course, ma'am," the voice said stiffly, as if offended by her tone.

Suddenly the hair on Kate's arms raised and the back of her neck felt icy cold. He was here! Bernie was here!

It wasn't a mental transfer this time, but like in the woods. It was a real presence—a threatening presence.

He would know how to get past the chain link fence, into the back yard. Had she locked the patio doors? She slammed down the receiver and ran to the back of the house. The door was part way open! She saw a heap of fur at the edge of the patio.

"Rasputin!" Tears welled up in her eyes. He had killed her cat, her only friend. She pushed open the door and ran to the cat, kneeling down to pick him up. He was barely breathing. She felt something tight around his neck.

Holding the cat close, she ran back into the house, her hand paused on the lock. What if he was inside? The thought made her legs tremble, but she had to see to the cat, he was so still and limp, like he hadn't any bones.

Kate held the cat in her arms while she ran around the house, turning on all the lights, afraid of shadowy corners. She took the cat into the kitchen, put him on the table and pulled out a knife from the drawer. If Bernie came near her, she would defend herself. Oh God! How could she plunge a knife into anyone, no matter what he'd done?

The cat had a thick rubber band tight around his neck. She carefully slid the knife under it. All the while her heart thudded, expecting Bernie to leap out at her from some hiding place. He could be hiding in the bedroom. But how did he get inside without her hearing him? The telephone. Bernie could have called her from the pay phone a short block from her house. While she'd stayed on the line trying to reach Richard and Captain Murphy, he must have slipped over her fence.

Kate breathed gently into the cat's nostrils, willing him to survive. Finally, he gasped and opened his eyes. His first tentative meow told her his windpipe hadn't been damaged. She carried him to the front room and laid him in his bed.

With the knife clutched in her hand, she walked from room to room, looking under beds and in closets. The last closet was the worst, she pulled back the coats, expecting him to jump out. He wasn't here now, she immediately felt his absence as she had felt his presence before. Why had he only meant to scare her? Was it a warning of the destruction he could do?

She needed to find Richard. He had to be at home by now. It was the only place he could go where he'd be alone and Bernie able to get to him.

Kate pushed the numbers with shaky fingers. *Pick it up, Richard. Pick it up.* On the fourth ring his answering machine kicked in. "Richard Slater here. Leave a message or call back." Short and to the point, just like him.

"Richard, I must talk to you. *He's* coming to kill you. Bernie is. He wants you dead." She talked fast, before the time was up. "I think he wants to kill me first so you'll know and then he'll come after you. He's been inside my house, he knows how to get to me. You're the only one who can stop him." She took a deep breath and continued. "Bernie said you should look in your own back yard. Do it, Richard. Maybe he's hiding there. He'd think that a great joke on everyone. But be careful."

When she heard the little zing of the end of the recording, she sat a moment, wondering what to do next. What would Bernie do? What had she unleashed when she told Richard to look in his back yard? Was that where Bernie was hiding? That would be so sick, just like something Bernie would think funny.

Kate plowed frantically through notes on her telephone desk. Richard had written his address on a piece of paper, ages ago when they first met. Usually so tidy, she hadn't taken time to file her desk contents in weeks. She came across his card, glanced at it briefly and threw it down, no home address there.

Kate thought of the telephone book but discarded that idea too. He'd told her Margaret insisted on an unlisted number and he'd never bothered to change it since she left. She looked at her watch. How much time had she wasted already? Had Captain Murphy received her message and would he give it any consideration? If he came, how long would it take? No need to call the police department for the sergeant's address, they'd never let it out over the phone.

Kate threw the phone book across the room in angry frustration. The number, where was the number? She discovered the last scrap of paper tucked alongside one of the cubbyholes in the desk. Recognizing Richard's writing, she prayed the address scribbled on the paper was his.

She reached for the phone again. It was wasting valuable time, but she had to leave word for Murphy to come to Richard's home. As soon as she made that call she ordered a taxi.

She had no plan, just the overwhelming need to get to Richard before Bernie did.

CHAPTER 26

The ringing of the phone jolted Slater out of his sleep. He stretched, forcing himself to wake up. His fist clenched tight around a tiny shoe. A delicate white shoe—like one Michelle might have worn. He threw it to the floor as if it had been white-hot.

The answering machine clicked on and he heard Kate's frantic voice. He listened, but didn't cut in, still dazed by the remnants of his headache, his drug-like sleep, and the reaction of seeing the shoe in his hand.

What was going on? Had he taken too many pills? He hated using the damn things. It was like a crutch, but it was the only way to get some rest.

What had Kate meant by her cryptic message? Was the killer stalking her? Or was he here? Thinking of her message, oblivious to any danger to himself, he opened the front door and went outside and around to the wrought iron gate leading to the back yard. Hesitating only briefly at the entrance, he pushed through cobwebs and thick shrubbery, emerging into a place he'd always avoided.

The heavy smell of earth and plants clogged his nose, his heart pounded loud over the oppressive silence of the back yard. Not a leaf stirred, not a bird announced its presence.

It reminded him of a park. Suddenly it reminded him of how much he feared parks.

A showering of sunlight sifted down through the overhanging branches and his captured gaze widened, his throat tightened so that he could barely swallow.

It was then he saw the shrine.

Slater fell to his knees, his open mouth expelled a cry of pure agony. Over and over his animal howls of pain resounded in the still garden until his voice left him and he could scream no more. He bent over, his forehead to the grass. Hoarse sobs tore from his ruined throat.

ᘓᘐᘓ

'That's right, fool. You finally figured it out. Took you long enough. I was sure the broad would guess. Maybe she did and didn't want to know. I'm the strong one, always have been. I finally got rid of the kid and got you by the short hairs. It's time you learned who you are and what you're a part of. Sure as hell that nosy dame is coming here to warn you. I'll waste her and let you see her dead. With that and what you know about the shrine, you'll never be able to surface again. I'm in charge now.'

Bernie clambered to his feet and wiped his knees of the clinging earth. He rubbed his sleeve against the tears on his cheeks with an ugly grimace of hatred. *'Cry baby, Jesus H. Christ, a fucking cry baby, just like the kid. Maybe that's where he got it from.'*

He glanced in smug satisfaction at the shrine.

'*A beauty, ain't it? I just wish you could appreciate it, but you're too goddamned dumb. When that creep at the home talked you into going to the police academy, I thought I'd shit green woolly-worms. Then I got to thinking, why not? It'd be a help to my plan, as long as I stayed in charge. And that never was in question. No way Jose. I can come out anytime, all it takes is one of your headaches. That's what gives me the edge.*'

He strutted around the yard, unmindful of the low branches striking his face, or the thorny bushes grabbing at his trouser legs. He wasn't the one afraid of the woods.

'*You tried to get me with those pills, those headaches and those stupid pain pills. Didn't you know I became immune to them? You only put yourself away to save me the struggle, so's I could get out easier, that's all, you poor, dumb bastard.*'

He picked up a shoe and dusted it carefully, holding it up toward the spare sunlight leaking through the canopy of trees. '*You almost caught me at the party. I was ready to get rid of that meddling lady friend of yours until you came back. You're strong, I'll give you that, but I'm in charge now. Then there's your daughter—you really piss me off about that. Don't you know she, of all the children, deserves to be protected? We still suspect Vincent, don't we, old man? You held me back all those years, but that's what began it all, what gave me the power to come out finally. We suspect him of evil. Everyone's evil.*'

He strutted toward the gate, shoulders back, young and cocky. He paused to look out onto the driveway. '*I'm gonna show you how strong I am, so's you'll know once and for all. I'll give you one last time outside and then you're history. I want you to know what's going to happen to your girlfriend—feel her fear when she finds out she's a dead woman. After that, you're finished. My life's ahead of me, I can do it alone now, I don't need you or the kid to help anymore. Maybe I'll arrange it for the lady to take the fall for us. They'll blame her and I'll move on. Go somewhere they don't know you.'*

When the gate opened, Slater staggered forward as if propelled by a force behind him. He stood in the driveway for a moment, his emotions and thoughts so tangled in his brain he despaired of sorting it out. Had he been inside a nightmare, hearing that voice?

He looked back once at the iron fence and shuddered. He couldn't go back in there, not for anything. He shuffled to the wide open front door and made for his chair in the sitting room, needing the comfort and solace of something familiar.

Once seated, his hoarse voice punctuated the silence. "I don't believe this shit. Someone's doing a number on me. No one's in charge of my mind or body, that's a load of crap." He thought of calling Murphy to get over here and collect some fingerprints.

Someone was screwing with his mind.

Bernie laughed, a very unpleasant sound. There was no one to hear it but him. *'You dumb bastard, guess you just won't give up, will you? I tried to do you a favor, letting you out to show you who's boss. I wanted you to admit I'm here, to recognize me. Well, here goes, one more time. That's all I'm gonna do to rub your nose in it. After that, adios.'*

Slater shook his head and looked down at his watch. Ten minutes had passed since he sat down. Where did those ten minutes go? He bent and retrieved something off the floor, turning it over in his hand. A photo of Michelle and Margaret, the glass broken, the gold frame bent as if someone had stepped on it.

His heart thudded in his chest, threatening to break through his skin. His throat burned horribly, it felt as if he was swallowing blood. This picture came from Margaret's father's home. He saw it on an end table the night of Michelle's birthday party. How did it get here?

The back yard—the shrine of shoes—did he dream all that? What did it mean?

Slater thought back to that day so long ago when he watched his daughter walk off with her new step father—a man she seemed to dislike and fear. Powerless to change anything, he had to let her go.

The same as with the twins.

Like a huge tidal wave forty feet high, his memory crashed down on him, the childhood he had successfully buried so deep for so long. The horrifying evil that had lain dormant in him until the helplessness he felt with Michelle had released the Bernies.

He leaned back against the fabric of the chair and absorbed the truth until it soaked through his body and brain like a sponge full of water.

CHAPTER 27

In the taxi on the way to Richard's, Kate was aware of an overwhelming sense of danger for herself and for him. The unseen menace frightened the hell out of her.

"Please. Can you go faster? I'll give you an extra twenty."

"Pay the speeding ticket too?"

Her panicked gaze met his surly stare in the rearview mirror.

"Yes!" Coming from the other direction she spotted a patrol car. The window wouldn't open and she waved frantically. She saw the frightened look of the cabbie in the rear view mirror and leaned back against the seat in defeat. There was no way to be sure the operator had tracked Murphy down to give him her message.

After her wild gestures toward the patrol car, the cabbie raced to their destination, as if afraid of what she would do next. The cab squealed to a stop and Kate stepped out. Was this the right address? Richard's car wasn't parked in the driveway, but the garage door was closed, windows painted over. She paid the driver and hesitating only briefly, told him to go.

Walking up the front steps, Kate first felt intimidated by the grandness of the house. Nothing Richard had ever said about his life prepared her for this. The door was ajar and she pushed inside.

She paused to catch the atmosphere, sensing Richard's presence along with something more ominous. Bernie had been here—was still here.

When she entered the sitting room, Richard's big, comfortable chair claimed her attention. She caught a sharp, quick flash of him sitting, head against the back, eyes closed, expression lost and defenseless.

Kate sat in his chair, feeling the material touch her skin, wrapping her hands around the ends of the chair arms. The warmth and feel of Richard's body gave off a protective aura and she basked in it for a moment, as if he held her, making her forget the danger. He'd been here, and not long ago.

The huge room also held a day bed, the pillow he used still resting on one end. He'd said he seldom went upstairs now that his family was gone. She reached for the damaged picture on the nearby table. Margaret and Michelle. Why was this broken? Had there been a fight? Nothing else seemed disturbed.

Kate closed her eyes and concentrated hard, but felt no immediate threat. Her instincts could be wrong, she dare not trust them one hundred percent. Reluctantly leaving the comfort of his chair, she moved in search of the kitchen. Kitchens always told a lot about a person. She pictured him sitting at a table, half asleep in the early morning, drinking a cup of coffee.

"Richard. Richard, please be here." Her whispered voice grated on raw nerves and she swallowed, not daring to call out again.

She pushed open the swinging door and entered the room. All the lights were on, as if someone had just left. Touching the countertop, she felt a presence, neither threatening nor benign, sort of a neutral feeling. Maybe Little Bernie had been here, but the older boy had said he was gone. For good.

She staggered back, frightened at the sudden flash of color and motion on the countertop.

The row of little girls appeared and in a blink of an eye, disappeared.

Kate's hands trembled when she picked up a container of pills to read the label. Richard B. Slater. Valium. Her throat tightened, making it hard to breathe. Was she losing it?

A shuffling, scraping noise sounded from above, upstairs. She hurried out of the kitchen, suddenly not liking the empty feeling in the large room. The stairs wound upward, darkly sinister at the top. She looked for a light switch, but didn't see one.

"Richard?" Her voice came out wobbly. If Bernie was up there, he'd know she was scared. No use going up there, wait for Captain Murphy, her inner voice counseled.

Ignoring the voice, Kate crept slowly up the winding staircase, expecting Bernie to grab her from behind or descend upon her from the top at any moment. Some hostile persona was here now. Kate felt its presence, hovering around her shoulders like a noxious atmosphere, harsh breaths, breathing in, breathing out. She felt the air moving in the stillness, the warmth against the back of her neck like someone standing close behind.

The bedrooms were empty as was the bath, each as pristine as a department store showroom. Toward the rear of the hall, a door was ajar. She heard the familiar little girl sing-song, so delicate, so fragile sounding, coming from the bedroom door. '*One...two...buckle my shoe.*'

She crept forward and flung it wide open

Michelle's room. Stuffed animals, mobiles on the ceiling, dolls of every description nearly crowded out the bed and dresser. Kate knelt and looked into a dollhouse, precisely scaled furnishings, elaborately decorated, perfect, with only a family missing.

Just like Richard's house.

She sat on the edge of the bed, reached for a teddy bear to hold and concentrated on the inside of her eyelids, as if it had been her computer screen. The hairs on her arms began to stir, sibilant breathing entered the room, the walls felt as if they inhaled and exhaled with a sensation of moving out and in. Her concentration deepened.

The teddy bear in her arms called forth the parade of little girls. They formed in front of her closed eyelids, one at a time until the last stood at the end of the line. Her heart beat faster to see two little empty wrapped cocoons of plastic at the end. As if ready for Jennifer and Michelle?

All the little dead girls had been in this room. The chorus of voices stunned her so she couldn't think any longer. She slumped over on the bed. Her head was pounding, feeling too large for her neck to hold it upright.

Her last doubts had erased completely, leaving her with a pulsing void in her middle that ached with cold emptiness.

Disregarding her fear of Bernie, she lay back on the bed and let her mind flow. She saw the children playing in the room with no sense of fear, delighted at all the new toys. Each little girl was separate, not touching the other, telling her they were on different time planes.

She saw the outline of a man, kneeling on their level, talking gently to first one child, then the other. She couldn't see his face—she didn't want to. The little girls liked him, trusted him.

A door downstairs slammed with a tinkle of broken glass, splintering apart the serenity she'd wrapped about herself. She pushed up from the bed, looking for a corner to hide in. "Don't come up the stairs, don't come up the stairs," she whispered.

Her mind was glazed over by what she had just witnessed in this room. Her head felt as if it might blow apart any moment, leaving her with a painfully empty shell on her shoulders. She needed to cry, great wrenching sobs—like Little Bernie—but Kate felt dry and used up, no tears left.

She tiptoed to the edge of the staircase and looked down, expecting any minute to feel strong hands clasp her shoulder or shove her down the stairs. Sensing a malignancy inside the house now, growing stronger every moment, pulsing into the atmosphere like a giant heart beat—a living organism—she crept down the stairs, looking as much backward as forward.

Racing to the door, she made it outside and considered running down the street, away from the terror—the sick feeling inside the house.

No. No more running. She had finished with running away. A resolve within her hardened. Kate knew she had to face her worst nightmare. There was no going back, there was no where to hide.

'*Go look in your own back yard,*' that was what Bernie had told Richard. She didn't want to go there, but she had to. This isn't the old Kate anymore, she told herself, dredging up every ounce of courage she possessed.

She pushed open the heavy wrought iron gate to the garden. Once inside, the malevolent feeling deepened, tucking around her like a smothering fog of darkness. Kate knew which direction to look, drawing on a reserve of courage she didn't know she had.

There was the shrine, just as it had appeared to her with the help of Little Bernie. A man knelt in front, his head bowed.

Richard.

Was it Richard or Bernie? That was when Kate realized that poor, defenseless Richard was the missing piece of the puzzle. Big Bernie was the evil personality. It had been Richard who so desperately called out to her for help through Little Bernie.

Tears streamed down her cheeks, but she barely felt them. Her heart shriveled up inside. Poor, dear, Richard.

But the man who rose to his feet and turned to face her was not her beloved Richard—she could see that in his eyes, the expression on his face. This was a stranger, a stranger with implacable hatred in his voice as he spoke to her.

"Bitch! You found me."

"Who are you?"

The man laughed. "You know the answer to that. I'm Bernie."

"Where's Richard?"

"I finally got rid of both him and that little shit. They'll never come back again. They wanted to stop my work."

"You didn't call me to help you."

"Hell no. They did."

That was the reason she'd been able to see the Bernies so clear in her computer. As a cop, Richard had locked away the experience of her finding her daughter until he needed it. He must have sensed something wrong inside him and couldn't figure it out. He zeroed in on her strength, the strength she hadn't known existed, the strength he helped her bring out of herself. He trusted her to help him without ever guessing about the Bernies.

"Does Richard know? You told him, didn't you?"

Bernie laughed again. The sound grated against her nerves, sending shivers over her body. She wanted to turn around and run.

Did Richard know he'd killed the children? Had he come out here to see this? What went through his mind when he discovered the truth? Her heart went out to him, so alone, so confused, so anguished about the pain and suffering his hands and someone else's mind had caused.

Had it given him even an instant of solace to think someone else pulled his strings? She didn't think so.

"The twins. That happened to Little Bernie."

"He couldn't face it. He was always a wimpy kid. He needed me."

That sickening scene with the father and the twin sisters had happened to Richard, when he was only eleven. Tears pulsed into Kate's eyes again, blinding her for an instant when she contemplated her own loss; the emptiness inside thinking of the life she and Richard would never have together.

She wiped the tears away. She had to be strong now, no time to dissolve. Was there any way to salvage anything here? Just as she had begun to open her heart to Richard, to let herself think love might come to her again.

"Richard! Come back. Come to me." Kate poured her heart into her words, knowing she'd lost this love before it began to bloom. She continued to say the words, calling to him, walking closer to Bernie, afraid, and yet hoping Richard was still strong enough to hear her.

In an instant, Bernie reached his hands out and grabbed her shoulders in an iron grip. She looked up into his eyes and stared at death. There was not a scrap of pity or kindness, only a calm, stony anger for her interference.

His hands crept toward her neck. Kate put her hands on his arms to pull him away but they were like steel bands, tight and rigid. She felt a pressure on her neck and her world turned black.

In her dreams she saw a form bending over her, touching her face. She didn't cringe away—it was Richard. She felt his fingers lightly caress her cheek, felt his hands on her neck and throat, smoothing and healing—gently touching her.

When Kate awoke, her head felt as if it was splitting apart, her brain in shreds, and her was so mouth dry she had a hard time swallowing. But she was alive!

She looked around carefully, before she sat up, to make sure Bernie wasn't waiting for her. He must have applied one of those karate things to her neck that cops probably learn how to do.

She sat up. Richard had been right all along. The killer had to be destroyed. No matter who was in charge of the body, whether Richard or Bernie, he couldn't be allowed to live—to go on meting out destruction. For Richard's sake, she would have to take up where he left off.

"It's the only way, dear Sergeant, you know it is. I wish to God there was something else to do." She spoke out loud, as if he were listening. "Bernie will take over the body, and that's why he didn't kill me. As Sergeant Slater, he'll claim I confessed to killing the children. It wouldn't be a problem to move the shoes to my house, hide them in a closet. Then he would be free to continue his sick work." She said the words out loud, as if he could hear her.

Leave, leave now, her inner voice pleaded. Big Bernie could change his mind about letting her live. It would be so easy for him to find her again and kill her this time.

Yet, if she escaped, if she left this instant, how impossible it would be to get someone to believe her. And the killings would go on. Kate knelt in front of the shrine to pick up one of the shoes, touching it to her cheek, feeling the soft presence of the little girl.

Grabbing up a shovel which lay propped against a tree, she dug furiously into the soft, loamy earth. Satisfied at the gaping hole, she scraped the shoes inside and quickly covered them before she changed her mind. Swiping the shovel several times across the mound brought it down to the level of the surrounding ground. She threw the shovel into the brush.

She looked at her handiwork, trembling at what she'd done. With her last resolve, she bent to scoop up dry, crackly leaves, scattered them across the mangled earth so that when finished, the terrible shrine was no more.

She held her hands together to stop the shaking. Destroying evidence and handing out judgment and punishment—how could she even think of it? It went against everything she believed in.

Yet if she didn't, who would stop the killing? How many more innocents had to die before Bernie was caught and Richard paid the ultimate price?

How would she do it? It would take planning, since Bernie didn't trust anyone. He was close, she felt it. It was only a matter of time before he came for her. He said he was through with Richard and Little Bernie, that he was strong enough to take over the body full time. He couldn't let her live either.

Kate brushed her dirty hands against her pant legs, straightening her shoulders with grim determination. The key was the Valium in the kitchen. The bottle looked full. She'd empty the contents into the coffee pot and wait. How many pills did it take to kill someone? She couldn't take a chance on any of the Bernies surviving. Would she be killing three people or only one?

Only one? Her calm acceptance made her stomach roll.

The noise of a car running intruded through her thoughts. Murphy! She wasn't ready for him yet. She had to get her hands on that Valium first. How to talk the captain into leaving? She could explain that she had called his office, worried because she couldn't find Richard, but he wasn't here.

In the front yard, she breathed a sigh, emptying her lungs of the cloying smells of the garden. No car parked in the street or in the driveway. The sound of a running motor came from the closed garage attached to the house.

Oh God! Bernie kidnaped Jennifer or Michelle and brought the child here to die. She jerked the garage door, tore her fingernails trying to pull the door upwards, but she couldn't budge it and lost valuable time with the struggle. She raced to the steps of the house. Her heart thudded almost out of her chest to see the closed front door. He could have locked it.

Kate leaned against the heavy door, which opened. Sparing a breath of thanks, she ran for the kitchen where she'd noticed a door. It had to lead to the garage. When she stepped down into the garage, exhaust fumes hit her in the face.

The outline of the car lurked behind a fog of gray smoke. Bringing her blouse up over her nose and mouth, she ran to the car door, prepared to jerk it open, expecting to see the body of a child inside. She coughed, her eyes watering until she could barely see through the window.

Richard sat behind the wheel. He turned his head slowly to face her, his eyes calm and sad.

In spite of her earlier resolve, Kate didn't want him to die. She held the material closer around her nose and mouth. Her eyes stung and burned with the effort to keep them open.

She grasped hold of the door handle. Her hand fell away as Richard slowly reached up to touch his fingers to his lips and then touched it to the window—his special kiss. She put her hand up against the window, the glass between them. Tears mixed with the acrid smoke from the sputtering car as she thought of his wasted life. Except for his daughter, he'd never known love, and now he never would.

Is this the way it has to end, Richard? I love you so much. Her lips formed the words and he heard them.

He smiled that small, secret smile. His eyes closed and he laid his head back on the seat. He trusted her to let him end it.

Kate didn't want to let go. But he was right, there was no other way. She went back inside the house. Passing his chair in the den, a strong need for comfort made her sit in it, one last time. She leaned back, and splayed her hands over the chair arms to wait. Time passed slowly but Kate knew when it was finally over and Richard's spirit departed. She wished for more cleansing tears but they had dried up inside her.

Tomorrow she would talk to Captain Murphy—tell him the entire story. He'd have to believe her. Then it was up to him if he wanted to call it a suicide and let the Bernies finally die along with Richard. Someday Michelle would have to know her father committed suicide, but if Murphy could close the files on the Shoe Man now, no one would ever have to know the whole truth.

Kate let herself out the front door and closed it firmly behind her. A feeling of peace blended with sorrow and loss as Kate heard Richard's voice telling her what she'd done was a righteous call.

Richard Bernard Slater's torment was over at last.

THE END

About the Author

Born in Phoenix, Arizona, Pinkie Paranya traveled all over the U.S., Alaska, and most of Mexico with her late husband. Ever since she can remember, writing has been her passion. After completing her fifteenth novel, trying to discover the genre she loved most, she still hasn't decided.

Paranya enjoys romances with their intrigue and uplifting happy endings, but she has also published two paranormal psychological suspenses, a cozy mystery, and an Early American Alaskan trilogy. To date, she has thirteen published novels.